A KAREN SKARYD MYSTERY

DEATH IN UTOPIA

PHILLIP VEGA

Death in Utopia (A Karen Skaryd Mystery, book 1)
Copyright © 2025 Phillip Vega
All Rights Reserved

First edition 2025
Published in Canton, GA, USA
by thewordverve (www.thewordverve.com)

eBook ISBN: 978-1-956856-84-2
Paperback ISBN: 978-1-956856-85-9

Library of Congress Control Number: 2025909482

Cover and paperback interior design by Robin Krauss
www.lindendesign.biz
eBook formatting by thewordverve

"I am the Lord your God, who brought you out of the land of Egypt, out of the house of slavery; you shall have no other gods before me."

— Exodus 20:2 NRSV

―――――――――――

"I believe the only way to reform people is to kill them."

— Carl Panzram (1891-1930), serial killer

PROLOGUE

Late fall clouds, inky black and streaked with crimson, loomed over the Pinellas High School football field as Det. Karen Skaryd stepped out of her department-issued Ford Explorer.

She'd just completed another ten-hour shift and was looking forward to the last few minutes of the regional finals between the Pinellas High Marauders and their crosstown rivals, the Treasure Island Hammerheads.

"Excuse me . . . pardon me . . . sorry," she said as she made her way past the cheering crowd to where her husband sat on the bleachers.

"Hey, babe." Brock said before shuffling over and handing her a cold hotdog and a flat cola. "Here you go."

Between bites, sips, and football action on the field, her husband of twenty-five years informed her that their youngest, Ellie, a high school senior and cheerleading captain, had just successfully hit a Scorpion maneuver, something she and her squad had been practicing for weeks.

"It was awesome," Brock boasted.

"Please tell me you recorded it."

"Of course." He smiled before handing over his cell phone.

Karen played the video, which showed a trio hoisting Ellie into the air. Balancing on her right leg, Ellie arched her back and held her left leg behind her back. Flawless.

"Jesus," she whispered, handing Brock his phone. A feeling of pride swelled within her.

"I know, right?" he said.

Ellie stood with the other cheerleaders on the sidelines shouting words of encouragement to their team on this chilly Clearwater, Florida, evening. The game was a close one in the final quarter. The Marauders were in the lead: 24:21—just two downs and 15 seconds away from heading to the State Championship . . . if their defense held the line.

Karen could taste the tension as both teams took their positions on the 38-yard line. Ellie's best friend, star linebacker Jackson "Jax" Rivera, known for his incredible athleticism and leadership stalked the offensive line like a panther.

"Come on, Jax!" Ellie screamed.

The Hammerheads' QB's voice could be heard over the crowd: "Red, fifty-seven. Red, fifty-seven. Set."

A salty Florida Gulf breeze blew across the field as the center snapped the ball. Oversized teens collided as the left guard and tackle created a gap, allowing the running back to rush forward with explosive speed. Two yards past the breach, Jax met him head-on.

The brutal impact caused the football to pop from the running back's hands and skid across the turf. Chaos ensued as players scrambled for the loose ball and created a pile-up.

A blend of cheers and groans filled the air as the officials blew their whistles, halting the play. Just 10 seconds left in the game.

The refs pulled the players off the pile, one by one by one ... Fans held their collective breath. Coaches on either sideline shouted instructions, and teammates helped each other up from the ground.

"Jesus, who has the ball?" a nearby fan asked no one in particular.

His question was quickly answered when the ref signaled a change of possession.

Marauders players and fans erupted in celebration while the Hammerheads crew groaned in frustration, wearing morose expressions. Between fist-pumps and high-fives, the detective's cell phone began vibrating in her back pocket, a reminder that a cop was truly never off duty.

Annoyed by the interruption, she gulped down the rest of her soda before retrieving her mobile to see who was bothering her during this crucial moment.

The screen read *Unknown.*

She was about to put the phone back in her pocket when she received a text.

It was a picture of Ellie, taken from the visitors' side of the field, cheering on her team—with the texted comment: *Cute.*

Had to be from one of the other moms. She was accustomed to receiving similar texts from fellow cheerleading parents. She smiled and brought her attention back to the game. Her phone buzzed again, and she pulled up the new text message.

A close-up shot of Ellie's crotch while mid-Scorpion—this time from her side of the field.

The message read: *I see London, I see France . . .*

What the—

Karen's heart rate increased, and her vision narrowed, as if only she and the phone existed.

Another image. This one of Ellie cupping her mouth while shouting something. The text read: *I wonder what else she uses that mouth for?*

Karen's jaw clenched, and she scanned the crowd, looking for—what exactly? Someone snickering and looking her way? Someone staring too closely at her daughter? Someone rushing out the exit during the celebration? All were possibilities. Or none were.

Brock leaned toward her. "Work problem?" he asked.

She raised her index finger in a give-me-a-minute gesture and stood, eyeballing the people around her—a full 360-degree scan. Would the culprit reveal themselves to her? If not now, when? What was going on here?

All she saw were enthusiastic fans packed tightly in the small stadium. Karen dropped back onto the bleacher, her eyes now on Ellie.

"Were you looking for someone?" Brock asked.

The clock hit zero. Game over. The noise in the stadium increased tenfold. Brock's attention went back to the field.

And the text messages kept coming.

Cheerleading images were soon replaced with Ellie wearing her Rosetti's Gelato uniform, scooping chocolate into a waffle cone. The comment: *Yummy.*

The next was an image of Ellie picking up a delivery package off their front porch with a laughing emojis and the comment, *What's in the box?*

The final text was of her daughter walking by a row of school lockers, chatting with Jax. The message read, *I hope she's not bearing false witness against a neighbor.*

Karen gasped, realization dawning. She quickly responded with a text of her own: *Moses?*

Miss me, Detective?

Furious, Karen bolted to the end of the bleachers, shouting back to her puzzled husband, "Keep an eye on Ellie."

"What's going on?" he yelled.

She stopped and turned back to him. "We have . . . a guest"

"Who?"

"Moses!"

Without another word, she was off again, leaving her startled husband to watch over their little girl.

CHAPTER 1

Five Months Prior

The mid-summer Caribbean humidity felt like a slap in the face as Karen and Brock Skaryd stepped out of the minivan under the portico at the all-inclusive Utopia Resort and Spa in Punta Cana, Dominican Republic.

Dressed in crisp, white uniforms, resort baggage handlers approached arriving guests, offering to take their luggage before guiding them inside to check in.

A well-groomed, dark-skinned young man named Jose, according to his nametag, stepped toward the Skaryds. In a respectful tone with slight Spanish accent, he reached for Karen's bag, "May I help you with your luggage?"

She quickly tugged back. "I've got it." She preferred to take care of herself. Always had, always would. And she could certainly handle her luggage.

Easygoing Brock, on the other hand, merely smiled and relinquished his carry-on to the young man. "Thank, Jose. Appreciate the help." He glanced at his wife and said, "We're on vacation, remember, Detective? Let it go."

She rolled her eyes and reluctantly handed Jose her bag. "Oh, are you a police officer?" Jose asked.

She nodded.

"Well, welcome to the Utopia, Officer . . ."

"Detective."

Brock held up a finger and interjected his correction, "Actually, this week, it's Mrs. Skaryd."

She chuckled. "He's right, Jose. No detective. Just call me Mrs. Skaryd."

"Skare-id?" Jose stammered.

The detective waved her hand. "Just call me, Karen."

"As long as you call me, Jose." He smiled warmly.

"You've got it."

"And if you need anything at all," he patted his chest, "just ask."

Brock smiled. "For Jose, right?"

"Exactamundo. Now, por favor, follow me."

They entered the lobby area, which was filled with oversized leather furniture, bright accent pieces, and lavish floral bouquets of all types, but mostly roses. Every part of the décor added to the tropical allure.

Overhead, a banner welcomed the Societas Internationalis Rosarum, one of two reasons Brock had booked this trip. The second was his and Karen's twenty-fifth wedding anniversary.

A plumber by trade, Brock's true passion, aside from his family, was roses. He spent many hours in the yard, caring for his babies. A dedicated rosarian, he was a finalist for his latest hybrid—a tropical tea rose named after his mother, Angela, who encouraged his floral fascination from an early age.

His "Angel Rose" was a large coral and orange flower with approximately thirty petals apiece. It was known amongst his fellow Tampa Bay-area rosarians for its intense fruity fragrance and stunning blooms.

The competition this year included his longtime rival, Diana St. James, a wealthy divorcee of a prominent human rights attorney. Diana currently served as the president for the Clearwater Chapter of the Florida Rosarian Society.

Known for her sharp wit and even sharper tongue, she was prominently featured in the advertising for the event, proudly showcasing her prized

"Peace Rose"—a hybrid celebrated for its large, fragrant yellow and pink blooms . . . and a subtle reminder of her carefully curated public image.

Ironically, despite her rose's reputation for resilience and beauty, Diana herself embodied the opposite. Known for her gossiping and antagonistic nature, she was the epitome of combative and hostile behavior. While her floral arrangements were admired for their vigor, Diana, who insisted on being called "Madam President," was more like a persistent virus—difficult to avoid and even harder to tolerate.

Upon seeing her face, Brock's smile soured.

Noticing his expression, Jose asked, "Are you here for the conference, señor?"

Brock looped his arm around Karen's waist. "That and our twenty-fifth wedding anniversary."

"Twenty-five years." Jose whistled. "Congratulations to you both."

"Thanks," Brock said. "I give her all the credit."

Karen chuckled. "Uh-huh, right."

Jose gestured to the front desk agent. "Dulce will check you in shortly. In the meantime, please make yourselves comfortable. I will deliver your luggage to your room once you finish with registration."

Brock handed him some cash and followed Karen to a nearby leather sofa to wait their turn. To pass the time, he hopped on his cell to play a game, while Karen took in her surroundings, including a sign indicating where to go to check in for the conference.

While waiting, a cocktail waitress arrived with a tray filled with white frozen concoctions.

"An Oasis Breeze," she offered. "Compliments of the resort."

"What's in it?" Karen inquired, taking hers off the tray.

"It's a resort specialty. A frozen coconut and rum cocktail infused with a hint of lime. It's very refreshing."

Karen took a sip, and Brock drained his in two gulps.

"Good?" the server asked.

"Very." Brock grinned. "Can I—"

"Have another? Of course, señor."

"Brock . . ." Karen started.

"What?" He reared back. "We're on vacation."

She smiled and swished her hand at him. "Okay, fine."

"And you, señora? Would you—"

"I'm fine with just one. Thank you."

"Sí, señora." The girl nodded before handing Brock another and moving on.

He held up his drink and toasted, "To us. Happy anniversary, babe."

She clinked his glass. "Happy anniversary."

He returned to his cell, while she sat back, reflecting on the good fortune in her life. Her successful career as a detective, her happy marriage, and of course, her beautiful children. She'd texted them with a status en route to the resort from the airport.

Richie, her eldest, and a junior at USF-Tampa, was the only one to reply: *Hey, Mom.*

She hadn't heard a word from Ellie and wondered if her daughter was still angry with her. She replayed their last argument in her mind.

"You're being ridiculous. We're just friends," Ellie had said. "Besides, it's not like you and Daddy are going to be home."

"That's not the point. It's not appropriate," Karen countered.

"It's just for the weekend. 'Sides, Jax's parents will be right next door."

"Ellie, I don't care. You're not sharing a hotel room with Jackson, and that's final."

"D-a-a-ad . . ."

"You heard your mother," he'd said. "The answer's no."

"Fine." Ellie had stomped away. "I can't wait to graduate and get the hell out of here."

And despite the good fortune in Karen's life, she couldn't help but think, *Get in line.*

CHAPTER 2

"Get a load of this sunset duo," Brock whispered, interrupting Karen's daydream.

She glanced over with, as her husband called it, her "detective eyes." Throughout her youth, Karen's father, Ricardo, a now-retired and decorated Suffolk County Police lieutenant, would put her through various exercises, from scenario-based role-playing to pattern recognition.

"Honey, never forget—a keen mind will always be your best tool," he'd often told her.

This twosome Brock had just pointed out were a caricature of a May-December romance. The gentleman, sporting silver hair and a trimmed beard, wore in a crisp, off-white linen suit, black Ray-Ban sunglasses, and a Panama hat. On his right wrist, a gold watch; on his left hand, a garnet pinky ring.

"Rolex and pinky ring," she mumbled to herself.

"Huh?" Brock asked.

"Nothing, babe."

"Doing the *detective eyes* thing again?"

"No," she lied.

He rolled his eyes and turned back to his cell phone while she sized up the older gentleman's companion—a curvy brunette in her thirties. She was clutching a designer handbag, inside which was a long-haired mini chihuahua. She cooed at the dog, "That's a good wittle Sable."

The woman looked like she had more plastic in her than a bucket of Legos and moved with the awkward elegance of a three-legged giraffe. Adorned with gaudy jewelry and flashing an unnervingly bright set of oversized teeth, she was the full spectacle.

A neatly dressed, dark-skinned Latina walked over and interrupted Karen's evaluation, "Señor y señora—?"

"Skaryd," Karen responded.

"Sí. Welcome to the Utopia. My name is Dulce. Por favor, follow me." And she led them to a massive wooden desk, intricately carved in a pineapple motif, at one side of the lobby.

"I will need your passports and a credit card for incidentals," she said.

Brock handed over his gold Visa and the pair's credentials. "Here you go."

Dulce made small talk while checking them in. "So, what brings you to our resort? Are you members of the Rose Society?"

"I am. She's not." Brock chuckled. "We're also here celebrating our twenty-fifth wedding anniversary."

Upon hearing the news, Dulce lit up, "¿Deveras? How wonderful."

Karen smiled. "Thanks."

"I've been married for six years," Dulce said. "You must share your secret."

"Patience," the detective snickered, elbowing her husband.

"That and choose your battles," Brock added.

Dulce nodded knowingly before pointing out the location for the conference registration area. "It is through the doors in back there, right past the water station. There are signs to guide you."

Karen glanced over her shoulder and noticed a young couple entering the lobby. The honey-blonde millennial held her phone up, narrating her entrance with every step, while her sandy-haired partner exuded a more reserved and traditional vibe in his casual tropics wear.

She cried out, "Cal, get a picture of me with . . ." and she turned toward the young man handling their luggage, "What was your name was again?"

"Eh, T-Tommy, señora," the nervous-looking bellhop said.

She playfully smacked his chest. "That's right. Honey, get a picture of me with Tommy for Insta."

"Sure, Chloe," Cal said with little enthusiasm.

The detective shook her head as Cal slung his leather satchel over his shoulder and snapped various poses. One with the blonde's arm around Tommy's waist. Another with her kissing his cheek. And a third with her toasting the camera with her recently acquired coconut cocktail.

Dulce slid back the Skaryds' credentials along with their resort room keys, then leaned forward and whispered, "I've upgraded you to Suite 1235, one of our premium twelfth-floor suites with a beautiful ocean view."

Brock's eyes lit up with appreciation. "Wow."

"Thank you," Karen said, smiling at the kind woman.

"My pleasure." Dulce winked, handing Karen a property map and list of daily activities.

"Do you recommend making dinner reservations?" Brock asked.

"Normally, I'd say no. Pero, with this week's event—"

"Understood." He nodded.

"You can always walk across the road to our little town," she informed them. "Here, I'll show you on the map."

Karen spread the map out on the desk.

"We have three restaurants and places to buy souvenirs." Dulce pointed them out.

"Is it all part of the all-inclusive?" Brock asked.

"The shopping, no," Dulce teased. "The restaurants, sí. If you like Italian, I recommend La Trattoria del Sol. I recommend their homemade meatballs."

"We'll definitely check it out."

Dulce directed them to their suite, then called on her next guest, allowing the Skaryds to kick off their vacation.

Had either of them known what was in store for that week, they might have grabbed their luggage and flown straight back home to Florida.

CHAPTER 3

On their way toward the exit, Karen noticed the benign Cal pluck a petal from one the many floral displays. While fingering foliage, he mumbled, "Hmm, nerium oleander."

"Geez, babe," Brock called out from the doorway. "Check out this view."

From inside the lobby, Dulce called for her next guests, "Señor y señora Reynolds?"

"That's us. C'mon, Cal." Chloe cried out as Karen wrapped an arm around Brock's waist to marvel at the view.

"Honey. This place is—"

"Right?" He shot her a big grin.

Before them were breathtaking azure waters, palm-fringed pools, and lush gardens. A warm tropical breeze blew as the pair slowly walked across Spanish tiles to a covered balcony.

Silently, they watched sun-soaked guests savoring the serenity and tropical delights of the aptly named "Utopia Resort".

Karen breathed deep, "Don't know 'bout you, but I'm ready to have some fun."

The broad-smiling Brock said, "Race you to the room."

Like giddy teenagers, the Skaryds made their way to their suite, walking past various signs promoting the Societas Internationalis Rosarum conference. On their way, guests dressed in beach attire greeted the pair as they walked by, putting a smile on both their faces.

Unfortunately, their joyful feeling didn't last long. From inside a nearby building, Diana St. James, Brock's nemesis, dressed in floral resortwear with matching gaudy earrings, stepped out with a cart filled with fragrant pink, red, and yellow roses.

They could overhear her bitching and complaining about who knew what to her brunette companion the moment they stepped into the Caribbean sun. Diana spotted the Skaryds right away.

"Bro-o-ck." She drawled with a feigned smile, causing him to wince.

Instead of addressing her with her title, he said with a curt, "Diana."

It caused her back to stiffen, which put a smirk on his face.

"Just arriving?" she asked.

He nodded.

"Beautiful roses," Karen said.

"Thank you, uh—"

"Karen."

"That's right. You're a crossing guard, correct?"

"Police detective, actually."

Diana waved her hand, "Meh, potato, po-tah-to. Anyway, my assistant here—" she pointed at the woman standing next to her "—and I are on our way to help set up the tent for the gala."

Brock stepped aside. "Don't let us get in your way."

"See you 'round," Diana said and turned to join arms with Bethany.

"Not if I see you first," Brock mumbled.

As the two women departed, Karen heard Diana saying, "... they're nobodies."

Karen put an arm around her husband. "C'mon, babe. Don't let her get to you."

He let out a breath. "Yeah, you're right."

Minutes later, they rode a creaky elevator up to the twelfth floor to their upgraded premium suite overlooking the aqua-blue waters of their Caribbean paradise.

"Wow," she whispered as they stepped inside.

Brock wrapped his arms around her waist. "Mommy like-y?"

"Very much."

"C'mon, let's check out the digs."

There was a large walk-in closet and a luxurious Spanish-flare bathroom. Ever the professional, Brock inspected all the plumbing fixtures, which put a smile on his wife's face.

"Wow, real copper pipes," he whistled. "Not that leaky polyethylene crap they use at those rub-n-tug motels down on Clearwater Beach."

Their suite included a spacious living room featuring plush sofas and designer chairs. Awaiting them in the master bedroom, behind French doors, was a California king-sized bed with bath towels shaped as swans.

A bottle of champagne chilled in a silver ice bucket on a nearby desk, with two plastic flutes, a covered-dish filled with chocolate covered strawberries, and a note, which read, *Happy Anniversary. Utopia Resort and Spa Staff.*

Brock popped the bottle . . . and the cork barely missed Karen's face.

"Oops. Sorry."

"Better than a bullet," she joked, taking her glass.

"Happy anniversary, babe."

Karen lifted her glass. "Happy anniversary."

"So, how'd I do, Mrs. Skaryd?" Brock asked with one eyebrow arched.

She placed her bubbly down and slid out of her sundress.

"That good, huh?"

"Shut up and kiss me."

Karen stretched her body across the sheets, like a satisfied cat in the sun. "Mmm, that was nice. What's next on the anniversary agenda, Husband?"

"How 'bout we head down to that swim-up bar?"

"Perfect."

CHAPTER 4

After spraying herself with sunscreen, Karen slipped into a conservative blue one-piece and tan caftan. Brock chose a faded Rush concert t-shirt and vibrant blue-and-white, knee-length swim trunks.

"Ready?" Brock asked, grabbing some cash.

"Sunscreen?" she offered.

"Nah."

"Okay, but if you get a sunburn . . ."

"Yeah, yeah." He quickly said. "Ah, hell . . . why not? Can ya get my back?"

She obliged, and they headed downstairs hand in hand.

As residents of Clearwater, Florida, the Skaryds were no strangers to people strolling around in beachwear. Still, it didn't stop Brock from commenting when he caught sight of a plus-sized woman in a thong, bent over a lounge chair.

"Jesus, I haven't seen that many divots since my last golf outing."

"Be nice." Karen smacked his arm.

"Don't blame me. I'm not the one wearing a bib instead of a tablecloth."

She ignored his comment and surveyed the pool area for a spot to place their things. Sadly, all the spots were occupied.

"I guess we got a late start," Brock said. "Sorry, babe."

"It's okay. Let's grab a bite, then try again later?"

From behind the pair, a familiar voice chimed in, "Excuse me, señor y señora..."

The pair turned and were greeted by the broad-smiling Jose, their bellman, now dressed in his poolside resort attire.

"Oh, hey . . . Jose, right?" Brock said. "Man, you're everywhere."

Jose smiled. "Is there anything I can help you with?"

"Nah, we're good. Thanks."

"Actually, Jose," Karen cut in, "we were looking for a place to put our things so we can relax around the pool."

"Not a problem," Jose said with a wave of his hand. "Would you prefer lounge chairs and an umbrella or a private cabana?"

"Now we're talking," Brock said. "Either works, I mean, if it's not too much trouble."

Jose waved his hand, "Not at all. Jose will take care of everything. Wait here."

Within minutes, a pair of cushioned lounge chairs and a circular table covered by a large patio umbrella with floral print were wheeled out next to the pool. After wiping down the chairs, Jose retrieved four beach towels, placing one as a pillow and the other at the base of the loungers.

"Wow. Thank you," Brock said.

"My pleasure, señor. Like I said, if you need anything—"

"Ask Jose." Brock slipped him some cash. "We'll remember."

As they got settled into paradise, Karen spotted the young millennial couple, Chloe and Cal, across the way. One of Jose's coworkers was setting up them up, and just like in the lobby, Chloe spent her time narrating the activity on her cell phone, while Cal stood idly by, acting more like her sherpa than her partner.

"Hungry?" Brock asked, cutting into his wife's quiet observation.

"Very," she said.

Karen placed her latest Richard Erlanger memoir—the author, a personal favorite—under her pool towel, and they walked to a nearby beachfront restaurant, the Yellow Fin, for an afternoon bite.

A hostess greeted them immediately, assuring them their table would be ready soon. Brock reviewed a specials menu posted on the wall while Karen took note of people wearing rose society lanyards while enjoying their lunches, including Diana and Bethany.

"Interesting menu," Brock commented as he returned to her side.

"How so?"

"It's flower-themed."

Karen cocked a brow.

"You'll see."

The hostess led them past a roped-off section to an oceanside table with a perfect view of the white-sand beach. Seated catty-corner from one another, they had the ideal vantage point to take in the romantic scenery, all while keeping each other close in conversation, unaware of events lurking beyond the horizon.

CHAPTER 5

The server arrived to take their order, "Hola, my name is Mario. I'll be taking care of you this afternoon."

Karen smiled. "Hi, Mario."

Gesturing to the menu, he went on, "As you see, we are celebrating a special flower-themed lunch."

"Yeah, I noticed," Brock said.

"Would you care to start with something from the bar? Perhaps one of our floral-infused drinks?"

After reviewing the menu, Karen ordered a lavender rose mojito, and Brock ordered a beer.

"A beer?" Karen teased, gesturing for the waiter to stay at their table.

"What?"

"I figured you'd try something rosy . . . like that rose-infused gin & tonic. No?"

Brock shook his head, "I'll stick with the beer, thanks."

"Sí, señor. I'll be right back with your drinks."

Time passed as the pair enjoyed their drinks and floral-inspired dishes. Karen opted for a grilled chicken salad infused with pansies, while Brock went for a barbecue-pork dish topped with honey-glazed hibiscus.

After a cautious first bite, he nodded appreciatively. "Hmm . . . not bad."

While enjoying their unique meal, Karen noticed that a hush had fallen over the restaurant, and the staff seemingly froze in place. Her eyes were to a corner of the room, where a rope separated it from the rest of the restaurant.

In diamond formation, four well-built body men, dressed head to toe in black, escorted an elegantly dressed, dark-skinned gentleman in a crisp, light-blue linen shirt, tan chinos and designer progressive lenses to a private table behind the rope. Karen detective's eyes immediately noticed the earpieces worn by the protective unit, along with bulges from concealed sidearms.

Like a bad car wreck, all the patrons stared, then looked away, then back again. The bodyguards strategically positioned themselves near their VIP employer.

"Talk about making an entrance," Brock joked.

"No kidding."

"Who do you think he is?"

Karen shook her head as a server approached the roped-off section. He seemed nervous, and Karen could swear she saw the water shimmying in the glass he held. One of the guards met him at the rope and gave him a quick once-over.

The elegant gentleman leaned over to a nearby body man and whispered something. With a nod, the brooding bodyguard joined his counterpart at the rope and allowed the server to enter unscathed.

Karen felt bad for this twentysomething young man, trying to earn a living without losing his life. She watched as he placed the glass down on the table, took the gentleman's order, and jolted from the section.

"That kid's gonna need a drink," Brock said.

Karen leaned closer to her husband. "He's not the only one. I got the jitters just watching."

Soon, the noise-level in the restaurant returned to normal. Seated nearby, Chloe narrated her lunch experience to her social media fans. On the other side of the Skaryds, a slightly inebriated Diana stood over fellow rosarian nominee, Kristen Montgomery and accused her of using dyes and preservatives to artificially enhance her hybrid tea rose.

"Everyone knows it," Diana alleged.

"C'mon, Diana. Sit back down, please," Bethany said, gesturing toward the chair that Diana had previously occupied.

"No." Diana jerked back. "Not until you admit it."

Kristen sat in silent mortification, her face gradually flushed as the confrontation and accusations unfolded. A server awkwardly attempted to diffuse the situation by offering the drink menu.

"Here we go again," Brock muttered.

"What?" Karen asked.

"She pulls this nonsense every year. Accuses someone of cheating so they'll either drop out of the competition, or if they win, people will question whether it was legitimate."

Karen was surprised to hear this, despite the unpleasant presence that she'd already noted from Diana. "Seriously?"

Brock nodded, his expression firm. "Yeah. She better not try that crap with me."

"I will not sit down," Diana continued. "There's no way you could have grown roses that perfect."

Like a stealth fighter, one of the bodyguards from the roped-off section approached Diana, his towering presence casting a shadow. Mid-accusation, Diana froze and turned, finding herself face to chest with the imposing man, who merely raised an eyebrow.

Diana's eyes widened. "Uh . . ."

He leaned in and whispered something to her, making her lower lip tremble. With a quick nod, she muttered what seemed to be an apology, then slunk back to her table as the entire restaurant watched the man return to his post at the rope.

Brock smiled and raised his glass to the elegantly dressed man who sat at the private table behind the rope. The man returned the gesture with a nod and a small smile of his own.

CHAPTER 6

The restaurant returned to normal, and the Skaryds were able to f inish their meals in peace. As busboys cleared tables, Mario entered the main dining area, pushing a dessert cart in front of him. His unfortunate first stop—Diana's table.

"Excuse me, ladies. Would you care for some coffee and dessert?" he asked.

A startled Diana put a hand to her heart. The drama. "Oh my God. You scared the hell out of me," she barked. "What do you want?"

"I'm sorry, señora, I didn't mean to—"

She waved him off. "Well, you did."

Bethany said, "Diana, he's just here with the dessert cart."

"Sí, señora. Perhaps you'd care for a rose petal sorbet?" Mario offered. "It's served with a side of fresh fruit."

"There are no nuts in it, are there? I'm allergic."

Mario looked caught off guard. "In the drink? Well, I do not think so."

"You don't think, or you don't know?" She scoffed and shook her head. "Do me a favor, Mario."

"Sí, señora." "Why don't you go into the kitchen and check to make sure," Diana said.

"Sí, señora, I will be right back." Mario nodded and shuffled away.

"Bad enough I've got to deal with this Kristen nonsense. Now I must worry . . ." On and on she went.

"No wonder she's single," Brock muttered.

"Be nice," Karen said, though she wasn't in disagreement. The woman was a bear. And not a cute, cuddly one.

"That *is* me being nice," he said. "Seriously. She bitches about everything."

"... and who the hell picked this resort, anyway?" Diana continued. "Next year . . ."

"See what I mean?" Brock said, waving his fork in her direction.

Mario then returned to Diana's table. "Señora, the chef said there are no nuts in the dessert."

"Good. I'll have that—" she pointed at one of the desserts on the cart "—and a coffee, too, but none of that last-of-the-pot stuff."

Bethany raised a hand. "Make that two."

"Sí, ladies. Dos sorbets y dos fresh coffees." Mario said before escaping.

That poor kid, Karen mused.

Brock lifted to his feet. "B'right back. Gotta pee," he said, kissing her hand. "Can you grab me a coffee?"

"Sure, hon. And I'll make sure it's none of that last-of-the-pot stuff."

He smiled at her joke and headed toward the restrooms, allowing her to sit back and enjoy the view outside versus the tumultuous goings-on inside the restaurant. On the beach, gulls flew about as visitors frolicked in the striking azure Caribbean water.

The scene reminded her of life back home in Florida, from her kids to the stack of investigations awaiting her return. Her most recent case involved the death of an African American seventeen-year-old girl, Aaliyah Andrews, who had been found stripped and dumped behind a convenience store dumpster.

The main suspect was Charlton "Charlie" Sasso, an allegedly jealous ex-boyfriend with a weak but solid alibi—a white baseball player at a nearby high school, with offers from Vanderbilt University, Louisiana State University, and UT Austin.

Amid a slow news cycle, an election year, and the salacious details surrounding the crime, Chelsea Delgado, an ambitious right-leaning district attorney with her eyes on higher office, seized the case with the intensity of a predator closing in on its prey, trying it in the court of public opinion to make a name for herself.

Pressure mounted for Karen and her partner, Terrell "T" Danielson, to solve the case. The DA accused the pair of incompetence. Citizens called for their heads. The Skaryds' daughter, Ellie, received threatening notes in her school locker and on her social media pages, which she eventually had to take down.

Karen and Terrell's boss, Lieutenant Woody David, had finally given in to the pressure.

"Arrest the kid," he'd ordered.

Karen argued that Sasso didn't do it.

The lieutenant shot back, "Did you follow the evidence?"

"Yes."

"What does it say?"

"That he slept with the girl," Terrell interjected.

"Then bring his ass in."

Karen pushed back. "Woody, we did. Twice. But my gut tells me—"

She was abruptly cut off. "First of all, it's Lieutenant, not Woody," her boss said. "Second, just give this fucking DA what she wants."

Karen still felt dismayed by the conversation. And disappointed. Ultimately, she and Terrell had no choice but to do as the lieutenant ordered.

Two days after his arrest, Sasso was found hanging from a bed sheet in his cell. His parents blamed the police, who in turn blamed the overzealous DA. This had occurred three weeks prior to the Skaryds' much-needed trip to Punta Cana. The wounds were still fresh in Karen's mind, despite the escape.

Mario appeared at her side, jolting her out of her morbid thoughts. "Señora. Would you and your husband care for some dessert?"

She looked up and smiled. "Two coffees, please."

"Sí, señora."

Moments later, Brock rejoined his wife.

"Better?" she asked.

"Much," he said as he sat. "I peeked into the kitchen on my way back. Those desserts look pretty good."

"I ordered us some coffee. Want me to call him back for some dessert?"

Brock thought for a moment. "Nah, maybe later. Wanna hang out by the pool after lunch?"

Before Karen could respond, chaos erupted a few tables over when Bethany shouted, "Oh my God, *Diana*!"

CHAPTER 7

Everyone's attention snapped to Diana as she clutched her throat, gasping for air. Bethany's frantic screams pierced the room.

Detective Skaryd moved swiftly. "Step back please. I'm a law enforcement officer!"

She wrapped her arms around Diana, performing the Heimlich as Diana's face turned crimson, panic flashing in her eyes.

The rose queen convulsed, and her bowels released as she appeared to have fainted. As Diana slid to the floor, Karen spotted something odd: a note written on the doily that had been under the coffee cup. She recognized the wording: Exodus 20:16. Foam dripped from the corner of Diana's mouth, hinting at something far more sinister than choking.

"Call an ambulance!" Karen barked, feeling a stab of regret that she hadn't packed Narcan.

One of the towering bodyguards appeared at her side, assisting with chest compressions as his boss was quickly ushered out, the scene spiraling into chaos. Despite their best efforts, Diana's final breath gurgled out, leaving the restaurant in stunned silence.

Karen's mind raced, cataloging details: the cryptic note, the foam—signs of poisoning, perhaps? She looked around the room, brimming with potential suspects.

"This is now an active crime scene!" Her voice cut through the chaos.

Brock, frozen in place, stared down at his wife.

"Brock, I need you!" she snapped.

Without saying a word, the bodyguard acted, efficiently roping off the area with the velvet ropes that had previously guarded the elegantly dressed man.

"Me llamo Wolfram," he said with a heavy Spanish accent. "Yo soy un retired cop."

"Detective Karen Skaryd, Clearwater Police," she said, eyeing him. His competence was evident, but there was no time for pleasantries.

"We need to handle this carefully," Wolfram muttered in a low voice. "The local team ... they are . . . como se dice . . . sloppy."

Karen frowned. "What?"

"They might not secure this scene properly. ¿Comprende?"

Having worked with various international law enforcement agencies throughout her career, she immediately understood. Meanwhile, so many questions ...

Who had poisoned Diana? Why the biblical reference?

Determined to unravel the mystery, Karen thought about questions she would need to ask the guests and staff. But the EMTs soon arrived, cutting off her queries, as her attention was drawn to them. The medics trampled through the scene, potentially contaminating the evidence, which included the note.

Karen's frustration flared. "What are you doing?"

Wolfram stepped in and got into a heated exchange with the lead EMT, whose name badge read, *Alberto Santiago.*

They exchanged rapid-fire words in Spanish, the tension palpable. Karen could sense a history between the two men. But there was no time for side arguments. Diana's death wasn't just an accident, and Karen's instincts screamed foul play. Stepping between the men, she asserted her authority.

"Enough," she ordered the men, eyes locked with Wolfram's. "We need to secure the body."

Santiago's sneer matched his words. "And you are?"

She didn't flinch. "I'm Detective Karen Skaryd, and if you don't step aside—"

Santiago raised his hands in mock surrender.

"Good," she said, forcing calm into her voice. She gestured to the remaining guests, some, like her husband, still stunned by the scene. "Now, why don't you and your partner be useful and take care of the witnesses? See if anyone needs medical attention."

Without waiting for his response, she turned her focus back to the crime scene. Santiago reluctantly moved on, approaching a distraught Bethany.

Karen pulled out her cell phone, snapping photos of the scene as former cop Wolfram continued with his own review of the scene. Fifteen minutes later, the local authorities arrived, led by Inspector General Rafael Montenegro, the lead homicide investigator for the Dominican Republic National Police, Punta Cana Division.

An imposing figure with a solid build, Montenegro's presence commanded attention. Wearing a tailored dark suit, with light-colored linen pants and a crisp, white button-down shirt. His salt-and-pepper hair and sharp dark eyes surveyed the scene.

His team consisted of two junior detectives, a forensic specialist, a crime scene technician, and a medical examiner. Like the EMTs, his detectives trampled the crime scene like amateurs.

Karen attempted to stop them. "You're contaminating the evidence—"

Wolfram waved her off, his expression weary. "It's no use. They won't listen."

Before Karen could respond, the imposing Montenegro strode over. He shot Wolfram a sharp look before addressing Karen.

"Inspector General Montenegro. And you are?"

"Karen Skaryd. Detective, Clearwater Police Department."

Montenegro gave her a long, scrutinizing glance. "Clearwater?"

"Florida," she said.

He nodded. "You're a long way from Florida, Detective. Here on vacation?"

"I was—" she gestured toward Diana's body "—until this happened."

Montenegro sucked his teeth and nodded dismissively. "Sí, well ... we'll handle this from here, no?"

Karen clenched her jaw, knowing she had no authority here. She stepped back, resisting the urge to argue.

"Alvarez, ven aquí," Montenegro barked, snapping his fingers,

Detective Maria Alvarez, medium height with an athletic build, rushed to his side. Her chestnut-brown hair was pulled back in a tight ponytail, and her piercing green eyes gleamed with eagerness.

She snapped a salute. "Sí, Inspector."

Montenegro pointed at Karen. "Take a witness statements from . . . what was your name again?"

"Skaryd. Detective Karen Skaryd."

"Sí, la señora Skaryd," he said, then back to his detective, "And escort them away from my crime scene."

CHAPTER 8

"Follow me, por favor," Detective Alvarez ordered, lumping Karen, Brock, and Wolfram together for statements—a rookie mistake.

Back home, Karen would have immediately corrected the situation. Here, she had no say. *Not my monkeys, not my circus*, she thought. She gave her statement first, followed by a shell-shocked Brock and, finally, Wolfram.

Karen noticed something—an unspoken connection between Wolfram and Alvarez. A subtle wink and smile passed between them.

Off to the side, Bethany's hysterical sobs cut through the air, accusing the waiter, "He did it! I'm telling you he poisoned her!"

Karen didn't dismiss the claim outright—experience had taught her not to—but she also knew better than to believe the first accusations thrown in panic. Wolfram's pursed lips told her he felt the same. Before exiting, Montenegro whistled sharply.

"Oye, Wolfram!" he pointed. "¡No te pierdas!"

Karen understood the message: *Don't get lost.*

Wolfram glared back briefly at Montenegro before donning his dark shades and leaving the scene without saying another word. Detective Skaryd wanted to chase after him but knew she needed to take care of her husband.

Even though Brock and Karen had been together for over twenty-five years, and despite Brock's experience handling his own version of messy situations as a plumber, he wasn't used to seeing a dead body—most civilians wouldn't be, even when married to a homicide detective.

She took his hand. "Come on, babe. Let's head back to the room and lie down."

Without a word, he nodded and took her hand as she led them back to their suite. As they approached the elevator, an unkempt young couple emerged breathless from a nearby room.

Their wide eyes locked on Karen and Brock like teenagers caught sneaking out after curfew. The girl tucked brunette locks behind her ear, and the guy shoved his hands deep into his pockets. His shirt clung loosely, wrinkled and untucked, like he'd rushed to dress.

Karen's gut tightened.

Something about their reaction felt . . . suspicious. She could confront them, but what was the point?

She was out of her jurisdiction and had zero authority.

Instead, she opted for a simple smile and nod. As they stepped into the elevator, Detective Skaryd took stock—male, mid-twenties, lean build, dark scruff on his jaw. Plain shorts, scuffed sandals. A simple silver thumb ring with a blue stone on his right hand.

The kind of accessory thrift-store hipsters liked.

The girl, also in her mid-twenties, wore a sundress that hung off one shoulder and an eye-catching heart-shaped pendant around her neck. Smudged eyeliner, flats, and an unmistakable look of relief as the door slid shut.

Karen didn't need to stop them.

She'd remember the details.

Once in their suite, the detective escorted her stunned husband to their bedroom and encouraged him to lie down.

"I'll grab you some Tylenol," she whispered, spotting the chilled champagne sitting in the ice bucket on the desk.

Hmm.

Like many with children, Karen prepared for most scenarios when traveling, from bandages to various medications. For this trip, she'd packed Tylenol, Pepto Bismol, Benadryl, and sleeping aids, just in case.

Instead of the Tylenol, the detective retrieved the Benadryl, along with a freshly poured glass of champagne. Normally, she wouldn't mix alcohol with medication, but in this case, she would make an exception.

"Here, babe. Take this." She handed him the pill and chilled beverage.

Within fifteen minutes, Brock was out like a light, allowing Karen to unpack and toss on running gear for a light jog around the property to clear her mind. She kissed her husband on the forehead and left the room.

Once downstairs, she knew she needed to stay clear of the scene.

Envisioning the property map in her mind's eye, the detective headed east past lush tropical landscapes toward the white-sand beach, reminiscent of Indian Rocks Beach, near her Clearwater home on the Gulf Coast of Florida.

Yet, unlike the familiar pines and palmettos of Florida's coast, here the vibrant bougainvillea, towering palms, and lush hibiscus filled the air with a distinctly tropical scent. The gentle sound of Caribbean waves lapped rhythmically along the shore.

Latin music played in the distance, helping to clear her mind. Winding through the resort's gardens and pathways, she found herself reflecting on the scene from the restaurant.

Fragments of information pieced together as the warmth of the afternoon sun grounded her in the moment. She recalled the well-dressed VIP and his overly protective entourage.

Karen wondered who the VIP was and why he needed such safeguarding. His demeanor suggested politics, but she'd dealt with high-level drug dealers before. He could easily be one or the other.

Or something else.

Would Wolfram, an ex-cop, associate himself with a criminal?

God, I hope not.

And what had caused Diana to choke moments after arguing with her fellow rosarian? The foam indicated poisoning. But who would have wanted her dead? And why? And what was the deal with the Bible note on the doily?

Beads of sweat formed on her brow as she tried to piece things together, sensing that the truth lay hidden in plain sight. Twenty minutes into her run, the resort staff began setting up a large white tent, placing powerful standing fans around the edges. A perfect opportunity to get out of the sun and ask a few questions.

Tiki torches were strategically aligned along the pathway leading toward the tent. Inside, a large banner over the dais read *Societas Internationalis Rosarum*, welcoming members to their prestigious event.

Tables were adorned with exquisite floral arrangements, fine linens, polished tableware, and plush chairs. Liquor-filled bar stations stood at each corner, and chocolate dessert fountains were strategically placed on opposite sides of the tent.

At a nearby table, staff members appeared to be gossiping about the scene at the restaurant. They immediately stopped when they noticed they weren't alone.

"Hola, señora. Can I help you?" asked a man whose nametag read *Juan*.

Karen fanned herself with her hand. "Looks like it's gonna be one heck of a party."

He nodded. "We hope so. Are you a member of the Society?"

"Me? Gosh no." She grinned. "My husband is, though."

"Understood, señora." Juan took note of her pallor. "Would you care for bottle of water?"

"Yes, please. Thank you."

He ducked behind a nearby bar to retrieve a cold plastic bottle.

"Here you go."

"Thank you," she said, applying it to the back of her neck before taking a sip.

"Por supuesto."

"You guys did a great job setting this up." Karen glanced around the tent. "I noticed there was a bit of commotion earlier at the Yellow Fin restaurant."

Juan tensed a bit.

"Did you happen to see anything unusual?" she asked.

While hesitant, he remained respectful, sensing the seriousness behind Karen's casual tone. He glanced around, as if to ensure his coworkers weren't listening, before leaning closer to her.

"I've worked here for a few years, señora. Today's been ... odd."

You could say that again.

Karen nodded.

"And now with la policía here, it has everyone on edge."

Before she could probe with further questions, Juan's supervisor entered the tent carrying a clipboard, ending the conversation. Normally, Karen would offer her business card and ask that he keep in touch in case he heard anything, but Juan had scooted away too quickly. Frustrating.

Karen drained her bottle of water, then checked her iWatch. She'd been gone for a while, and Brock might awaken any time now. It would take her at least another twenty minutes to get back to her suite.

So much for clearing my head.

On her way back to the room, she passed by the marina, which featured a gleaming display of sleek yachts and elegant sailboats, a far cry from the charters her neighbor Ed ran back home for deep sea fishing trips.

She chuckled at the memory of how rank her son's clothes smelled after working summers for Ed. Every time, she'd hold her nose and send Richie straight to the laundry room before going any deeper into their home.

As she approached, Karen's gaze landed on Wolfram, who stepped out onto the deck of a yacht. They shared a brief wave, but his attention was pulled back inside almost immediately, disappearing as if summoned.

Something I said?

Shrugging off his rudeness, she went wound her way back to the hotel, through the lobby and up to the room, where her husband still slept soundly. Not wanting to disturb him, she stripped off her sweaty clothes in the bathroom and stepped into the luxurious rainfall shower, letting the warmth ease her tension.

Fifteen minutes later, feeling refreshed, she slipped into a plush resort bathrobe and matching slippers, wrapped her hair in a towel, and checked on Brock. Still sleeping. Despite them being married for twenty-five years, she knew he still hadn't grown accustomed to the shadow of death that seemed to follow her.

Karen made herself a cup of rich Dominican coffee, which she took out onto the balcony, along with the remaining chocolate-covered strawberries.

While sipping her coffee and gazing at the Caribbean, Karen's mind raced over the details of Diana's death, starting with the VIP guarded by Wolfram and his men. Also, could the server, Mario, have accidentally— or intentionally—tainted Diana's dessert? And what about the cryptic message on the doily?

She knew rumors would spread quickly among the resort staff. She wanted to keep investigating this, though it was well outside of her jurisdiction, but she would need to be subtle, discreet about her approach. Under the radar—even when it came to her husband. At least as much as possible.

Her thoughts were interrupted as the sliding door opened and Brock stepped outside, looking rested but still shaken.

"Good nap?" she asked.

He rubbed his eyes and nodded, and the movement reminded her of their children as toddlers.

"Took a shower, huh?"

"I did. Went for a jog to clear my head, so when I got back, I jumped in."

"How was it?"

"The jog or...?"

"The shower."

Once a plumber . . .

She smiled, "Awesome."

Brock settled into the lounge chair beside Karen, and they shared a quiet moment, munching on strawberries and taking in the view. She took his rugged hand, caressing it gently, hoping to ease his lingering tension. Finally, he broke the silence.

"How do you do it, Ka?" he asked.

She knew exactly what he meant, but said, "Do what, honey?"

The weariness on his face reflected the weight of Diana's recent death.

"Deal with all that . . . death?"

Karen removed the towel from her head, pausing to absorb the depth of his question. Memories came flooding in—of dismembered bodies found in the remote swamps of Brooker Creek Preserve, of back-alley victims with gunshot wounds, and of Aaliyah Andrews, whose terror-stricken face haunted her still. That case had been closed when the suspect committed suicide.

"Honestly, honey, it never gets easier," she admitted. "I've just learned to compartmentalize and focus on the job."

He tilted his head, as if trying to grasp her reality.

"It's like a puzzle," she continued. "If I let emotions take over, I'll never find the answers."

He squeezed her hand. "At least you have us to come home to. A place where you can let it go ... or try to."

She smiled, grateful for his support. "Why don't you shower while I finish my coffee? Then we can decide what we want to do for dinner."

Brock kissed her, then went inside, leaving Karen alone with her thoughts once again. She knew she should let go of Diana's death, but deep down, she also knew that she wouldn't.

CHAPTER 9

After Brock's shower, they reviewed the list of various dinner restaurants available at the resort and zeroed in on one of the three open-air restaurants, nowhere near the crime scene—La Brisa Bistro.

No reservations required.

"What do you think?" Brock asked.

"Sounds perfect." Karen said.

She wore a breezy, tropical-print maxi dress, sandals, her gold necklace with a cross, and light make-up with a touch of perfume. Brock tossed on a maroon-and-white striped polo shirt, khaki shorts, and a pair of Nike sneakers. When they stepped outside, the slight breeze was enough to chill Karen. She decided to go back to the room to grab her cardigan.

"I'll get it for you," Brock said.

"I know exactly where it is. Easier for me to go. Enjoy the scenery," and she left him standing in the portico.

While waiting for the elevator to arrive, the same young couple she'd seen earlier stumbled out of a different ground-level suite—looking disheveled-looking as before. Like rabbits caught in the gaze of a predator, the two froze when they spotted Karen, just like they'd done the first time.

Before saying anyone could say a word, the elevator pinged, the doors opened, and out stepped the selfie-taking millennial with Cal in tow.

"Oh, excuse us," Chloe said, as they exited.

Karen moved out of the way, allowing them to get out of the elevator. As they did, the other couple hightailed it out of there.

The detective took a deep breath and muttered to herself, "Leave it alone, Skaryd. You're on vacation."

After retrieving her sweater, Karen met Brock in the portico and they strolled to the restaurant, which hummed with activity.

Seated near the entrance was that May-December couple from the lobby. The scantily dressed female companion rested her ample bosom on their table as she sipped red wine.

Karen's attention turned toward the hostess, who had just approached the reception podium. "Welcome to La Brisa Bistro," she said cheerily. "Do you have a reservation?"

Surprise flashed across Brock's face, "The, uh, brochure said we didn't—"

"There's about a forty-five-minute wait at the moment. Would you like to add your name to the list?"

Brock was clearly disappointed at the news. "I don't suppose you can recommend another restaurant?"

"Well . . . with all these rosa guests—"

"We'll just have to wait," he cut in.

She nodded. "I'm sorry."

"What do you want to do?" he asked Karen.

"Room service?"

"May I offer a suggestion?" the hostess asked.

"Please do," Karen said.

"You may want to try Utopia Town across the courtyard near the lobby entrance."

"The place with the meatballs, right?"

"Sí, they also serve burgers and pizza."

"What do ya think?" Brock asked his wife. "Not as fancy as I'd hoped, but . . ."

"Honestly, I don't care. I just need to eat something other than strawberries."

He turned back to the hostess. "We'll take your suggestion. Thank you. I'd like to go ahead and get our names on the list for tomorrow night."

She scanned the reservation list and nodded. "What time?"

"Six o'clock," Brock said. "Under Skaryd."

"S-ska—?"

He spelled it for her.

"Gracias, señor. I have you down for tomorrow evening at six."

Nestled on the grounds just across from the lobby was a charming small town. It was advertised as a delightful haven for guests seeking simple culinary experiences with a touch of local flair. It featured four casual restaurants and a variety of shops.

A strategically placed map outside the town entrance guided visitors to the culinary and retail adventures awaiting them.

"Here we go," Brock said, reading from the list of eateries. "Burger Bliss, Pizza Paradiso, Casa del Sabor, and Trattoria del Sol."

"We haven't had good meatballs in a while. That Trattoria place?"

"Works for me," he said.

Boutique shops lined cobbled streets, offering an array of local crafts, souvenirs, and curated treasures. The Trattoria del Sol was nestled between the burger joint and a boutique selling an assortment of t-shirts, gifts, and other tchotchkes.

Each restaurant posted a menu outside. This one featured typical Italian fare, along with an assortment of delectable desserts. While the Skaryds scanned the selections, a couple exited the restaurant. The aroma of garlic and herbs filled the air.

"Mmm, yes please." Brock smiled as he held the door open for his wife.

They were greeted immediately.

"How many?"

"Two," Brock said.

"Follow me, por favor."

The Skaryds were seated at a six top, one of two tables available.

Brock opened the wine list. "Want a little vino?"

"Sure. We're not driving," she joked.

As they began to peruse the menu, something caught Karen's attention at the front of the restaurant.

Wolfram.

Clad in all black clothing, right down to his shoes, he walked past the hostess stand and directly toward the back of the restaurant. The hostess hurriedly followed behind him. He stopped, turned toward the hostess, gesturing at an occupied table. She nodded, then he spoke into his iWatch.

Moments later, Wolfram's boss, the elegantly dressed gentleman from earlier, walked through the front door, surrounded by the rest of his security detail. Or maybe they were assistants—Karen couldn't tell for sure.

The hostess quietly explained to a couple of four that she needed their table and would seat them elsewhere. "We will provide you with another round of cocktails and dessert on the house," she said, and it was loud enough that Karen could hear. "Por favor, follow me." One of the guests at that table looked like he was about to complain, but when he saw Wolfram waiting nearby with a cocked eyebrow, the gentleman nodded and encouraged his friends to follow the hostess to the new table.

After the party of four departed, a busboy and server swiftly cleared, wiped down, and set the table. Wolfram's boss bowed in thanks then took his seat, and his associates strategically positioned themselves nearby.

"Who is that guy?" Brock whispered.

"He's clearly a somebody."

"Ya, think?"

They glanced back again, this time catching his eye. The detective smiled at the man, who returned their gesture, though his smile didn't reach his eyes. The lack of joy there cut right to Karen's heartstrings.

She whispered, "Aw, Brock, he looks so lonely."

"He's fine."

"I'm just saying—"

"Mm-hmm."

"What?"

"You're 'I'm just saying' means you want me to invite him to join us."

"And?"

"Babe, c'mon," he said. "Let's just order some appetizers."

"Fine," was her curt response, and she sipped her water.

An unmistakable chill now filled the space between the Skaryds.

Brock sighed and placed his napkin on the table. "I'll be right back."

He made his way toward the man's table, an action that immediately put his security guys on alert. Three of the four bodyguards formed a triangle between their principal and the approaching target. Even the restaurant staff seemed to be wary of the move, on edge.

Wolfram intercepted Brock. "Can I help you, señor?"

Karen hurried over to her husband's side. "Brock, maybe it's best that we leave it alone, like you said."

As if Karen hadn't said a word, Brock held out his hand, which Wolfram only glared at. Brock brought his arm back to his side. "My wife and I would like to invite this man—" he motioned "—to join us for dinner."

"Hi, Wolfram." Smiling, Karen wiggled her fingers at the big guy.

A slight nod. "Detective."

"I hope you don't mind us offering," she said. "It's just—"

Wolfram cut her off. "He appreciates the offer, Detective, pero, no thank you. Why don't you return to your seats?"

"Shouldn't you ask him?" Brock said, motioning again at the man seated at the table, who was expressionless.

"There's no need. Senator Ortiz dines alone."

Senator, huh? Well, that answers a few questions.

The hostess walked over. "Is there a problem?"

"No," Karen said, then took her husband's hand. *We don't need this shit.* "C'mon, Brock. Let's just go back to our table. We did the right thing, and they've declined. Moving on."

As they turned to walk away, Karen heard the senator say, "Wolfram, ven aquí."

She and Brock slowly turned around. It was the first time they had heard his voice—an authoritative whisper with a Spanish lilt. Like someone who had enjoyed too many cigars.

Wincing like a child about to get in trouble, Wolfram moved to the senator's side. The two men exchanged words while the hostess and the Skaryds stood about fifteen feet away and waited. Moments later, the gent stood and, with an air of seasoned authority, approached the couple. Wolfram followed close behind him.

Then Wolfram stepped up and said, "Señor y señora, allow me to introduce you to mi jefe, Senator Juan Carlos Ortiz, de la Provincia La Altagracia, retired."

Karen almost curtsied, the introduction was worthy of royalty. Brock wiped his hand on his shorts—and she knew he was suddenly feeling nervous—before extending it to Senator Ortiz.

"It's a, uh, pleasure to meet you. My name is William Skaryd, but everyone calls me Brock. And this is my wife, Karen."

"Un placer conocerte," the senator said and shook Brock's hand. "Señora . . ."

Like any professional politician who'd performed this act a thousand times, he took Karen's hand and kissed the back, causing her cheeks to flush.

"Oh, well, yes . . . thank you, Senator—"

"Por favor, call me Juan Carlos."

"Juan Carlos it is," she said. "Please, won't you join us for dinner?"

"As you Americans say, it would be my pleasure." He took Karen's outstretched hand and escorted her to the Skaryds' table, Brock and Wolfram in tow. The other three bodyguards repositioned themselves, and the wait staff kicked it into high gear, setting down another place setting.

Juan Carlos held Karen's chair for her as she sat and waited for Brock to do the same before taking his own seat across the table.

"Thank you for inviting me to join you."

"Any time," Brock said.

"You seemed—" Karen started, then bit her tongue. She couldn't tell this distinguished man that he seemed lonely.

"Sí?" the senator pressed.

Oh hell. In for a pound . . . "You seemed so . . . I don't know exactly how to say it."

"Alone?"

"Yes," she whispered, feeling sheepish.

This observation appeared to amuse the retired politician. His chuckle diffused any tension that lingered at the table.

"The life of a retired politician," he said with a hint of melancholy. "And as they say, I've been called worse."

Brock laughed, which elicited a genuine smile from their guest.

"A former colleague once told me that solitude is often a friend of those who have seen much. One must learn to embrace it. And in public life, you are rarely alone, but in retirement . . . you realize how much of yourself you've given away."

The table got quiet as they digested the senator's political wisdom.

"Yet, here I am with new friends," he added, spreading his arms wide. Then he turned his attention on Karen. "Wolfram mentioned that you are a policía back home."

"Yes, a homicide detective." Karen said.

"She's also a former FBI agent," Brock interjected.

Senator Ortiz raised his brows. "That's very impressive. And what about you, mi amigo? Are you also in law enforcement?"

"Me? No, no." Brock chuckled. "I'm a plumber. I own a plumbing business."

"So, an officer and a tradesman," Ortiz said.

"That's us." Brock smiled, squeezing Karen's hand with affection.

A server approached with a bottle of cabernet, but Wolfram intercepted him and examined the bottle. Seconds passed, then a nod, apparently a signal that the nervous server could proceed to the table.

After the server poured a small sampling of wine into the senator's glass, Juan Carlos swirled, sniffed, and tasted the red liquid with practiced ease. "Very good," he said, and the server filled their glasses.

Juan Carlos raised his glass. "To never truly being alone."

The Skaryds returned the gesture. Karen took a sip of the cabernet and found it smooth but unremarkable, with the kind of bite that reminded her why she usually stuck to beer. Brock, ever the polite connoisseur, smacked his lips appreciatively, more than likely following the senator's lead.

They slipped into casual conversation, the wine acting as a social lubricant.

"What's it like being a senator?" Brock asked, swirling his glass of vino.

Juan Carlos paused, a thoughtful expression forming as he leaned back, his fingers loosely cradling the stem of his wineglass.

"Being a senator was, how you say, complex. It was like being both el capitán and un pasajero—a captain and a passenger."

"How so?" Karen asked, intrigued.

"Every day brings new challenges. It's about listening—truly listening—to the voices of the people, understanding their needs, hopes, and dreams. Like this wine," he added, raising his glass, "it's a balance—knowing when to lead and when to let the moment guide you."

Karen nodded slowly as she soaked in his viewpoint, holding her own glass between the fingers of both hands, the layers of the cabernet mirroring the layers of their conversation.

"And yet," Juan Carlos added, "you must navigate the undercurrents of policy, of politics ... balancing expectations with reality. It's a delicate dance."

"What's the hardest part?" Brock asked.

Juan Carlos chuckled. "Ah, the hardest part? Well, one might say it's keeping everyone happy. But in truth, it's finding the balance between staying true to your values and adapting to the ever-changing tides. Leadership is, how you say . . . fluid, you understand."

"And what's one decision that stands out to you?" Karen asked. "Anything definitive?"

The man offered a small smile, a glint of amusement in his eyes. "Every decision is significant, mi amiga. In the moment, you weigh options, consider outcomes, and then you move forward. Each choice shapes the future in its own way, though rarely in the way one anticipates. You learn to trust the process, and in time, the path reveals itself."

"So, no regrets, then?" Brock asked.

Juan Carlos took a measured sip of wine, his expression serene. "Regrets are part of life's journey, amigo. But as for politics? One must focus not on what could have been, but on what can still be done. There's always another horizon, another opportunity to make things right, if one is lucky."

"You politicians sure know how to talk around a question," Brock joked.

Juan Carlos grinned, raising his glass again. "Ah, but isn't life itself about navigating the questions we're not ready to answer?"

Karen lifted her glass with a knowing smile.

Even though none of them had placed an order, servers arrived with a fresh antipasti salad filled with local cheeses, marinated olives, and grilled vegetables, along with a charcuterie board featuring cured prosciutto, spicy Calabrese salami, dried mangoes, figs, locally sourced honey, and rosemary-infused crackers.

Brock's eyes widened, as did Karen's, though her expression was far less obvious. Brock was an open book, and that was one of the many reasons she loved him. Though sometimes . . . she wouldn't be opposed to him being less open.

Her husband rubbed his hands together. "Now that's what I call a spread."

"Brock ..." she started.

He raised his hands. "Wha?"

"It is all right, Detective."

"Karen, please."

He bowed respectfully. "Por supuesto, Karen. Let him enjoy."

"See? He wants me to enjoy," Brock said, reaching for the prosciutto.

"Fine, but remember what your doctor said about your cholesterol."

"Babe, we're on vacation."

Juan Carlos casually lifted his glass toward the server—the signal for more wine. Brock filled his plate with vigor. Karen chose only a few morsels for herself. She didn't want to ruin her appetite for the main course, whatever that might be.

As they savored the local flavors mixed with Italian classics, the conversation turned to the Skaryds' meet-cute story.

"Tell me, Brock. How did you meet your delightful esposa?"

"Prison," he joked, causing Juan Carlos to nearly spit out his wine.

"He's kidding." Karen gave her husband a warning look as she smacked his arm. "Tell him you're kidding."

The senator wagged his finger, chuckling. "That was very funny, mi amigo."

"Seriously, though, we met at a local park," Brock said. "She was out jogging. I was playing softball with some friends."

"Deveras?"

"Yes," Karen took over. "A foul ball nearly hit me, and this guy here came running over to retrieve the ball."

"And to check on your well-being," Brock added.

"Uh huh. Anyway, one thing led to another—"

"And we've been together ever since," her proud husband finished for her. "Married twenty-five years this month."

"Veinticinco, wow," Juan Carlos said. "Muy impresionante."

"And what about you? Is there a missus senator?" Karen asked.

Before he could answer, the main course arrived along with another bottle of wine. A selection of veal osso buco with sprigs of rosemary, grilled branzino with herbs, and garlic-rubbed lamb chops.

This guy doesn't kid around, Karen thought, feeling a moment of gratitude for how this evening had unfolded.

Brock seemed to approve of the spread as well, nodding and saying, "That's what I'm talking about." Yet, as he continued to scan the plates on the table, there was a shift in his demeanor. *Is he disappointed with something?*

"What's the matter?" she whispered.

"Ah, nothing," he said, but she knew it was a lie. "It's just . . . all this fancy stuff, and no meatballs."

She could barely contain an eye roll. *Him and his meatballs.* "You'll survive."

"Is everything okay?" Juan Carlos asked.

"Yes, everything looks perfect, right, Brock?"

A quick glance at Karen, then he put on a fake smile. "Yeah, no, everything's perfect."

The senator eyed his guests, understanding dawning in his expression. "Well, I may not have FBI training or a detective's badge, but I am a father of four, so I know disappointment when I see it. What's wrong? We will make it right."

Karen looked down at her lap, shaking her head. Brock cleared his throat, then, "I was just hoping to see their famous meatballs."

Juan Carlos raised his index finger, and a server appeared. Within minutes, fresh meatballs smothered in red sauce were delivered to the table.

"Much appreciated," Brock said, spearing a meatball, then another.

Karen said, "Juan Carlos, you didn't need to do that, but thank you."

He spread his hands. "Ah, it is my pleasure. Just look at his face."

She glanced at her husband, who waggled his eyebrows and took a big bite of his favorite Italian add-on.

CHAPTER 10

Their pleasant meal lasted a couple of hours, after which Juan Carlos offered the couple an opportunity to join him on his yacht the following day. "If you don't already have plans, of course."

"No, yeah, I mean . . ." Brock stammered.

Karen placed her hand on her husband's wrist. "What he's trying to say is, we'd love to."

Juan Carlos gestured for Wolfram to come closer, and the big guy leaned down for further instructions. They were spoken quietly into Wolfram's ear, and Karen couldn't catch a single word.

The senator then stood. "Wolfram here will provide you with all the details. Until tomorrow."

"Until tomorrow," Brock said.

The exchanged handshakes, and Juan Carlos left, as quickly as he'd entered, surrounded by three of his four body men. Wolfram stayed behind briefly to share the details of tomorrow's adventure.

"We will sail out in the late morning."

"What time exactly?" Karen asked.

"Be there at half past nine."

"And what should we bring . . .?"

"Just yourselves." He smiled. "Trust me."

"If you say so," she said.

As Wolfram made his way to the exit, Brock called out, "Hey, Wolfram. You never told us which boat."

He glanced back at them and said, "She knows."

"Of course she does," Brock whispered, earning a smile from his wife.

The following morning, after sharing a light continental breakfast, the Skaryds arrived at the docks at 9:30 on the nose. A salty breeze filled the air as they walked toward Juan Carlos's sleek yacht named *Libertad*—Spanish for *Freedom*.

"Wow, wow, wow." Brock marveled at the luxury boats lined up along the marina.

Karen noticed his gaze lingering on a catamaran. On the dock beside it, a skimpy-bikini-clad Chloe and shorts-and-T-shirt-wearing Cal were about to set off for their own adventure. A sexy, bare-chested Latino stood confidently on the boat, grinning widely—apparently, their captain. The man's laidback, jovial demeanor promised an unforgettable day at sea. A gold cross and chain glinted against his tanned chest, catching the sunlight with every movement as he gestured for Chloe and Cal to board.

"Looks like we're not the only ones heading out today," Karen said as they approached a steep gangplank to the deck of Juan Carlos's yacht.

As the pair stepped onto the *Libertad*, they were welcomed aboard by Wolfram, Captain Alejandro, and an attendant named Camilla, who was holding two flutes of champagne.

The captain, standing tall in a crisp white uniform, had large brown eyes that conveyed both professionalism and a hint of curiosity as he welcomed them with a polite bow and a firm handshake for each.

"El señor y la señora Skaryd, on behalf of my crew, it's an honor to have you join us."

Karen took a deep inhale of the salty air. "Thank you for having us."

Brock, on the other hand, seemed a little less sure as he tread carefully, his arms outstretched, as if he were walking along a balance beam. "Uh, yeah, thanks."

No sea legs for my husband. Maybe he'll get the hang of it before the trip ends.

Dressed elegantly in a chic nautical outfit, Camilla stepped forward with a genuine smile and handed a glass of champagne to each of them.

"Bienvenido—welcome," she said in a lilting Dominican accent, "Please make yourselves comfortable. If there's anything you need today, do not hesitate to ask."

Camilla's eyes lingering on the Skaryds and then on their surroundings, Karen noted, suggesting the hostess was taking in every detail so as not to miss a potential need.

Wolfram wore dark shades, further adding to his mystique. Still in all black clothing, he stood a few steps back with his arms crossed, offered a silent nod, subtly asserted his protective presence.

Easy there, cowboy.

Captain Alejandro gestured toward the deck's lounge, while the yacht crew moved seamlessly into action, making it clear that Karen and Brock were about to experience a day of refined hospitality—but under a watchful eye. Nothing on this yacht would be left to chance.

"Will Juan Carlos be joining us?" Karen asked as she and Brock each sunk into a well-cushioned lounge chair.

As if on cue, the smooth, yet authoritative voice of the senator drifted across the deck. "But of course," Juan Carlos said, appearing from a shaded doorway, holding a glass of champagne.

Dressed in a white linen shirt and tailored slacks, he moved with relaxed confidence, clearly in his element.

"I wouldn't miss this for the world," he continued, nodding to Camilla, who quickly arranged a chair beside the Skaryds' lounge chairs. "After all, what's a day at sea without good company?"

He settled into the chair, gesturing toward the view of the sparkling blue water. "I trust you're ready for a day you won't forget."

Camilla handed out an elegantly printed itinerary. While reviewing her copy, Karen appreciated the level of detail, from weather expectations to a personalized menu. She glanced up to find Juan Carlos watching her, and she adjusted her sunglasses and smiled. "It's wonderful," she said.

"Music to my ears. Think of today as an extension of last evening," the senator said, lifting his glass of champagne as the engines came to life. "May this day bring us laughter, adventure, and perhaps a few surprises—because life, like the sea, is always richer with a touch of the unexpected."

Brock lifted his glass. "To the journey ahead."

"Salud," Juan Carlos said, his eyes glinting with a hint of mischief and mystery.

CHAPTER 11

The yacht pulled away from the dock, gliding over the azure waters off the Dominican coast. Karen settled back onto her plush lounger, a sense of contentment filling her as her husband did the same. The clinked glasses, then turned their faces to the sun and the gentle breeze.

Juan Carlos, ever the gracious host, shared the day's itinerary. They would cruise along the coastline, stopping at scenic locales, while he attended to a few personal matters.

"You have full use of the yacht, and Camilla will see to your every need."

Brock perked up when he heard this comment.

Karen held back a giggle. *Easy, tiger.*

Their first stop was Isla Catalina, a small island known for its stunning beaches and coral reefs. They were provided with snorkeling gear, and Captain Alejandro gave them a few pointers on the best spots.

"If you swim out about fifty feet, you'll come to the Wall," he informed them.

"You mean like Pink Floyd?" Brock asked cheekily, causing Juan Carlos to cock an eyebrow.

Captain Alejandro chuckled. "Not quite, señor. It's a reef that drops about a hundred feet. Ideal for seeing fish up close."

"Cool," Brock whispered.

"The other spot—" the captain gestured toward the shore "—is called El Aquarium."

"Really? How come?" Karen asked.

"The water is very calm and offers excellent visibility. It will feel like you're swimming in a fishbowl. You'll see."

"Enjoy, mis amigos," Juan Carlos said before departing on a tender boat with three of his four body men. Wolfram stayed behind.

The Skaryds spent a few hours exploring the vibrant underwater world, teeming with colorful fish and coral, while Juan Carlos attended to his business. Though Karen enjoyed her time swimming, she found herself wishing her father and children could have been there to share in the experience.

"Missing the kids?" Brock asked as he swam toward her with his swim mask and snorkel on top of his head.

"What makes you say that?"

"You might be a detective, but you're not the only one who notices things."

"Whatever." She playfully splashed him. *He knows me all too well.*

"I thought so," he said. "Ready to swim back?"

"Yep."

Camilla offered the pair refreshing hibiscus-infused water glasses and lightly chilled towels upon their return to the yacht.

"Lunch will be ready in an hour," she informed them. "In the meantime, we've arranged a relaxing massage on deck. Come this way, por favor."

"Massage?" Brock whispered. "Hot damn."

They stretched out under the shade of the yacht's canopy as expert masseuses worked out any lingering tension. Between the massage and the luxurious surroundings, Karen felt herself relaxing in a way she hadn't in ages—and in particular, the tension from Diana's recent death momentarily eased.

For lunch, the staff outdid themselves, offering a selection of locally inspired dishes: lobster grilled with lime and garlic; ceviche made with freshly caught fish; and Dominican-style empanadas filled with spiced beef and cheese.

For dessert, they enjoyed tres leches cake topped with caramelized mangoes.

"Jesus, Ka, does it get any better than this?" Brock said while sipping on a chilled Dominican rum concoction.

"It does not," she said.

While they lingered over lunch, basking in the gentle sway of the yacht, Karen noticed a sleek catamaran passing in the distance. Chloe and Cal, the millennials from the resort, were aboard. Chloe was laughing and taking selfies with their bare-chested captain, while Cal gripped a nearby rope for dear life.

"That poor kid."

Brock followed her gaze. "Ah, he'll be fine. But I have to admit, there's a big difference between what we've got here, and what he's dealing with over there. Yeah, you're right: that poor kid."

As the afternoon wore on, Juan Carlos reappeared, looking refreshed and in good spirits. He invited Brock to join him for a cigar and rum, while Camilla offered to accompany Karen to the salon for a manicure. Wolfram followed the ladies.

"Babysitting duty?" Karen quipped, glancing back at her shadow.

Wolfram exhaled quietly. His irritation was subtle but unmistakable.

"Ay, mija! These hands," Luz, the manicurist, exclaimed as Karen settled into the chair.

Karen flushed. "Yeah, it's tough when you're busy chasing down criminals."

Intrigued, Luz paused. "¿Eres policía?"

"A detective."

"Whoa, impressive. But even detectives need pretty nails, no?"

"Well, my hands have been through a lot."

Luz waved her off playfully. "Let's see if I can work my magic."

She began massaging Karen's fingers with fragrant almond oil, the soothing aroma helping Karen relax. Across the room, Wolfram sat, ever alert, his gaze flicking occasionally in Karen's direction.

Karen called out to him, "So, Wolfram … any thoughts on that incident yesterday?"

"A few, Detective," he said coolly.

Luz raised an eyebrow but continued the manicure.

"Care to elaborate?"

A brief pause, then, "Not here."

He gestured toward the deck and left the salon.

Okayyy. I guess I'm following him.

When Karen excused herself mid-manicure, Luz clicked her tongue in disapproval, reminding the Detective of her own Dominican mother. "Ay, Dios mío. Leaving already? I'm not done making your hands beautiful."

Karen offered an apologetic smile. "I know, Luz, and trust me, I know I need your magic. I promise to be back pronto to finish what we started."

"Mm-hmm, I'll hold you to that, mija," Luz said with a playful yet stern look. "Don't make me track you down. Even detectives need a little pampering."

"I wouldn't dare cross you, Luz," and with a wink, Karen went to find Wolfram.

CHAPTER 12

Karen stepped out onto the deck—the ocean breeze caressing her face and Wolfram up ahead. She decided to let him take the lead, resisting the urge to interrogate him like a suspect. Experience had taught her that, sometimes, silence was the best way to get someone to reveal the truth.

Wolfram leaned up against the railing, looking out over the water. The soft hum of the yacht's engines provided a degree of privacy. She mimicked his position.

Leaning toward her, he spoke in a low tone. "That's our next stop." He gestured out over the water to a coastline—a picturesque blend of terracotta roofs, sleek yachts, and bustling dockside activity, framed by the lush cliffs of Altos de Chavón.

"Wow, looks like someone dropped the Hamptons into the Caribbean."

"It's called, La Marina Casa de Campo. I caught my first homicide there as a subcomisario de DICRIM—that's a deputy commissioner with the Central Directorate of Criminal Investigations."

"Oh yeah?"

"Sí. Robbery gone wrong—a shopkeeper stabbed to death. I was so green," Wolfram reflected. "My boss was Manuel Espinosa . . . a real cop's cop, you know?"

Karen smiled and nodded slightly, reflecting on her own experience with supervisors she'd admired over the years.

"He yelled at me to stop stepping over the evidence. Just like you told the people in the restaurant yesterday. Anyway, that homicide . . . well, the shopkeeper's lifeless eyes haunted me for weeks, and I nearly lost my lunch on the scene."

"Been there."

"Reminded me of tu esposo's reaction."

"Yeah, you'd figure someone who's been married to a cop for twenty-five years could handle those types of things by now," Karen said. "Especially a plumber who's used to dealing with . . . well, you know what."

"Sí. Pero death is different than mierda," he said.

"Let me ask you," Karen began, her tone light, "is this kind of hospitality typical for the senator? Inviting strangers onto his yacht, treating them to five-star luxury?"

Wolfram's lips twitched into a faint smile. "Juan Carlos has a reputation for generosity. Especially when he's cultivating relationships."

"Cultivating relationships?" Karen repeated, raising an eyebrow. "Sounds like a euphemism for something less than pleasant, no?"

"It depends on who you ask," Wolfram said cryptically, his eyes scanning the marina. "He's a man who values connections. They say his influence extends far beyond this island."

Karen leaned casually against the railing, letting the lull of the waves set the rhythm of their conversation. "And does his generosity usually extend to strangers who happen to be staying at a resort where someone mysteriously dies?"

Wolfram's gaze flicked toward her, sharp but measured. "You have quite a direct way of asking questions, Detective."

"It's a gift," Karen smiled. "But seriously, what's the word on what happened? Someone like you must have heard something."

He hesitated, his gaze drifting out to the water. "People talk. Especially when they're nervous. But it's mostly whispers—nothing solid. Yet."

Karen nodded, not wanting to push too hard. "Whispers have a funny way of growing louder when the right ears are listening."

Wolfram chuckled softly. "I'll keep that in mind."

Karen nodded, and a silent understanding passed between them. Wolfram didn't reveal any specifics, but it was clear he had an inside source, someone who could be pivotal to the investigation.

"Perdon, señora Karen," Camilla said, breaking the moment as she approached, a blend of charm and efficiency. "We will be docking soon."

"Okay, Camilla."

"Y el senator has offered to give you a personal tour of the marina and insists on showing you the best spots himself."

Wolfram excused himself. "I better get ready. You're in for a treat."

The yacht docked smoothly at La Marina Casa de Campo, its polished deck gleaming under the Caribbean sun. Karen stepped onto the pier, taking in the scene. The marina buzzed with activity—luxury yachts moored side by side, boutique-lined streets bustling with well-heeled shoppers, and the scent of fresh seafood mingling with salt air.

Across the way, that same catamaran caught her eye. Chloe and Cal were in the process of disembarking. Chloe had layered a vibrant sundress over her bikini, posing dramatically in front of the boat with the captain at her side. Then she entwined her arm with the captain's and they ventured off into town, while her husband, Cal, trailed behind like a dutiful lapdog.

As Karen turned her attention back to the marina, she spotted the wealthy May-December, and she couldn't help but wonder at the fact that everyone from the resort seemed to be here.

The couple walked toward an upscale jewelry store, and Karen chuckled, shaking her head.

Looks like someone's getting another pretty bauble.

"Karen, Brock . . . over here," the senator called out, gesturing toward a path flanked by armed guards.

He led the Skaryds through the marina with effortless authority, pointing out fine dining spots and private lounges. His protection unit shadowed him, their eyes scanning every face and alley.

"This place is incredible," Karen began casually. "It's easy to see why people come here for a sense of security ... and privacy."

Juan Carlos pointed at a boutique just up ahead. "Casa de Campo prides itself on being a haven for the elite. Some might say that privacy is its currency."

Karen tilted her head thoughtfully. "I imagine that privacy is sometimes complicated, especially when things go wrong. Like what happened yesterday at the resort—a woman dies suddenly."

The senator paused, his faint smile not quite reaching his eyes. This time, though, she didn't see loneliness, but more of a calculating stare. Maybe she'd pressed a hot button. "Sí, a most unfortunate incident."

His polished response was expected, but the hesitation beforehand was telling, which added to her growing list of clues.

Juan Carlos's cell phone rang, its distinct tone cutting through the marina's ambient hum, interrupting their conversation. He glanced at the screen, his expression briefly tightening before he stepped aside, the phone pressed to his ear.

"Sí," he murmured, his voice low but sharp, the polished veneer slipping for just a moment.

Karen's brow arched. *Hmmm...*

With his back turned to Karen and Brock, the senator spoke rapidly in Spanish, his tone alternating between terse and commanding. Karen couldn't make out the words, but the urgency in his posture was unmistakable.

"What's going on?" Brock asked in a low voice, probably picking up on her alert posture.

"Shh, not now. I'll tell you later."

The senator's free hand gestured subtly, and one of his guards stepped closer, murmuring something into his wrist mic. Moments later, Juan Carlos ended the call and returned, his usual composed smile firmly back in place.

"Mis disculpas," he said smoothly. "Something urgent has come up. I'm afraid I must leave you in the capable hands of Wolfram for the rest of your tour and ride back to the resort. Enjoy the marina—I'm certain we will speak again soon."

Without waiting for a reply, he signaled his team and strode off, his guards flanking him tightly, leaving Karen with more questions than answers.

Wolfram's body language also spoke volumes. She knew he hated playing babysitter. After watching his team walk off, he released a slow breath, turned to the pair, and tossed on a fake smile.

Brock apparently saw right through it, not that it was difficult to do. "Dude, look—" he started.

Karen held up her hand, cutting him off. "Honey, let it go."

"No, I won't. He clearly doesn't want to do this. And that's all right," Brock said, turning back to Wolfram. "We're adults. We can find our way around without you escorting us."

"Wolfram, he's right. We do appreciate your time," she said, her tone neutral, but her intent was to probe. "I'm sure you've got plenty of other duties, though. Hmm?"

Wolfram hesitated, his gaze darting back to where the senator had disappeared. Karen noted the flicker of unease in his usually controlled demeanor.

"Not at all," Wolfram said finally, though his words lacked conviction. "Let me show you the private galleries. They're reserved for high-profile guests."

Karen exchanged a look with Brock, curiosity sparking between them. "Lead the way," she said, following Wolfram as he guided them toward a shadowy corridor between the boutiques.

CHAPTER 13

The gallery was elegant and understated, the walls lined with art that exuded wealth and exclusivity. The Dominican art burst with bold colors and depictions of local life. On the other hand, the more minimalist designs showcased muted sophistication and European elegance.

Karen allowed herself to admire the pieces briefly before turning her attention to Wolfram, whose nervous energy was palpable.

"Wolfram," Karen began, her voice low, "you've worked with the senator for some time, haven't you?"

He stopped abruptly, turning to face her. "Why do you want to know?"

"Just curious about the man of the hour. Even though he's retired, he still seems . . . influential."

"That is one word for it," Wolfram muttered under his breath. He started to say something else—perhaps to smooth over his obvious slip—but instead he shook his head and looked away, moving toward the grouping of art.

Brock and Karen glanced at each other with raised eyebrows, then followed. Just as they were about to enter the next gallery, Wolfram's phone buzzed, the sharp tone breaking the quiet of the space. Karen noticed his reaction—tense, almost startled. He looked at the screen, his jaw tightening.

"Excuse me," he said, quickly stepping back the way they'd come. "Go on ahead without me, please."

Another glance between husband and wife, then Karen shifted her focus to Wolfram, who had moved near a sculpture, his back to them. Like Juan Carlos's tone earlier, his was low but urgent, speaking in rapid Spanish.

Karen strained to hear, and though she couldn't pick up the words, it was the tone that unsettled her—an unmistakable edge. Panic? Anger? No . . . more like someone managing a crisis.

"Everything okay?" Karen asked upon his return.

Wolfram pocketed his phone and rocked back and forth—heels to toes, heels to toes. "That call . . . it was from my, uh, mole at INACIF. That's the National Institute of Forensic Sciences."

"Oh really? Sounds important. What is that exactly?" Brock asked.

"It's our version of, how you say, the coroner's office," Wolfram said. "Preliminary autopsy results just came in for la rubia."

"The blonde?" Brock said, surprising both Wolfram and Karen. "What? I took Spanish in high school."

"Anyway, you were saying?" Karen prompted Wolfram, her expression sharpening.

"Two things. First, when they brought her in, an earring was missing."

Karen's eyes narrowed.

"Sounds like sloppy police work," Brock chimed in.

"With this team investigating the case, it's possible, yes."

"Maybe." Karen replied. "What's the second thing."

"She was poisoned," Wolfram said quietly. "They haven't figured out what type of toxin yet, but it was fast-acting, likely administered just before her collapse."

Brock whistled softly. "So, someone *really* wanted her dead. Do they know who?"

Wolfram shook his head. "No suspects yet, but they're actively looking for a server named Mario and the woman the victim argued with before she died."

"Makes sense, but you say 'actively looking.' Can they not find the server and that woman for some reason?"

"I didn't say that."

"It was very implied in the words *actively looking*." She crossed her arms.

"I just meant they are going to question them, I guess. I don't know all the details. But . . ." His voice trailed off and he didn't finish his thought. Instead, he pursed his lips. *Zipping it*, so to speak.

Karen rolled her eyes. "Come on, Wolfram. Spill it. But what?"

"But . . . those two are not the only ones the cops want to speak to."

Brock jumped in with, "Oh, yeah? Who else is on their list?"

"Usted, señor," Wolfram said flatly.

CHAPTER 14

Karen instinctively gasped, and Brock stiffened beside her. "Wait. Are they trying to pin this on me?" he asked.

"I'm sure that's not the case," Karen said, placing a gentle hand on his arm. "Stay calm. I'm sure they want to talk to all the rosarians. Right, Wolfram?"

The man hesitated. "Maybe, sure."

"So far it's just Brock?" she pressed.

Wolfram blew out a long sigh. "A witness claims he was seen talking to her earlier in the day. I would say it's just routine questioning."

"Routine, my ass," Brock countered. "Do I need to get a lawyer?"

"No," Wolfram said firmly, "but your wife knows how these things work. They're chasing every lead, and you are part of the timeline."

Karen's mind raced with angles and theories. "Poisoning means premeditation. Someone planned this, likely with access to the resort's staff or amenities. Did the mole mention anything else?"

"Not yet," Wolfram said, glancing toward the marina entrance. "But this ... uh, changes things."

No shit.

"We should head back," Brock said. "Let's go, babe."

"We will, okay? But give me a minute first," she said, her tone firm yet calm. "Let's take the scenic route back to the yacht. I need to think, and maybe I'll pick up a little thank-you gift for Senator Ortiz while we're at it. After all, he went out of his way to host us."

Brock sighed but nodded, his posture still tense. "Fine, but let's make it quick."

As they strolled back through the marina, Wolfram walking quietly behind them, the setting sun cast golden hues across the water. Karen's sharp eyes caught the May-December couple from earlier, the older man now standing outside an upscale clothing boutique, apparently waiting for his much younger companion who was shopping inside. Karen slowed her pace, observing the scene with interest.

"Looks like someone's getting more goodies," Karen murmured under her breath.

"What's that?" Brock asked.

Karen shook her head. "Nothing. Let's keep moving."

A few steps later, Karen noticed another familiar sight: Chloe, Cal, and the catamaran captain. Chloe was draped over the captain, laughing and snapping selfies with her perfectly manicured fingers. It was a loud and carefree moment, as if the world were hers alone. As always, it seemed, Cal followed behind them, his posture slouched and his hands shoved deep into his pockets. He looked up briefly, catching Karen's gaze, then quickly looked away.

"Chloe certainly wastes no time," Karen remarked.

Brock scoffed. "That Cal kid looks like he's ready to swim back to the resort."

As they approached the dock where their yacht was moored, Karen tugged Brock's arm. "Wait here a second. I'm going to pop into that boutique over there and find something for Juan Carlos."

"You're serious?" Brock asked, exasperated. "Can't this wait? The resort has tons of shops."

Karen turned to him, her expression resolute. "No, this can't wait. We need to play this smart."

"What do you mean?"

"First, we need to thank Juan Carlos for his kindness. Second, depending on the way things go, it's crucial that we keep someone like him on our side."

Brock threw up his hands. "Fine, but hurry up."

Karen darted into a boutique, her eyes scanning the carefully curated displays of fine cigars, luxury pens, and ornate cufflinks. She settled on a box of expensive Dominican cigars, rich and earthy, wrapped in a velvet ribbon.

Perfect.

When she rejoined Brock, he was leaning against a post, his jaw tight as he stared at the yacht. Wolfram had gone ahead of them and now stood by the gangplank, his expression unreadable.

"Got it," Karen said, holding up the gift bag.

"Great. Can we go now?" Brock asked, his patience clearly gone.

They boarded the yacht, and the unspoken tension between the three of them seemed to make the air heavier. A totally different mood from when they'd arrived. The hum of the engine was soothing, but Karen couldn't stop her runaway thoughts. The May-December couple, Chloe's antics, the poison—all the threads of the day tangled together in her mind.

Brock broke the silence. "So, what's your plan?"

Karen leaned against the railing, the salty breeze brushing her face as she stared out over the water. She absently ran her fingers over her partially manicured nails.

"First, we get back to the resort. Then, I start pulling at the loose threads. Whoever poisoned Diana planned this carefully, but killers like that always leave something behind, despite themselves."

"And if they try to drag me into this?"

Karen pushed off the railing and hugged her husband. "They won't. Not if I can help it."

Before Brock could reply, Camilla approached, her voice cutting through the hum of the yacht's engine.

"Señora Karen," she said, her tone apologetic, "the manicurist, Luz, was asking about you. She wants to know if you're ready to finish your nails."

"I guess I better before she hunts me down. Besides," she added, glancing at Brock with a wry smile, "I think better when my hands are busy."

CHAPTER 15

The steady rhythm of the boat's engine blended with the soft, precise movements of Luz as she resumed Karen's manicure. Her focus and efficiency mirrored Karen's growing clarity. Karen flexed her hands, admiring the precision of her neutral-toned nails, which complemented her Latina complexion to a tee.

"What am I missing?" she murmured to herself.

"Qué, hija?" Luz asked.

"Hmm? Oh, nothing. I'm just thinking out loud."

Luz smiled. "Mis hijas do the same thing."

"How many daughters do you have?"

"Quatro. My youngest is expecting her second."

"Wow. Congratulations."

They continued their chitchat until the resort's lights came into view, glittering against the golden hues emerging in the late afternoon sky. Just the sight of the resort felt like a weight on Karen's shoulders as she thought about her husband's unexpected situation with the law.

As the yacht glided into the marina, Karen's mind churned with details . . . dots she couldn't quite connect. Luz packed up her tools, giving Karen a warm smile.

"Buena suerte, hija. Whatever is on your mind, you'll figure it out."

Karen returned the smile, grateful for the brief distraction. She retrieved the gift bag with the cigars for Juan Carlos. She placed it on the yacht's polished dining table alongside a handwritten note:

Juan Carlos,

Thank you for your hospitality and generosity today. This is but a small token of our gratitude. We look forward to our next conversation.

Warm regards,
Karen and Brock

Satisfied, she turned to Brock, who had been pacing near the railing. "Ready to go?"

"More than ready," he muttered, his jaw tight.

They disembarked and made their way through the resort, the fading light casting long shadows on the cobblestone paths. By the time they reached their room, the weight of the day hung heavy in the air.

Karen headed straight for the closet, pulling out a soft teal wrap dress.

Brock dragged a clean shirt from his suitcase. "I don't like this, Ka," he said, breaking the silence. "Being dragged into whatever this is—it feels like a setup."

She adjusted her earrings in the mirror, her expression thoughtful.

"Honey, listen. Panicking won't help. We simply stick to the facts and let them chase the shadows."

Brock grumbled but nodded. He knew better than to argue when it came to her cop logic.

A short walk brought them to La Brisa Bistro, for their six o'clock reservation. Like the previous evening, the place hummed with business, and the warm breeze carried the scent of salt and freshly grilled seafood.

The hostess recognized them instantly and seated them immediately. As they approached their reserved table, Karen's sharp eyes caught sight of the millennial couple from earlier. To her surprise, they weren't alone.

Chloe, radiant from her day at sea, was laughing animatedly. Her phone in hand, she snapped selfies with the catamaran captain seated at Chloe's left-hand side. *How many of those damn selfies does she need?* The captain's rugged, sun-weathered face showed amusement as he leaned into the frame. On the other side was Cal, somberly nursing a glass of wine and glancing at his wife with a mix of affection and resignation.

Karen's brows furrowed, and all she could think—again—was, *Poor guy.*

"Come on, babe," Brock said, gently pulling her toward their table. He held the chair for her, and she sat, trying to stay in the moment and not let her thoughts about the day sidetrack her.

She accepted the menu from the hostess with a thank-you, as did Brock, and when their waiter arrived, they ordered drinks—heavy on the alcohol and quickly.

As the night deepened, the bistro's warm lights twinkled like stars. The tension in Karen's chest had begun to ease . . . until her phone vibrated in her purse. She glanced at the screen.

It was a message from Terrell, her partner back home: *Call me when you have a moment.*

Her blood ran cold. He would never interrupt their vacation unless it was something critical. An emergency.

And she had some idea what it might be.

She placed her napkin onto the table, her appetite vanishing. She showed Brock the message and excused herself.

The resort's lush landscaping muffled the chatter and clinking glasses of the bistro as she found a quiet spot near the edge of the terrace. Her fingers hesitated over the WhatsApp call button before she pressed it.

The line barely rang once.

"T, what's going on?" Karen asked.

Terrell Danielson's familiar baritone came through the line, carrying a weight that instantly set her on edge.

"Karen, I hate to interrupt your vacation, but we've got a development."

Her stomach tightened. "It's about the Andrews case, isn't it?" It was an investigation they'd been working on when she left, the victim found near a dumpster behind a convenience store.

"Yeah, and it's worse than we thought," he said, his tone grim. "Charlton Sasso didn't kill her."

Karen froze. "How do we know?"

"We just got back the DNA results from scrapings beneath her nails. It wasn't his."

Karen's mind raced. "Whose is it?"

"We're running it through the system now, but . . . there's more."

"Hit me."

"I think whoever killed the girl also killed Sasso. It wasn't a suicide."

Her breath caught. "But he was in custody . . . hanging from a bed sheet."

"I know, I know," T said. "His parents blamed us, the DA blamed the cops, and LT made us close the case."

Karen's voice sharpened. "I remember it well. What about it?"

"Yeah, well, I had some free time, and I went back through the reports. There were some inconsistencies in the autopsy. Bruising around his neck didn't fully match the ligature marks from the sheet. And get this—the guard on duty that night? He disappeared a week later."

Karen gripped the railing, the cool metal grounding her as the weight of T's words settled.

"Are you saying this was a setup? That someone staged his suicide to keep him quiet?"

"It's what I'm thinking, yeah. We might be dealing with someone who's cleaning up loose ends."

Karen exhaled slowly, her mind shifting gears. "What about the DNA results? Have we compared them to that of guard?"

"Not yet. Like I said—"

"You're running it through the system."

"Yeah, but here's where it gets even stranger."

"How so?"

"The lab tech flagged something unusual about the sample. It's connected to a larger database tied to international activity."

Karen's instincts screamed at the implication. "What kind of activity, T?"

T hesitated. "Trafficking."

The word hit her like a punch to the gut. Her gaze drifted back toward the bistro, where Chloe, Cal, and the boat crew laughed over drinks. She saw Brock sitting at the table, sipping his drink, looking back at the door. For her.

"And Karen," T continued, his voice taut, "there's a name linked to the database—someone who shouldn't have any connection to a small-town murder."

Karen swallowed hard, already knowing she wouldn't like the answer. "Who?"

"Senator Juan Carlos Ortiz."

But she hadn't expected that.

CHAPTER 16

Her knees nearly buckled. "The retired senator from down here in the Dominican Republic?"

"One and the same," T confirmed. "We're still trying to piece it together, but his name and fingerprints are all over this. If he's involved, this thing is way bigger than just a girl behind a dumpster."

"Shit," she hissed. "I had dinner with him last night and spent the day sailing around the island on his big-ass yacht."

"Must be nice."

Karen pulse picked up speed as she pieced together fragments of conversations, odd glances, and buried unease. Something about this wasn't adding up. Not the murder, not Charlton's death, and certainly not Juan Carlos Ortiz's involvement.

The phrase "Keep your friends close, but your enemies closer" looped like a mantra. Questions clawed at her, relentless and sharp.

Did Juan Carlos know about her involvement in the Andrews/Sasso investigation? The senator's polished veneer and calculated charm suddenly seemed far more dangerous. His name tied to Charlton Sasso's alleged suicide wasn't just a coincidence—it was a thread, and Karen was tugging at it with every breath.

And then there was Wolfram. She thought of his steady composure aboard the yacht, the way his words danced just shy of transparency. Was Wolfram connected to this? Did he know more than he let on? His loyalty to Juan Carlos seemed genuine, but in Karen's line of work, loyalty was often a façade.

And what about Diana? Her untimely death at the resort, poisoned in the lap of luxury, felt like the work of someone meticulous—someone with a motive that was still obscure. To her at least. Was there a link between that case and the murder back home? Or were the two just parallel lines destined to collide in the most unexpected way?

Karen's fingers instinctively curled around the edge of the terrace railing. *What am I missing? What do I need to see?* The questions were a drumbeat, steady and insistent, and yet no answer emerged from the haze.

"Karen . . ." T's voice snapped her back to the present. "You good?"

"Define *good*," she muttered, forcing herself to breathe deeply. "This all feels so personal somehow."

"Can't argue that," T said. "But listen, you've got to be careful. If Ortiz knows who you are . . . well, this isn't just about solving a case. It's about staying alive."

Karen nodded to herself, scanning the terrace. The laughter and clinking glasses from the bistro felt distant, a faint echo of normalcy she could no longer touch.

"I hear you, T. But I'm not letting this go. Not now."

"Didn't think you would. Just make sure you don't get tangled up in their game. Play it smart. And if you need me to come down there, I will."

"I'll let you know," she said. "In the meantime, stay on it."

"I will. And if I find out anything new, you'll be the first to know."

"Thanks. Hey, before you go—" Karen adjusted her grip on the phone "—I need a favor."

"Name it," T said, the rustle of papers faint on his end of the line.

"There's been a bit of a complication here," Karen began, carefully choosing her words. "A woman at the resort, Diana St. James, was poisoned. Local authorities are investigating, and they've made it clear they want to question Brock."

There was a beat of silence before T spoke. "Why?"

Karen sighed, her frustration bubbling to the surface. "Apparently because he was seen talking to her. I don't know . . . seems lame. But they're also both members of this rose-grower society, call themselves rosarians, and she and Brock were pretty competitive. There's a big conference for the society here at the resort—I may have mentioned it. It's part of the reason why we're here . . . and to celebrate our twenty-fifth. It's ridiculous, T. He barely spoke to her, but now he's somehow tangled up in this."

"Sounds like they're grasping at straws, to be honest. But I suppose they have to cover all their bases. What do you need me to do?"

"I need you to dig into the lead investigator, Inspector General Rafael Montenegro," she said. "See if there's anything in his background that could be cause for concern—or worse, if he's tied to Juan Carlos Ortiz."

"Montenegro. Got it."

"Maybe I'm just being paranoid."

"Paranoia keeps you alive, Ka. You taught me that. I'll run a check and see what I can dig up. Anything else I should know?"

"Maybe . . ." She paused. Was she grasping at straws? "I've also noticed some tension between Montenegro and Juan Carlos's right-hand man, a guy named Wolfram. Could be personal, could be professional. I don't know yet, but it's enough to make me wonder if there's more under the surface."

T chuckled dryly. "Sounds like you've landed in a soap opera."

"Tell me about it," Karen muttered. "But I need to know if Montenegro's clean or if I should be worried about him or anyone on his team stacking the deck against Brock."

"I'll dig into Montenegro and his connections. Give me a day or two. Watch your six."

"I always do," Karen said, a faint smirk touching her lips, despite the weight of the situation. "Keep me posted, right?"

"Count on it," he said. "And hey, don't let them rattle you. You're the best at untangling this kind of mess."

Karen ended the call, slipping her phone into her pocket. If there was one thing she knew for certain, it was this: the truth always left a trail. It didn't stay hidden forever. She just needed to follow that trail, no matter how many twists and turns it took.

CHAPTER 17

Karen rejoined Brock at the table, her movements deliberate. She tried to maintain a calm-and-cool mask, but her husband didn't buy it for a second.

"What's up?" he asked quietly. "Everything okay?"

"Fine," she said smoothly, the lie leaving a bitter taste in her mouth. "Just work stuff."

He cocked an eyebrow as he took a sip of his drink, his eyes on her. "Mm-hmm."

She waved a dismissive hand. "I'm serious. It's fine. What are we ordering?"

"Not sure yet. I was waiting for you." He opened his menu, and though she did the same, her gaze drifted toward the millennial couple and the catamaran crew. Same snapshot as before: Chloe all over the captain and Cal looking like a third wheel.

Karen lifted her cocktail to her lips and stared at the menu, though the words blurred as her thoughts lingered on her conversation with Terrell and all that had transpired since arriving at the resort. The puzzle pieces were still scattered but starting to align. That phrase repeated in the back of her mind: *Keep your friends close, but your enemies closer.* The problem was, she wasn't entirely sure which was which.

Dinner at La Brisa Bistro was exceptional, but Karen was so distracted she struggled to enjoy it. She toyed with the grilled lobster tail on her plate, slicing it into perfect bites, most of which she never lifted to her mouth. She knew Brock had noticed, but he didn't press her—his own tension was vying for attention. They'd ordered a bottle of merlot to go with the meal, and he drained first glass quickly before pouring another.

"Babe," Brock said, breaking the silence, "what do we do if they come for me?"

She screwed up her face and shook her head. "Why would they?" Karen said. "And if they try anything shifty, they'll have to get through me."

Brock shrugged. "You sound so sure, but . . . we're out of country, and these guys—"

Karen lowered her voice. "Honey, look, I may not know the local players, but I know the game. Trust me. Please."

Brock leaned back with his arms crossed. "You're not going to tell me what's going on in that head of yours, are you? And that phone call has only made it worse."

"I'm trying to connect dots, okay?" she said. "But there are too many moving pieces, so it would be difficult for me to explain right now. I do have T digging into that Inspector Montenegro for me. I'll know more soon."

Before he could respond, a familiar voice interrupted.

"Señora Karen. Señor Brock. Good evening."

Senator Ortiz stood at their table. His tailored linen suit was impeccable despite the humid Caribbean air. A faint smile curled his lips, but Karen didn't miss the sharpness in his eyes.

"Juan Carlos," Karen said, recovering quickly and offering a polite smile, "what brings you here?"

He gestured toward his bodyguards. "I had a meeting earlier and saw you dining here. I thought it only polite to say hello."

"Care to join us?" Karen asked.

"You wouldn't be intruding," Brock added, forcing enthusiasm into his voice. "Please, have a seat."

The senator hesitated briefly before sliding into the chair beside Karen. His bodyguards stepped back to a discreet distance.

"How has the evening been treating you?" Juan Carlos asked, his tone upbeat and casual.

Karen put on a pleasant expression she didn't feel. "It's been a lovely evening. The food here is excellent."

"And your day on the yacht? I trust it was enjoyable?"

"It was great," Brock said quickly, reaching for his wine. "Thank you again for inviting us."

"I hope it helped ease the unpleasantness of yesterday."

Karen's grip on her fork tightened. Every word he spoke felt calculated.

"Yes," she said lightly. "It was a welcome distraction."

The senator motioned for a server, and a vintage Rioja was presented in no time. Raising his glass, Juan Carlos offered a toast. "To friendship."

Karen and Brock exchanged a glance before lifting their new glasses of wine. "To friendship," they echoed.

The detective remained hyperaware of every subtle shift in Juan Carlos's demeanor. He was charming, attentive, and completely unreadable—a dangerous combination.

"Tell me, mi amiga," he said. "How does a woman of your talents unwind on vacation?"

Karen's smile didn't falter. "The same way anyone does—a good book, some sunshine, and maybe a little wine. Today certainly topped my list."

"I'm glad to hear this." Juan Carlos chuckled. "But surely your sharp mind never truly rests. Once a detective, always a detective, no?"

"You'd be surprised," Karen said coolly. "Even sharp minds need a break."

Juan Carlos leaned back, thoughtful. "A wise philosophy."

He then steered the conversation toward Brock's work as a plumber and his passion for hybrid roses. Karen used the opportunity to observe Juan Carlos without the pressure of direct interaction.

When Brock mentioned Diana St. James, Karen caught it—a flicker in Juan Carlos's eyes. It was brief, but it confirmed what she suspected: he knew more than he was letting on.

Eventually, he rose, his presence commanding. "Thank you for the company—and the cigars. I'll savor one this evening."

Karen shook his hand firmly. "And thank you for today."

Brock also shook his hand, and with a subtle nod, Juan Carlos disappeared into the night, his bodyguards gliding silently behind him.

Brock let out a low whistle. "What the hell was that about?"

Karen's eyes narrowed. "I don't know yet, but I intend to find out."

As the pair prepared to leave, the bistro's hostess approached, her expression strained. "Señora Skaryd, there are some gentlemen here who wish to speak with you."

Karen turned to see Inspector General Rafael Montenegro standing with two officers at the entrance. Karen knew the night was far from over.

She told the young lady, "Thank you for letting us know," and the hostess scurried away.

"Looks like it's showtime," Karen muttered.

Brock paled. "What do we do?"

"We play their game—for now."

CHAPTER 18

Karen stood with a composed expression, despite the knot tightening in her stomach. Brock rose hesitantly beside her, his hand trembling as it brushed against hers.

"Let's go," Karen said softly, her tone steady.

They walked to the bistro's entrance where Inspector General Rafael Montenegro waited, his presence as commanding as ever. His dark suit was immaculate, his polished shoes reflecting the dim lighting. Behind him, the two officers stood stiffly, their hands resting on their belts.

"La señora Skaryd, El señor Skaryd," Montenegro greeted them with a formal nod. "I trust I am not interrupting your evening?"

Karen's detective instincts flared. The inspector's politeness felt rehearsed, his tone oozing false civility. She offered a tight smile. "Not at all. How can we help you?"

Brock stepped forward, his voice shaking slightly. "What's this about?"

Montenegro's smile was thin. "It is a routine matter, I assure you. We have some questions about your interactions, señor, with the deceased, la señora Diana St. James."

Karen stepped between them, her tone sharp. "If this is routine, it can wait until morning. We are on vacation and enjoying our meal."

Montenegro's gaze didn't waver. "With all due respect, señora, the sooner we resolve this, the better for everyone involved."

Karen didn't flinch. "Obviously you don't care much about the fact that we are in the middle of dinner."

"I'm sorry for that, señora, but time—."

She held up a hand. "Time is of the essence, yes. I get it. But my husband is not going anywhere without me."

Montenegro studied her for a moment before nodding. "Very well."

Karen and Brock glanced at each other. She tried to convey her reassurance without words but with her eyes, and Brock seemed to understand. He nodded and pulled in a long breath. She turned back to Montenegro who gestured toward a sleek, black SUV idling at the curb. "If you both would accompany me."

Karen's gaze flicked to the SUV, then back to Montenegro. "Now that I think about it, is there some reason we can't answer your questions here?"

Montenegro's expression went cold, the formal politeness gone. "This is not a request. For your sake, I hope you will cooperate."

Karen's jaw tightened. She had no jurisdiction here. No allies, aside from Juan Carlos—and even that connection felt sketchy. She glanced at Brock, whose wide eyes silently pleaded for guidance.

"We'll come," she said, her words clipped. "But I expect this to be brief."

Montenegro inclined his head, seemingly satisfied. "Of course."

The ride in the SUV was tense. Karen sat stiffly as she watched Montenegro from her position in the back seat. Montenegro was in the passenger seat, his posture relaxed, though his eyes occasionally flicked back toward her, studying her.

One predator observing another.

"Diana St. James appeared to be a fascinating woman," Montenegro said suddenly, breaking the silence. "Did you know her well?"

"I'd met her a handful of times. My husband knew her better, of course, through the Rosarian Society."

Montenegro turned to better face the us in back seat. "Is that so, Señor Skaryd? You were close?"

"I, uh . . . I wouldn't say we were close," Brock said, his cheeks flushing.

"We just ran in the same circles through the society. She was, uh, passionate about roses."

"Indeed," Montenegro murmured, his tone noncommittal. "Her death is a tragedy—a loss for your floral community, I imagine."

Karen could feel the trap closing in. Montenegro wasn't asking idle questions; he was probing for weaknesses. She redirected the conversation. "Inspector, if you have something specific to ask, I suggest you get to the point."

Montenegro's eyes glinted with amusement. "Patience, señora. We're nearly there."

The SUV pulled into a government building surrounded by high walls and armed guards. Karen's stomach churned. Whatever this guy wanted, it wasn't going to be a simple conversation.

They were escorted into a dimly lit interrogation room. The air was stale, the walls bare except for one side that held what she suspected was a two-way mirror. The furniture was interrogation room chic—folding chairs positioned around a rectangular table. Montenegro motioned for them to sit, and he took a chair opposite them at the table.

"Señora Skaryd," he began, his tone sharp. "Your reputation precedes you. A decorated detective from the States, renowned for solving complex cases. But here, you are out of your element."

Karen met his gaze evenly. "That doesn't mean I don't recognize a setup when I see one."

Montenegro chuckled, a low, humorless sound. "And what would make you think that?"

"Because you're not asking about Diana St. James. You're testing how much we know."

Montenegro leaned forward. "Then tell me, señora, what do you know?"

Karen took a minute to decide how to respond. Revealing too much could be dangerous, but playing ignorant might be worse. Before she could answer, the door swung open.

Juan Carlos Ortiz strode in, his presence commanding as ever. His bodyguards flanked him, their expressions unreadable.

"Inspector," Juan Carlos's tone carried a faint edge. "I wasn't aware my guests were being detained."

Montenegro rose, his expression darkening. "Senator Ortiz, this is an official investigation. I suggest you—"

Juan Carlos held up a hand, silencing him. "Your investigation does not grant you the authority to harass tourists, especially those under my protection."

Karen's eyebrows lifted slightly. *Under his protection?*

Montenegro's jaw clenched, but he said nothing. Juan Carlos turned to Karen and Brock and smiled. "Come. You've had enough interruptions for one evening."

Karen hesitated, but Brock was already on his feet, eager to escape. She followed, her mind filled with countless questions and concerns.

As they stepped into the night, Juan Carlos leaned toward her, keeping his voice low. "You're welcome, Detective. But be careful. The inspector general plays for keeps."

"And you don't?" Karen shot back.

Juan Carlos's smile didn't falter. "Let's just say our interests align—for now."

Before Karen could respond, her phone buzzed. She glanced at the screen and froze. The message was from Terrell:

Found something on Montenegro. Call ASAP. Trust no one.

Karen's grip tightened on the phone as she stared into the dark street. The game had just shifted, and she wasn't sure who the players were anymore—or what side they were on.

This didn't feel routine at all, despite Montenegro's assurances. This was the first move in a dangerous game, and Karen knew the stakes had just been raised.

CHAPTER 19

Back at their suite, Karen sat on the edge of her hotel bed, her phone pressed against her ear. T's voice crackled on the other end, the urgency in his tone cutting through the ambient hum of the air conditioner.

"So . . . I dug deep on Senator Ortiz. It's worse than we imagined. His name is tied to human trafficking—money trails, offshore accounts, and a venture with Diana St. James's ex-husband, Nathaniel."

Karen glanced toward the bathroom door, where Brock's shadow moved behind the door, unaware of the storm unfolding. "What kind of venture?"

T exhaled sharply. "Some non-profit called 'the Horizon Initiative.' On the surface, it looks legit—offering housing and employment for displaced families. But Karen, that's the front. The real story? They're funneling people into human trafficking rings."

Karen's grip on the phone tightened. "And Diana?"

"Not sure. She may have discovered the truth and confronted her ex," T said grimly. "These guys have everything to lose if she talked. That's motive, Karen—damning motive."

Karen's pulse quickened. Diana's murder suddenly felt less like a tragic coincidence and more like . . . a silencing. The pieces clicked into place. A sprawling conspiracy hidden behind a humanitarian façade.

Before she could press her partner further, a sharp knock rattled the hotel door. Karen's head snapped toward the sound, her instincts on high alert. "T, hang on," she whispered, moving through the suite toward the door.

Her heart thudded in her chest as she peered through the peephole. On the other side, the friendly familiar face of the bellman, Jose.

She opened the door, and the young man handed her a folded note. "This was left for you at the front desk, Señora Skaryd."

Karen thanked him, closed the door, and unfolded the note. The words scrawled on the Utopia-branded paper sent a chill down her spine: *Exodus 20:15.*

She picked up the phone again. "T, something's happening here. Stay on Ortiz. This isn't over."

The next morning, over breakfast, Karen barely touched her coffee as she replayed Terrell's revelations in her mind. The bright sunlight streaming through the restaurant window felt almost cruel against the storm of uncertainty brewing inside her.

As Brock returned with his second plate of eggs and pastel de guayaba, a commotion near the entrance area caught Karen's attention. A cluster of staff hovered near the maître d stand, their expressions somber, worried even. Curiosity propelled her forward. She approached a staff member clutching a towel to her chest, her face pale.

"What's going on?" Karen asked.

"Guests found . . . dead," one woman stammered. "A young couple in one of the recently vacated suites."

Karen's heart sank.

She returned to their table. Not wanting to alarm her husband, she told him that she forgot her book in their suite and would meet in a few minutes down at the beach.

His mouth full, he gestured with his fork, mumbling something that sounded like, "Sounds good."

She headed toward the suite but diverted her path at the last moment, heading instead to the building next door, where a small crowd of resort staff hovered nearby, their hushed tones and nervous glances signaling something was very wrong.

Officers were swarming the suite, their hurried movements suggesting a lack of coordination. She'd seen this type of haphazard work before, and it rarely led to answers.

At the entrance, she recognized a familiar face: Officer Alvarez. The same Alvarez who had been present at the scene of Diana St. James' murder. She stood on the threshold, her posture stiff but alert, her hand resting lightly on her holstered weapon.

"Officer Alvarez," Karen called out.

Alvarez turned, her sharp eyes narrowing briefly before recognition dawned. "Señora Skaryd," she said, her tone a mix of surprise and suspicion. "You seem to have a knack for showing up at crime scenes."

Karen gave a tight smile. "Or maybe I'm just in the wrong place at the wrong time. What happened here?"

Alvarez crossed her arms. "I can't discuss an ongoing investigation."

Karen glanced past her into the dimly lit suite. "May I see the scene? If it's who I think it might be . . . well, I'd like to make sure."

Alvarez's stance didn't budge. "This is a police matter, señora. You're not authorized to enter."

Karen shifted tactics, her voice firm. "I'm a senior homicide detective in Florida with years of experience, and I am offering my assistance."

Alvarez raised an eyebrow. "Detective Skaryd, you are not in Florida. You're in la Republica Dominicana, and unless you have your badge and jurisdiction with you, I can't let you in."

Karen's stomach tightened. She'd left her badge and gun locked in her safe back home, never expecting she'd need them on vacation. She took a deep breath, keeping her frustration in check.

"Officer, if it's who I think it is, those victims aren't strangers. I've seen them sneaking around the resort, which means there's may be more to this than meets the eye."

Alvarez's eyes searched Karen's face. Then the officer sighed and rubbed her temples. "I understand your concern, but I must follow protocol. Please stay here while I speak with Inspector Montenegro."

CHAPTER 20

Before Karen could protest, Alvarez turned on her heel and disappeared into the suite. Karen clenched her fists at her sides, frustration bubbling beneath the surface. From the doorway, she scanned the scene—wineglasses left half full, a phone charger dangling in an outlet. The curtains were drawn but uneven, and the open patio door carried a faint ocean breeze that did little to mask the smell of something darker.

She could hear the murmur of voices and the shuffle of boots over carpet. A crime scene, yet again. The resort was turning into a graveyard dressed in five-star luxury.

A few minutes later, Alvarez returned, her expression unreadable. "Inspector Montenegro will see you."

Karen stepped inside. The atmosphere was heavy with tragedy, the kind that seeped into the walls. The suite was immaculate, apart from the two lifeless bodies sprawled across the bed.

It was them—that couple she'd seen sneaking out of different suites before stepping onto the elevator these past few days. Now, their final act was frozen in time, as if sleep had overtaken them mid-embrace—instead of a messy excrement and vomitous-fueled death often associated with a drug overdose. Karen had seen too many death scenes to accept that façade. This one was too picture perfect. She approached slowly, absorbing the details like pieces of a fractured puzzle. The woman lay on her side, her head resting gently against the man's shoulder. His arm draped loosely across her waist. A bottle of red wine rested on the nightstand, with pills scattered like breadcrumbs across the sheets.

Staged, she thought as her eyes drifted to their faces—serene, except for their death pallor and faintly blue lips. She glanced at the man's right hand and frowned. A distinct tan line circled his thumb, but no ring.

Karen kept that observation to herself, tucking it away for later. This wasn't the first time something had gone missing.

Diana St. James had been wearing gaudy novelty earrings at lunch, Karen remembered. But when the medical examiners retrieved Diana's body, one earring was missing. Wolfram had chocked it up to sloppy police work. Now, it felt more like a subtle signature.

Montenegro stood at the foot of the bed, his dark gaze landing on Karen as she approached.

"Señora Skaryd, you do have a knack for finding yourself in the middle of my investigations."

Karen met his stare, unflinching. "I wouldn't have to if you solved them faster."

Cocking an eyebrow, Montenegro scoffed. "Charming. Do you think this connects to Diana St. James?"

Karen turned back to the bodies. The scene was too pristine. No forced entry. No struggle. *Orchestrated.*

"I think this resort is holding more secrets than the guests are willing to pay for."

Montenegro stepped closer, and she feel his breath on her neck when he said, "You should tread carefully. Pushing too hard, too fast—"

"Isn't that the point?" Karen spun around to face him. "The truth doesn't wait for invitations."

Montenegro's jaw tightened. "You're not in your jurisdiction, Señora. You don't want to make enemies."

Ignoring the implied threat, Karen scanned the nightstand. A glass sat empty, condensation pooling beneath it. Next to it, partially hidden under the base, was a folded piece of paper.

She gently slid it out, flattening it against her palm.

Exodus 20:15 – You Shall Not Steal.

Karen's breath hitched. The same verse that was delivered to her door the night before.

Montenegro read it over her shoulder, and she glanced at him. His stoic expression cracked slightly, suspicion flickering briefly in his eyes.

"Do you still think this is a coincidence?" Karen whispered, eyes narrowing.

Montenegro said nothing.

Karen hesitated, then reached into her purse, pulling out the folded note she'd received the previous evening. She handed it to Montenegro. He unfolded it carefully, eyes narrowing as he read the identical biblical verse.

"Where did you get this?" His voice was cold, edged with suspicion.

"A bellman delivered it to my room last night," she explained quickly. "I don't know who sent it."

Montenegro's suspicious gaze remained fixed on her. "And you didn't think to immediately inform me or my investigators?"

"I'm giving it to you now," Karen replied evenly, meeting his skeptical stare.

He held her gaze a moment longer, clearly unconvinced, before finally placing both notes into separate evidence bags.

Karen glanced again at the male victim's thumb, the missing ring lingering heavily in her mind. What else had been taken? This killer wasn't just covering their tracks—they were collecting trophies.

"This isn't a honeymoon gone wild. It's staged, and you know it," Karen insisted firmly.

Montenegro's gaze hardened. "Thank you for stating the obvious, señora. I think you are done here."

"This isn't just about me. Or you. This is about finding the truth, no matter how inconvenient it might be."

Montenegro snapped his fingers, calling over Alvarez, "Por favor, escort la señora from my crime scene."

Karen raised her hands in a defensive posture. "No need. I'm leaving. Your monkeys, your circus."

"Gracias," he said, ignoring her insult. "Y señora—"

Karen turned. "What now?"

"Not a word to the other guests."

Once outside, Karen pulled her cell out and quickly texted her partner back home: *Two more victims. Same biblical signature. Find out everything you can about Ortiz's ties to this resort. Time is running out.*

Slipping her phone back into her pocket, she cast one last look at the room. The killer wasn't just sending messages—they were escalating. And Karen knew she was racing against the clock before the next Bible verse was left behind.

With a gloomy heart, she made her way to the suite, where she would retrieve her book, as promised. The salty breeze did little to clear the heavy sense of dread clinging to her. The sun blazed overhead, cruelly indifferent to her inner turmoil. She couldn't shake the nagging feeling that Montenegro knew more than he let on.

As she rounded the corner, a shadow moved in the periphery of her vision. She stopped short, scanning the area all around her, then did it again. Nothing. Just a stray breeze rustling the nearby palms. She shook her head and kept walking, her mind whirling with theories and dead ends.

The resort's cheerful chatter continued as if nothing had happened, but Karen felt like unseen eyes were following her every move. She quickened her steps.

CHAPTER 21

Karen pushed open the door to the suite, surprised to see Brock seated on the balcony, his iPad in hand. He looked up, his brow furrowed.

"Brock, oh hey. I thought I was meeting you at the beach."

"Yeah, that was the plan. I came back to the room to grab this." He held up his tablet. "I was surprised to find that you weren't here. Must have crossed paths. Where ya been?"

Karen licked her lips as she thought about what to say. She hadn't intended to involve Brock in any of this. But there he was, his concern etched plainly on his face. There was no avoiding it now.

"I, uh, went to the building next door," she said cautiously, closing the door behind her. "There was another . . . incident. A couple was found dead in one of the suites."

Brock's eyes widened, his grip tightening on the iPad. "Murder?"

She shrugged. "Looks like it."

"Ka, what the hell is going on?"

Karen moved closer and wrapped her arms around him for a long second. Then she stepped back, holding him at arm's length. "I'm not sure, honey, but I think it's all connected. To Diana, to Senator Ortiz, to Montenegro . . . The couple—they're not just random victims. It was purposeful, just like before. Only this time, they left a different verse behind."

"Different verse? What are you talking about."

She joined him on the balcony and explained to him how she'd seen the note left with Diana when she was poisoned at the restaurant and now the new one left beside as the couple lay strewn, lifeless, across the bed.

Brock's face paled, and he set the iPad down on a nearby patio table. "This is insane."

"I know." Karen said. "And I think whoever is behind this knows I'm asking questions, and between these texts and biblical verses, they're clearly trying to send a message."

He raked a hand through his hair, anxiety flickering in his eyes. "Screw the messages. What about me? How does all this affect *me*? The police were already looking at me for Diana's death—or at least enough to bring me in for questioning. If they think I'm somehow involved in these latest murders . . . Oh God." He plopped into a chair and dropped his head.

Karen stepped forward, placing a hand on his arm. "I won't let that happen. I'll clear your name if it comes to that. But for now, I need you to stay calm and stay out of sight. Don't give them any reason to focus on you."

Brock stared at her for a long moment before exhaling shakily. "You always have to get involved, don't you? Even on vacation."

Karen offered a weak smile. "It's who I am?" More a question than a statement.

"Yeah, whatever." He shook his head, his expression softening slightly. "Just . . . be careful, okay?"

"I will," she promised, adding, "I need to check on a few things. Stay here, lock the door, and don't answer it for anyone except me."

"Some vacation," he muttered, then, "Just be careful and come back in one piece. Please? I still want to hit the beach with you."

"Okay, honey. Thanks for understanding," and she scooted out into the hallway, quietly shutting the door behind her. A couple of steps down the hall, and with barely enough time to compose herself, she nearly collided with Wolfram. His sudden appearance startled her, and she instinctively took a step back.

"Detective," he said, his tone softer than usual, laced with something close to concern. His impeccably tailored outfit and unruffled demeanor seemed out of place against the resort's humid chaos, but it was his expression that caught her off guard.

"Wolfram?" she managed, eyeing him warily.

"I heard about the deaths," he said. "Are you okay?"

Karen blinked, unsure how to respond. This was a stark contrast to the detached man she'd spoken to yesterday.

"Brock and I are fine," she said cautiously. "Why do you ask?"

He hesitated for a moment, as if weighing his words. "When I heard what happened, I thought of you. Two more deaths. It seemed prudent to check in."

His sudden concern felt misplaced. "I appreciate it," she said, "but you don't strike me as the type to rush in out of worry. What's really going on, Wolfram?"

"Let's just say I know how dangerous secrets can be, and this place seems to be . . . full of them."

Her eyes narrowed. "That wasn't really an answer, but okay, I'll play. What secrets? Care to share?"

Wolfram's expression shifted, his features tightening ever so slightly. "The autopsy results came in earlier than expected. For Diana St. James. They are officially ruling it a homicide. Someone wanted her silenced."

Karen's breath caught. She'd suspected as much with the poison and all, but hearing it confirmed sent a chill through her. She asked the question she needed to ask but didn't want answered, "Who's their main suspect?"

Wolfram shook his head. "They don't have one. Not officially."

"Meaning?" she pressed. His carefully worded response was not lost on her.

He didn't answer right away, but instead looked past her down the corridor, as if searching for the right answer.

"I think," he said slowly, "this is bigger than Diana. Bigger than that couple they just found. Or you and me, for that matter. I . . . You should just be careful."

This would be the second time in a matter of minutes that someone advised her to stay vigilant and watch out for herself, causing her frustration to bubble to the surface.

"You keep dropping breadcrumbs, Wolfram. If you know something, say it. Why are you here? What do you want?"

CHAPTER 22

Wolfram tilted his head to one side, then the other. "Maybe I'm just trying to keep you alive, Detective."

"Don't give me that bullshit," she said with a roll of her eyes.

Instead of engaging her further, he straightened, his usual composed demeanor returning like a mask.

"I'll be around," he said lightly and began to walk away, but Karen wasn't ready to let him go.

"Wolfram."

He paused, glancing over his shoulder.

"Why do I feel like you know more than you're telling me?" she asked, her voice steady despite the turmoil roiling inside her.

His lips curved into a small smile, barely there. "Because I probably do."

And with that, he walked away, leaving Karen standing outside her suite, the chill of his cryptic words causing her to shiver. Wolfram's sudden shift in demeanor, his warning, the subtle implication that he was protecting her—it all felt like pieces of a puzzle she couldn't quite fit together. And, of course, that's exactly what it was.

Her phone buzzed in her pocket, breaking the spell. She pulled it out and read the message from her partner in the States: *Ortiz has ties to an offshore account under Nyssa Holdings Intl, a division of the Horizon Initiative. It's a network, Ka. Bigger than we thought. I'm still digging.*

Karen's heart pounded as she stared at the screen. Wolfram had said the same thing—this was bigger than Diana. But how much bigger? And why was Wolfram suddenly so invested in her safety?

As she slipped her phone back into her pocket, her gaze drifted down the corridor. Wolfram was no longer in sight.

If he was protecting her, as it seemed, she wondered, *From what? Or whom?*

Instead of heading to the first crime scene, Karen turned and headed back inside her suite. Her mind set on one thing. Whatever Wolfram knew, she would find out. And she wasn't going to wait for him to decide when to share it.

Brock was lying on the sofa, his iPad face down on his chest. Probably about to enjoy a catnap. Upon hearing her enter, though, he shot straight up and said, "Wow. That was quick."

She raised her hand—a signal that she needed time to think—and marched past him to the patio without saying a word. T's message . . . *Nyssa Holdings Intl.* The name itself felt innocuous, almost too clean for the sinister underbelly it supposedly hid. But the connection to Senator Ortiz, the cryptic messages with the Bible verse, and Wolfram's evasiveness painted a picture that was anything but innocent.

She came back inside and grabbed her laptop, the screen illuminating her face. Sitting in chair at the desk, her fingers flew over the keyboard as she typed the business name into every database and search engine she could think of.

Articles on shell companies, vague business dealings, and mentions of offshore assets tied to Central America began to surface. A handful of records linked Nyssa Holdings to human rights initiatives and environmental ventures.

Plausible enough to pass a cursory glance, but Karen wasn't buying it.

Her phone buzzed again, interrupting her search. Another message from T: *Found a name associated with Nyssa—Gregor Volkov. High-level figure in trafficking ops. Connected to Ortiz and a European network. This goes global.*

Her pulse quickened.

Gregor Volkov.

She knew the name well.

Karen's FBI training kicked in, narrowing her focus despite the adrenaline surging through her veins. She had learned long ago that panic only clouded judgment, and right now, clarity was her greatest ally.

Brock came to her side, concern etched deep in his everyman features. He had every right to be worried—this was spiraling out of control.

"Ka, what's going on?" he asked with furrowed brows.

"I just heard from T," she said, her words clipped. "Things are getting more complicated."

"Complicated how?"

Karen didn't look up from the screen. "The name T just sent me—Gregor Volkov. He's not small-time. He's a big player in international trafficking. And somehow, he's connected to Ortiz. To Diana. And to Nyssa Holdings."

"Nyssa Holdings," Brock repeated. "What's that?"

"It's a front—a division of something called the Horizon Initiative. Most likely a shell company used to hide dirty money and mask illegal operations, likely tied to Ortiz and his network."

"Jesus . . ."

"Tell me about it. And now I'm standing right in the middle of it."

"You mean, *we're* standing in the middle."

Karen let out a slow breath, her hands gripping the arms of her chair. "Babe, listen—"

"No, Ka, you listen. If these guys are as dangerous as you say, then you're not handling this on your own," Brock said. "Better yet, you should leave this to—"

"To whom?" she snapped, cutting him off. "The local police? The same talent who bungled that crime scene in the restaurant? No. I need to figure this out before more people end up dead."

Brock made something like a growling sound, but his silence was a tacit acknowledgment that she was right. They stared at each other for a moment.

"Okay. I'll stay in the suite—" he pulled his phone out of his pocket "—and keep tabs on any news that comes through while you do whatever it is you're planning to do next."

Karen didn't argue. She appreciated Brock's pragmatism in the face of danger. It was one of the reasons she loved him. But this wasn't a team effort. It couldn't be. Not with the stakes this high.

She grabbed her phone, the weight of it oddly comforting. Volkov's name stared back at her from T's latest message. A high-level trafficker. Connected to Ortiz. She couldn't afford to wait for T to send her breadcrumbs. She needed answers now.

Karen stood and paced the room. "If Volkov's involved, he won't be operating in the open. He'll have layers of protection, false identities, maybe even diplomatic ties. But everyone, even him, leaves a trail, even if it's faint."

"Meaning?" Brock asked.

She stopped, staring out the patio door at the beach below. Sunshine glittered as resort guests frolicked in the azure waters. Off to the side, the pool with its swim-up bar. A restaurant. The neighboring building of suites filled with vacationers. All of it masking deadly secrets just waiting to make themselves known. Because the truth couldn't stay hidden forever.

"Meaning . . . I need to start at the beginning and check out the first crime scene."

CHAPTER 23

Karen adjusted her ponytail in the bathroom mirror, her reflection revealing the steely determination she often tried to suppress during family trips to Disney or the local parks back home in Florida. But today, it was impossible.

Diana St. James's death gnawed at her, a puzzle piece just out of reach. And now there was a second one . . . well, two. Added to that, the information from T and the hints from Wolfram.

In the back of her mind, she could hear her father whispering to her, *"Karen, if you get lost in an investigation, retrace your steps. Start at the beginning."*

And that's why she was going back to the first crime scene.

Exiting the bathroom, Karen found Brock seated on the edge of the bed, his shoulders hunched, worry etched on his face.

"You're not seriously thinking of going back there, are you?" he asked, voice heavy with concern.

"Babe, I gotta," Karen said, slipping on a simple pair of sandals. "I just know if I see it again, something will pop. It's needling me, like a splinter in my mind."

"You're out of your jurisdiction, Ka. This ain't Clearwater."

She gave him a tight smile. "That's why I'll be subtle. If anyone asks, I'll say I dropped an earring, came back to look for it. You of all people, a plumber, know how women hate losing jewelry."

Brock sighed, rubbing his temples. "Still, with that young couple found dead in the other building, the cops are crawling all over the place. Aren't you putting yourself at risk of interfering with an investigation?"

"That's why I need you to act normal," Karen said, stepping toward him and placing a hand on his arm. "Go down to the beach, and see if that kid, Jose, can find us a couple of chairs so we can lie low. If you don't act calm, you'll make them suspicious, and that's the last thing we need right now. I'll meet you at the beach. Go."

But he didn't go. He stood towering over her, his brow furrowed. "I get it. You're in cop mode. I've lived with it for twenty-five years. But they're watching me in relation to Diana's death—and who knows, maybe the other two deaths as well. This ain't a game. You scurrying around the crime scene isn't going to help."

She opened her arms and hugged him tight. "Trust me. I'll be careful. And I won't let anything happen to you. Or us."

He hesitated, then blew out a sigh of resignation. "Fine. I'll head to the beach. But promise me you'll meet me there in an hour. No heroics, okay?"

"No heroics," she promised with a kiss.

CHAPTER 24

The resort was eerily quiet, with only the faint hum of ocean waves and the distant chatter of resort staff breaking the silence. Karen stuck to the shadows, moving swiftly but cautiously toward the restaurant where Diana had collapsed.

Police tape still cordoned off the entrance, but the patrol presence had thinned, which she attributed to the more recent deaths. It was times like this she missed having Terrell at her side. He could distract witnesses. Keep people at bay while she investigated the scene.

Karen circled to the rear entrance, avoiding the main path. Inside, the restaurant's once-vibrant atmosphere had been replaced by a cold sterility and silence. Tables had been cleared, and the staff had abandoned their posts.

The daylight cut a narrow beam through the darkness, allowing her to step into the kitchen for a pair of rubber gloves before retracing her steps to Diana's table.

It was still there, though the scene had been stripped of most evidence. She crouched beside the table, her eyes scanning the floor. A faint smudge near the base of the chair caught her attention—a whitish powder, almost invisible to the naked eye.

She grabbed a tissue from her purse and carefully collected a sample. The incident played over in her mind. Diana's convulsions and foaming mouth. Wolfram had confirmed it was poison, but what kind? And what was the point to citing Exodus 20:16?

Karen stood, sweeping her gaze one last time—and that's when she saw it.

Something she'd seen before.

The doily was crumpled and dirty, peeking out from beneath the chair. *Sloppy police work, indeed. They'd missed it.* She leaned in and picked it up with gloved fingers. The delicate lace edges were smudged with faint footprints, carelessly trampled by the investigators. She flipped it over, confirming it was the same doily she'd seen at Diana's table the night she died—Exodus 20:16, written in black ink. Karen had left it there, not wanting to tamper with evidence and assuming, wrongly, that the investigators would have seen it.

Well, damn . . .

Karen moved quickly. She grabbed two baggies from the kitchen—found behind a roll of foil—and slipped the doily into one, careful not to disturb it further. She retrieved the tissue with the powder residue and placed it into the second bag. Evidence, fragile but crucial. She sealed both bags tightly and tucked them into her purse.

She snapped a few photos with her cell phone, documenting the current state of the now vacant restaurant, then she left the restaurant. No one had spotted her, as far as she could tell. Walking along the beach, the ocean waves turned into white noise against her thoughts. She spotted Brock waving at her from under a beach umbrella. She headed that way.

"So?" he asked as she plopped into the chair beside him.

Karen pulled out the evidence bags just far enough for him to see. "Found this under Diana's table. A doily with *Exodus 20:16* written on it. And some white powder, which I picked up with that tissue there."

Brock looked up the verse on his phone. "'You shall not bear false witness against your neighbor.' That was Diana all right. Talk about hitting it on the nose."

"Regardless, she didn't deserve to die." Karen said. "I need to get these to T for processing."

Brock's eyes narrowed. "How? He's back home in the States."

"This is a resort. They have to offer delivery services for their guests, so I'll send it overnight. He'll do some tests and then we'll know more than we do today. Hopefully a lot more, like what the hell is going on around here."

Brock exhaled sharply. "Karen, whoever's behind this isn't playing. You're walking a fine line."

Karen nodded, her gaze fixed on the horizon. "I know. But whoever they are, they left that message for a reason. And I'm going to find out why."

Somewhere in the shadows of the resort, Karen knew someone was watching—waiting.

And she'd be ready for them.

CHAPTER 25

Karen's legs still trembled slightly as she watched the waves roll in, the tissue-wrapped powder and the doily heavy on her mind. She hated that Brock's frustration with her wasn't misplaced. He had every right to be concerned. Their peaceful getaway to Punta Cana had turned into a nightmare, and she wasn't just watching it unfold—she was stepping directly into its heart.

Brock reclined beside her, sunglasses on, his fingers clutching the edge of his towel with a tension that belied his relaxed posture. She wanted to comfort him, but a voice in her head, likely her father's again, urged her to focus. The killer wasn't going to wait for her emotions to catch up.

"What's the next move?" Brock asked.

"Observe," Karen said without hesitation. "Whoever is behind this, they're here, somewhere, blending in."

"Great," he muttered. "So now we're surrounded by potential killers. Sort of takes the joy out of a resort vacation."

Karen didn't respond, scanning the faces of the resort guests. The laughter of a couple splashing each other in the water. The sharp pop of a volleyball against bare hands. A waiter weaving between chairs with fruity drinks in hand. Everything seemed so normal.

But normal didn't explain Diana St. James's sudden death or the eerie note left behind. Nor did it explain the bodies of the young couple found staged in the suite the next building over—and with the same note on the nightstand. Or why someone would send Karen the same note.

Her eyes landed on a man sitting alone several rows down. He wore a Panama hat pulled low, concealing most of his face. Unlike the other guests, who appeared engaged with their surroundings, his head barely moved. He wasn't wearing sunglasses, and she could see that his eyes scanned the beach, left to right, right to left.

Karen leaned toward Brock, pretending to adjust her chair as she whispered, "Don't look now, but there's a man in a Panama hat two rows down. Do you see him?"

Brock didn't flinch. His years as a plumber—handling everything from hysterical homeowners to being knee-deep in someone else's mess—had given him a practiced ability to remain calm under pressure. "Yeah, I see him. Why?"

"He's watching," Karen said. "Not the beach, not the water. The people. He's watching them like he's taking inventory."

"Maybe he's just a weirdo."

"Or maybe he's someone I need to keep my eye on."

Karen leaned back in her chair, her sunglasses sliding slightly down her nose as she discreetly observed the man in the Panama hat. His movements were precise and methodical. Every so often, he would pause to scribble something quickly in a small notebook before slipping the pen neatly back into his pocket.

Karen casually lifted her phone and took a selfie, angling it carefully to capture him in the background. She frowned slightly as she checked the image—his face was obscured. It was time for Plan B.

"I'm going to check something out," she said abruptly, standing and brushing sand from her legs. "I won't be long."

"Karen . . ." Brock began.

Damn, it's like he can read my mind.

"Two minutes, tops, and then I'll be back. You stay here and relax," she said, giving his shoulder a reassuring squeeze.

"Will do," he said, smiling and turning his face to the sun. "Just stay out of trouble."

Holding her sandals loosely at her side, Karen walked toward the water, careful to maintain an angle that allowed her a discreet glance at the man's notebook. As she passed, she caught a brief glimpse—rows of tiny, intricate marks. Symbols or numbers, perhaps, but nothing she could immediately decipher.

The man never looked up.

She continued along the beach a bit farther, pausing briefly to admire a collection of seashells, then turned back toward the resort. Nearing a waiter who was handing out bottled water, she smiled warmly.

"Could I get a couple of those?" she asked.

"Por supuesto, señora," the waiter replied, reaching into his cooler and handing her two chilled bottles, their condensation glistening in the sun.

Leaning in slightly, Karen kept her tone casual yet conspiratorial. "Mind if we take a quick selfie?"

Before he could reply, she wrapped a friendly arm around his shoulder and angled the camera just right, this time successfully capturing a clear shot of the man in the Panama hat behind them.

She reviewed the photo, and satisfied, she showed it to the waiter, asking, "Do you know that man in the background—the one in the Panama hat?"

The waiter's brow furrowed as he studied the image on her phone, then glanced over her shoulder. "Him? He's been here for a few days. Always alone. Never orders much."

"Is he a guest here at the resort?"

"Creo que sí," the waiter said. "Pero I don't know which room."

Karen nodded, thanking him as she took the bottles and made her way back to Brock.

"Anything?" he asked.

"Not yet," Karen said, settling in beside him. "But something about him feels off."

The man stood suddenly, folding his notebook and tucking it into the pocket of his cargo shorts. He strolled away from the beach, heading toward the main building with measured steps.

Karen's sixth sense flared.

"I'm going to follow him," she said, already standing. When Brock started to protest, she shook her head and said firmly, "Stay here. If anyone asks, I went to the bar for a drink. You're just enjoying the beach."

Brock sighed heavily but didn't argue, except to say, "This is getting old, Ka."

She carried her sandals, slipping them on when she was clear of the sand, and followed the man at a safe distance, weaving between guests and staff to avoid detection. He headed for the side of the resort that bordered the marina.

The man paused near a maintenance door with a sign that read: *Closed for Repairs*. After glancing over his shoulder briefly, he disappeared inside. Karen quickened her pace, slipping into the shadows to avoid being seen.

She waited a moment before approaching the door he'd entered. It was slightly ajar, and she heard the faint sound of papers rustling.

Karen leaned against the outside wall, listening carefully.

A man—she presumed it was the same one she'd been following— muttered to himself. She strained to understand the words but couldn't. Next, the sound of a zipper. Karen's pulse quickened.

She was determined to learn who this man was and what he was doing. The doily under Diana's table, the powder, the notes—it all had to connect.

This guy wasn't just another vacationer, that much she knew.

And whoever he was, he'd just become a prime suspect on her list.

When she heard no more sounds from the room, she dipped back into the shadows and waited for him to leave. But he didn't. Or at least, not through the same door.

Was he still inside? Perhaps there were multiple rooms connected to this one. A labyrinth, and he was making his way through it.

Dare she check?

CHAPTER 26

Karen gave it another full minute, then scooted back to the wall just outside the door, which was still ajar. Pressing her hand against the cool metal, she eased it open a little bit more so she could peer inside. The room beyond was dimly lit, a stark contrast to the vibrant sunshine of the resort.

Industrial shelves lined the walls, stacked with cleaning supplies and maintenance tools. In the center of the room, the man stood with his back to her, hunched over a table cluttered with papers.

I have to know who this guy is.

No, Karen. It's too risky.

I'll pretend to be just a Nosy Nellie looking around the resort.

That won't work.

Yes it will. I'm doing it.

When she was done arguing with herself, she bit her lip and stepped inside. Her rubber-soled sandals were silent against the concrete floor. The man continued to shuffle through documents, his movements sharp and deliberate, unaware of her presence.

The man reached into his pocket and pulled out the small notebook she'd noticed earlier. He flipped it open, jotting something down before glancing at one of the papers on the table. Karen strained to see, but his body blocked her view.

Then he spoke, his accented voice low and steady: "You think you're clever, don't you?"

Karen froze, her heart pounding. Was he talking to her? She slipped behind a tall shelf and pressed herself against the wall.

Her heart was pounding so hard she worried he might hear it.

Careful not to make a sound, she peeked around the edge of the shelf. The man wasn't looking her way—he was staring at the board in front of him, a grim mosaic of faces, locations, and scribbled notes connected by threads of string.

Karen's eyes darted over the board. Her heart sank when she spotted her own picture pinned near the center, a bold question mark scrawled next to it. Brock's face was there too, similarly marked, along with photos of Wolfram, Senator Ortiz, his bodyguards, various resort staff, and a new face she didn't recognize. Beneath it was a name she'd only heard in whispers.

Gregor Volkov.

Her blood ran cold. She now had a face to match the name—a gaunt, sharp-featured man with piercing eyes that seemed to stare directly at her, even from the grainy photo.

The man in the Panama hat stepped back from the board, tilting his head as though admiring his handiwork. "You're all connected," he murmured, his tone matter-of-fact. "Some more than others, but it doesn't matter. Loose ends get tied up one way or another."

Karen's chest tightened. Good guy or bad guy? She wanted nothing more than to confront him, to demand answers, but her training told her to stay hidden. Making a move too soon could put her and Brock in even greater danger.

The man pulled out his phone, snapping a picture of the board before tucking it back into his pocket. He grabbed a duffel bag from the floor, slung it over his shoulder, and turned toward the door. Karen willed herself to be as tiny as possible, so quiet, out of sight. She held her breath as he walked past.

The sound of the door clicking shut was deafening in the silence that followed. Karen exhaled slowly, her body trembling as she straightened. She waited a moment, listening for any sign that he might return, before stepping cautiously toward the board.

Up close, the photos and notes were even more overwhelming. Strings connected Diana St. James's picture to Ortiz and the resort staff, while another line stretched to the young couple found on the bed in one of the resort's suite. Each connection was labeled with dates and cryptic symbols, like a web spun from chaos.

Karen's eyes locked on a note beneath her own picture. It read: *Why here? Why now?* The questions mirrored her own unease. Why had Volkov's network turned its gaze on her and Brock? Was it because of her past cases? Or was it something else entirely?

Like many in her profession, she didn't believe in coincidences. Her fingers traced the strings leading to Gregor Volkov's face. Beneath his picture was a single word—*Mastermind*.

Karen's breath quickened. This wasn't just about the murders at the resort. This was part of something much larger—an operation so meticulously planned that even the investigators were being watched.

A faint scuff outside the door snapped her out of her thoughts. She froze, her ears straining. The doorknob rattled briefly, then stilled.

He's coming back.

Karen snapped a quick photo of the board with her cell phone, making sure to capture every detail, then slipped back toward the rear entrance. Her heart thundered in her chest as she eased the door open and slipped out into the blinding sunlight.

By the time Karen returned to the beach, she was breathless, her heart and mind racing like wild horses. Brock was right where she'd left him, in the lounge chair, earbuds in, his head tilted back. The picture of relaxation. But she knew he was anything but relaxed.

Karen sat down beside him, her hand trembling slightly as she pulled out her phone. She plucked out his earbuds. "We have a problem," she said quietly.

He sat up and turned to face her. "What now?"

She handed him the phone. "This isn't just about Diana or that couple in the suite. It's bigger. Look."

Brock's face paled as he scrolled through the photos. "Is that . . . us?"

Karen nodded. "Whoever this guy is, he's not just watching us. He's tying us to Volkov, Ortiz, and everyone else involved. And Volkov . . . well, he's not just a name anymore. I think he's here."

Brock stared at her, eyes wide. "What are we going to do?"

Karen took a deep breath, and her resolve hardened. "We need to get ahead of this. Find out what they know and why we're on that board. If we don't . . ."

Her words trailed off as she glanced toward the main building. The man in the Panama hat was standing at one of the many strategically placed balconies throughout their all-inclusive paradise, which allowed guests to enjoy the view of the crystalline sand and azure waters below.

And his gaze seemed to be fixed directly on her.

She could be mistaken. Overly paranoid.

She removed her sunglasses and looked again, squinting against the sunlight.

He casually tipped his hat towards her, before turning and leaving.

Karen's stomach dropped.

She felt certain: he knew she'd been in the room.

CHAPTER 27

Panama Hat Man's arm returned to his side. His stance casual, leaning against the railing as if enjoying the view, but his sharp gaze was locked on her. It was the same look she'd seen a hundred times before in suspects—calculated, assessing, dangerous.

Brock followed her line of sight. "Is that him?" he asked, his voice low but urgent.

Karen gave a slight nod, keeping her expression neutral. "Yeah. The guy from the boiler room."

Brock's jaw tightened. "You think he knows you were in there?"

"He just pointed at me."

"Are you sure?"

"No. But it just . . . it feels like he knows. Or is wondering about it, anyway," Karen said, forcing her voice to steady. "If he was absolutely sure, we wouldn't be sitting here right now."

"Yeah, well, I don't feel like testing that theory," Brock muttered, pulling the brim of his baseball cap lower. "What's the play, Ka?"

Karen didn't answer immediately. She knew she had to stay calm, keep her movements deliberate. Any sudden action might spook him—or worse, confirm suspicions.

"We wait," she said finally, her voice firm. "We act normal, just like before. He's watching us, so we give him a show. Nothing out of the ordinary."

"Normal?" Brock's voice rose slightly, though he quickly lowered it again. "You mean while he's up there deciding whether or not to call his friends to take us out?"

Karen placed a hand on his arm, her grip firm. "Trust me. He doesn't know what I saw, and we need to keep it that way. We planned a day at the beach, and we're going to do just that." She lay back on her chair and lifted her face to the sun. Out of the corner of her eye, she saw Brock shaking his head, but he eventually stuck his earbuds in and settled back in his chair.

One minute went by.

Two minutes, then three.

She couldn't stand it any longer. She stood up and sprayed herself with sunscreen, giving her a chance to glance at the balcony.

He was gone. For now.

"He's gone," she said, plopping back into her lounge chair and releasing a long sigh of relief. Brock simply nodded and took her hand in his. They sat there in silence, the sound of the waves and the distant chatter of resort guests a thin veil over the growing sense of dread.

Finally, Karen stood, brushing sand off her legs. "Let's head back to the room."

Brock removed his buds. "You said we shouldn't—"

"That was then. Now we need to regroup. Besides, I've had enough sun and sand for the day."

"Make sense," he said, and they packed up.

Walking back to their suite, Karen constantly scanned the area for any sign of Panama Hat Man. The sun was beginning to dip toward the horizon, casting long shadows across the resort. By the time they reached their door, Karen's unease had shifted into a cold, focused resolve.

Once inside, she locked the door behind them and pulled the curtains shut. "We need to break this down," she said, pulling out her phone and sitting on the edge of the bed.

"As if you haven't been already?" Brock flopped onto the couch.

"It's wise to refresh," she said.

"What exactly are we dealing with here, Ka? Because this isn't just a killer stalking his next victim. It's . . . well, it's a damn international situation."

"Agreed." She stared at the photos she'd taken of the board in the maintenance room. "Human trafficking, murder, political corruption, who knows what else—it's all connected."

She scrolled to the photo of Gregor Volkov's face, the name beneath it bold and damning.

"This guy—Volkov—is at the center of it. He's orchestrating it, and he's pulling strings to control people in power. Ortiz, the resort staff, even Wolfram . . . I believe they're all part of his web."

"And us?" Brock asked, leaning forward.

Karen's jaw tightened. "We've certainly been pulled into this, so . . . yeah. Us too, for some reason I've yet to discover. Maybe it's because of me—my past cases, my connections. Or maybe it's something else. Either way, we're in the crosshairs."

Brock rubbed his temples, frustration bleeding through his voice. "So, what do we do? Go to the authorities? Call the embassy?"

"Not yet. We don't know who we can trust. Volkov's reach is too wide. If we make the wrong move—" She looked at him with raised eyebrows.

Brock nodded, understanding the stakes.

Karen paused for a beat, then stood. "I need to take care of something. I'll be back in ten minutes."

"Where are you going?" Brock demanded, his voice sharp. "We need to know where each other is at all times."

"Probably not a bad idea. I'm going to the front desk," she said. "I need to send these evidence bags to T, and I don't want to wait another second."

"Be careful, Ka. I don't want our twenty-fifth to be our last."

The lobby was quieter than usual, the tension in the air palpable as guests trickled out with their luggage. Karen approached the front desk, where

Dulce, the manager who had checked them in, offered a polite but strained smile.

"Señora Skaryd," Dulce began softly, "I hope everything is okay. I want to apologize for the inconveniences these last few days. I promise you, this kind of thing . . . well, it never happens here."

"I understand, and we're not leaving, so don't you worry about that."

Dulce let loose a heavy sigh. "Unlike many guests."

"I'm sorry to hear that, but you can't get rid of us that easily." Karen winked, which elicited a big grin from Dulce. She couldn't imagine the kind of stress Dulce was under trying to manage a renowned resort under the shadows of murder. "I do need your help with something, though. Does the resort offer a delivery service to the United States? I have a package that needs to be sent overnight."

Dulce brightened, eager to be of service. "Yes, señora. We use international couriers. Overnight delivery is available. Where will it be sent?"

"Clearwater, Florida," Karen said. "You wouldn't happen to have like a padded envelope, would you?"

"Yes, of course. My treat." She chuckled. "The envelope at least."

Karen couldn't resist joining him in the laughter—and it felt good. A little levity in all this sadness.

Dulce excused herself to retrieve the envelope from the back office. Upon her return, she handed Karen the envelope. Karen placed the evidence bags inside, sealed it, then addressed it.

"The shipping fee is seventy-five US dollars, señora. Would you like this charged to your room?"

"Yes, please." Karen handed over her ID and watched as Dulce carefully prepared the courier documents, placing the envelope securely into a pouch.

"The courier will collect it tonight, and it will arrive tomorrow afternoon," she assured her.

"Thank you so much," Karen said, tucking her ID back into her wallet. "Things will get better soon, Dulce. Don't give up hope."

"I won't, Señora Skaryd. Thank you for saying that."

Back in the suite, Karen found Brock pacing restlessly. "It's sent," she announced, her voice steady. "T will have it by tomorrow."

"Hopefully it will lead to some answers," he said. "I'm ready to start enjoying ourselves without looking over our shoulders."

"Indeed." But deep in her heart, she doubted that would happen.

The shadows had deepened outside, and they moved to the window to take in the magical view. Karen instinctively scanned the grounds with her detective's eye. Somewhere, she knew, the man with the Panama hat—or worse—was watching.

Message received.

For now, she would wait.

CHAPTER 28

Karen's phone buzzed, and she stepped away from the window, glancing at the screen. Her stomach flipping when she saw the message.

The text was accompanied by a photo—Brock sitting on the beach, a red circle drawn around his head.

She put a hand to her mouth, but a small whimper escaped.

Brock rushed to her side. "What is it?"

Karen didn't want to show him, but she couldn't keep him in the dark. Not about something like this. She showed him the screen.

His face paled as he stared at the message.

"Son of a—" Brock began, but Karen cut him off.

"We can't panic, Brock. That's what they want."

"They're threatening me, Ka. How am I supposed to *not* panic?"

"Please, honey. Please listen to me. I've protected witnesses from worse than this, people who had nowhere to turn, and I never let them down. I'm not about to start now—not with you."

Brock stared at her, his jaw working silently. "I'm still going to panic."

"Low-key panic, please." She punched up T's number, her own panic roiling under the surface of her calm demeanor. "I need T on this."

Brock dropped onto the couch, rubbing his temples as Karen propped her phone against a glass of water and waited. After a few rings, T's face appeared on the screen, his hair as wild as ever, eyes sharp and alert.

"What's going on," were his first words. The man knew how to read a room.

Karen didn't waste time. "I need your eyes on something. I've sent you two bags of evidence via overnight delivery. It'll be there tomorrow afternoon, and I need you to process it as soon as it arrives."

T frowned. "Evidence? What are we talking about?"

Karen leaned over, carefully explaining, "It's from the first crime scene. One of the bags is contains remnants of a poison, we think—but I need confirmation. It's on a tissue."

T nodded, his expression hardening. "I'll ask the lab to run a chemical analysis."

"Sounds good. And please stay on top of them," she said. "They're always telling us they're too busy. No shortcuts."

"I'll do what I can to make it priority. See if they can tell us exactly what we're dealing with. If it's a known compound, we'll trace it. If not, I'll dig deeper."

Karen then mentioned the doily with Exodus 20:16 scrawled across it in ink. "It was left behind at the scene. The locals missed it. I want it processed for prints, fibers, anything."

"I'll check for oils, trace skin cells, or any DNA. An ink analysis will tell us the brand and type of pen. It's a long shot, but as you always say, 'small details can crack big cases.'"

The tension in her shoulders eased slightly. "That's what I needed to hear. Thanks, T."

"No need to thank me," he said. "Besides, I've done more with less."

"You sure have. Don't mind me, but I'm counting on you again."

"It's nice to be needed." He leaned closer to the screen, his expression dead serious. "But, Ka, whatever you're dealing with, it appears to be very precise."

"Yes." She pursed her lips. She knew what he was getting at.

He continued, "The kind of deliberate moves that only come from someone who knows what they're doing."

Karen's thoughts churned as she sent him a text. "I agree. And that's what worries me. Check out the pics I just sent. The first is of the board I found in the boiler room. The second is of the guy who set it up."

"Looking . . ." He let out a long whistle. "Holy . . . This looks like something from a task force office."

"That's what I'm trying to figure out," Karen said, glancing at Brock, who sat silently now, playing a game on his cell phone. She knew it was to keep his mind busy, keep himself from panicking—not a lack of interest. He was listening to every word.

T paused, studying the screen carefully. "Karen, I've seen your boards. I've worked with you for years. This? This looks like something you'd do, to be honest."

Karen blinked. "So, you think this guy's an investigator? A cop like us?"

"It makes the most sense," T said with a shrug. "Look at the precision, the connections. He's tracking Volkov, Ortiz, and the resort staff. But here's the thing—he's got you and Brock pinned on there with question marks. My gut says he doesn't know what side you're on yet."

Karen leaned back, her mind spinning. "So, he's suspicious of me."

T shrugged. "Wouldn't you be? If you're this guy—some investigator neck-deep in Volkov's operation—and suddenly a Clearwater cop shows up asking questions, you're gonna wonder why."

Brock, still playing on his phone, muttered, "What about the threats? The photo of me? That doesn't sound like a good-guy move."

"Did Brock say threats? What's he talking about?"

"Sending them now," Karen said forwarding those images to T as well.

T's face tightened as he reviewed the additional data. "Geez, I don't know, Ka. There's something off here."

"Ya think?"

"No, what I mean is, this isn't adding up."

"What's not adding up?"

"How do we know this Panama hat guy sent these pics?" T asked.

"We don't."

"Okay, let's assume he did. Why would he? What's his endgame?"

"For me to mind my own business."

"Okay, and . . .?"

"And if I don't, there could be consequences. Deadly ones."

"Maybe, but I'm not buying that last part. Look, cops like us are... territorial. We hate sharing our toys, let alone having a cop outside their jurisdiction, sticking their nose into our investigation.

Karen nodded in agreement.

"If this guy's an investigator, this might be his way of backing you off. A scare tactic, not an actual threat."

She rubbed her temples, absorbing the new angle. "If you're right, and this guy's investigating Volkov, then he's a *resource* for us. But if you're wrong—"

"He may be playing both sides," T finished. "Partner, you need to stay sharp."

"Sharp's my middle name."

"I thought it was Constanza?" T teased.

Karen pursed her lips, and flipped him the bird, the way a sibling would respond. "Anyway, the package is on its way. Process it as soon as it lands. Also..."

"Put this guy through facial recognition. See if I get a hit. I'm already on it."

"Thanks, T."

"Always." He smiled.

She disconnected, leaving the room thick with tension.

"Whatever T finds out," Karen said, slicing through the heaviness, "I'm not letting this guy control the board."

Before Brock could respond, her phone buzzed again.

She checked the screen.

And froze.

The text read: *You think you're safe because you're smart. But smart isn't enough. See you soon.*

Attached was a grainy photo of Karen herself, taken earlier that day.

Brock leaned over her shoulder, his face pale. "Ka—"

"It's only a warning," she said quietly. "Same as the one about you. I'll forward it to T." And she did.

As she typed, Brock asked, "A warning for what?"

"That he's watching. But that's fine, because now we're watching him too."

CHAPTER 29

Karen leaned against the balcony railing, sipping coffee and contemplating her life. The salty morning breeze tugged at her hair as she stared out at the endless blue expanse of the ocean. With T working the forensic angles, it gave her some room to breathe—but not to stop.

Her phone vibrated in her hand, a text from T confirming receipt of the package.

Samples delivered. Processing now. Poison results later today. Doily—working prints/DNA. Will update.

Karen grabbed her bag from the desk chair and tucked her phone inside. Brock, still half-asleep, cracked one eye open as she moved around the suite.

"Where're you goin'?" he croaked, his voice still gravelly with sleep.

"Out for supplies," Karen said evenly. "I need to start piecing this together."

"Supplies? For what?"

Karen slung the bag over her shoulder. "I need a board. Pins, index cards, markers—something to map out what's happening. I need to see it all in front of me."

"Ka, please. This isn't Clearwater. You're a cop without a badge here."

"What else am I going to do? Relax and ignore the danger?"

"Nooo."

"Exactly. This ain't my first rodeo. Sleep in. I'll be back soon."

Before he could argue further, she was out the door, calling for a cab at the front desk.

The drive took her far beyond the manicured facade of the Utopia. As the cab rattled down the uneven streets, the pristine beaches and luxury villas disappeared, replaced by a starker reality. Here, the Dominican Republic wasn't a glossy image on a travel brochure—it was raw and unfiltered.

Makeshift homes, some built from patched tin and crumbling bricks, lined the dusty roads. The air was heavy with the scent of wood smoke, street food, and unrelenting heat. Barefoot children darted across the road, laughing and shouting, while stray dogs wandered aimlessly.

Karen watched it all, a familiar ache settling in her chest. Poverty wasn't new to her—it had been part of countless cases back home—but seeing it like this, in the land her mother once called home, cut deeper than usual.

Her mother had grown up in Santo Domingo, the capital city. Karen had grown up hearing stories of the disparity between the haves and the have-nots in the DR—stories of inequality masked by palm trees and postcard beaches. But her mother had been one of the fortunate ones. Her grandparents were both educated, hardworking professionals who had managed to provide—even during the global economic turmoil of the 1920s and '30s.

After her mother graduated college, she'd immigrated to the United States, met her father, and together, they built a good life together. He, as a decorated police officer, and she, as a bilingual elementary school teacher in the Three Village Central School District, teaching for nearly three decades.

Her mother's passion for education and language helped her bridge cultures—especially for immigrant families—and allowed the family to maintain a comfortable, middle-class life in suburban Long Island.

They'd succeeded, but those early stories never left Karen. Now, watching it unfold outside her cab window—not through her mother's memories, but with her own eyes—left a bruise on her spirit.

This wasn't the resort's curated version of the island.

This was the Dominican Republic her mother rarely let slip past nostalgia's filter.

And for Karen, it was a sobering reminder of the difference between surviving and thriving.

"You okay, señora?" the cab driver asked, glancing at her in the mirror.

Karen met his gaze and nodded. "Sí. Estoy bien."

Eventually, the cab pulled up to a small, weathered store called Haribo's. The sign hung crooked, its paint peeling from years of neglect. The driver hesitated. "Are you sure this is what you are looking for?"

"It's perfect," Karen said, handing him a twenty-dollar bill. "If you circle back in fifteen minutes, you'll get another one of these."

He shrugged. "Sí, señora."

Inside, the store was dim and dusty. It reminded her of those dollar stores back home with their shelves overflowing with random items—wrapping paper, cleaning products, children's toys—but Karen spotted what she needed immediately.

She grabbed a large corkboard, brushing away a layer of dust, then scooped up boxes of push pins, a pack of 4x6 index cards, rolls of tape, black and red markers, and a pair of scissors. A cheap notebook sat by the register, and she grabbed that too.

The shopkeeper, an older man with tired eyes, gave her a weary smile as she approached the counter. The total charge was 1,076 Dominican pesos.

Karen arched her brow and handed over a fifty-dollar bill, earning a small nod of approval. "Gracias," she murmured before hauling the supplies outside.

The cab driver gave her another look when she climbed back in. "¿Projecto grande?"

"Sí, something like that."

When she returned to the suite, Brock raised an eyebrow at the load in her arms. "Geez, you weren't kidding about supplies."

Karen said nothing and got straight to work. She shoved the dining table against the wall, then propped up the corkboard. Methodically, she laid out the pins, index cards, tape, and markers in front of her like surgical instruments. Her movements were sharp, practiced, driven by instinct and urgency.

"Three deaths," she muttered. "Diana St. James—poisoned in the restaurant. The young couple—staged in the suite next door."

She wrote each name on a card—labeling the couple as Doe 1 and Doe 2 for now—and pinned them to one end of the board, linking them with a single red strand.

Below Diana's name, she taped a note: *Exodus 20:16 – You shall not bear false witness.* Under Doe 1 and 2: *Exodus 20:15 – You shall not steal.*

"Symbolic murders," she said, circling both verses with a thick stroke of the black marker. "But what's the connection? Why these people? Why now?"

Behind her, Brock leaned in, studying the growing web. He tapped the space between the victims. "What if the note and doily are the key? Maybe this Moses guy thinks Diana lied about something which wouldn't surprise me. And that the couple stole something. It's like his bizarro version of justice."

Karen turned, the faintest smile tugging at her lips. "That's some brilliant deduction. And that *Moses* monicker? Yeah. I like that. That's what we'll call him for now."

Brock smiled with pride as she took a step back, assessing the board. The layout struck a chord. It mirrored the one in the boiler room—the web she'd seen assembled by the man in the Panama hat.

She grabbed her phone again and compared the two photos side by side. The resemblance was uncanny. Had her subconscious borrowed from his board? Or had they both arrived at the same conclusions—two investigators following the same deadly trail?

In both boards, one name loomed largest.

Gregor Volkov.

Karen pinned his name at the top, like the grainy image she'd captured from the boiler room. She drew new lines—connecting Volkov to Diana, to the couple, and to Senator Ortiz.

"This all comes back to Volkov," she whispered. "He's the linchpin. Whatever's happening here—he's at the center."

Her phone buzzed, jolting her.

That sound hadn't meant anything good lately.

She took a deep breath, picked it up, and read the new message.

Tick-tock, Detective. You're running out of time.

Attached was a photo—of her newly assembled board. Taken from a drone or telescopic lens.

CHAPTER 30

"Damn it."

"Now what?" Brock asked, stunned by her outburst.

She tossed her phone and ran to the balcony. She scanned her surroundings including the sky. Nothing. Just clear skies, and people frolicking on the beach. After a few minutes, she returned inside, closing the curtains behind her.

"Jesus, Ka. We're on the twelfth floor. How the hell did they get this?" he asked, handing her phone back.

"I don't know. A drone maybe?"

Brock shook his head in disbelief, as Karen composed herself, and returned to study her board. Red threads crisscrossed the cork like arteries, leading from one name to the next, with Gregor Volkov's anchored at the top. The names Diana St. James and the young couple, seemingly staged in a final moment of passion, stared back at her, silent questions hanging in the air.

She brushed her hair back, trying to ignore the dull ache forming at her temples. The unanswered clues, and damn text messages. A photo of her board—the warnings that they were watching. But who were "they"? Who was sending these texts? Was it Volkov's people? The man in the Panama hat? Friend, foe, or someone just as tangled in this mess as she was.

"Ka?" Brock's voice pulled her from her thoughts. "You're staring at that thing like it's about to solve itself."

"If it only worked that way."

"Remember, we've got a luncheon at noon with the Society folks. After what happened with Diana, everyone's expected to show. I can't miss this, and I'd like you there with me. Oh, *and* we have the awards banquet coming up too."

The Rosarian Society's gala was two days away. His hybrid "Angel Rose," named after his late mother, had put him on the map among Tampa Bay rosarians. This ceremony was important to him—personally and publicly.

Karen nodded, her mind already moving. "I'll be there. More than anything, we need to keep up appearances that everything with us is normal. No one can suspect what's going on behind the scenes."

Brock sat on the arm of the sofa, "What are we gonna do with the board?"

"What do you mean?"

"What if housekeeping comes in and sees it?"

Karen's lips pressed into a tight line. That was a problem—one she had already started working through. A murder board wasn't exactly a subtle decoration, and the last thing she needed was a curious maid stumbling across it.

"This should take care of things." She said, taking the Do Not Disturb sign and placing it on knob outside their front door.

Brock gave her a skeptical look. "And if they ignore it?"

Karen furrowed her brows in thought as she hung the sign. Then she walked to the corkboard and pulled it from the wall, carefully moved it into the closet, and propped it against the back corner, facing the wall.

"Hey, toss me those throw pillows," she said. He did, and she wedged them in place to secure the board and to cover it up. "That'll do for now."

Brock drained the last of his coffee, "Okay, we've got the board stashed and a fancy lunch to get to. What about the local cops? You know they'll have more questions."

"They always do," Karen said, slipping her notebook into her bag. "But I'll handle them later. For now, we go about our lives."

Brock gave her the thumbs-up. "Nothing to see here."

She grinned. "That's the spirit."

The luncheon was held at a sprawling, open-air pavilion near the resort's main gardens. White linen-draped tables, sparkling crystal, and bright floral centerpieces made the event look like something out of a magazine. The powerful scent of roses reminiscent of a florist shop, filled the air, mingling with the sharp tang of salt carried in from the sea.

Karen and Brock arrived together, her hand resting lightly on his arm. The chatter around them was polite, but she could feel the undertone of whispers as guests cast discreet glances their way. Diana St. James's absence was so palpable, it almost seemed like she was actually there.

"Brock, good to see you." A tall man with a shock of silver hair approached them, a glass of champagne in hand. His nametag read *Brady*. "Quite the tragic news about Diana."

"Yeah, that was certainly unexpected," Brock said with a shake of his head. "She'll be missed."

And so it went. Brock chatting with fellow rosarians as Karen eyeballed the crowd. No one looked out of place—well-dressed retirees, horticulturists, and socialites mingled beneath the soft hum of string music. Yet Karen couldn't shake the feeling that eyes were on them even here at the luncheon, unseen and calculating.

When Brock went to grab them each a cocktail, Karen caught sight of Panama Hat Man near the garden's edge. He was dressed well enough to blend in, but his posture was rigid, his gaze fixed on the crowd in a way that didn't quite fit.

Kinda like me.

She turned casually, keeping him in her peripheral vision. He didn't move, but as usual, something about him sent a chill up her spine. How long had he been standing there? Had he seen her yet?

"Ka."

Brock's voice startled her, and she turned as he approached with two wine spritzers.

"Everything okay?" he asked, noticing the sharp look in her eyes.

"Yeah," Karen said softly, forcing a smile. "Just thinking about Diana. And the award. It could be a big day for you."

Brock nodded, his expression softening. "Honestly, it's not the same without her here, even though she was a pain in the ass."

Karen glanced back toward the garden's edge. The man was gone, but she knew he wasn't done with . . . whatever he was doing.

The clock was still ticking.

CHAPTER 31

Later, back in the suite, Karen pulled out her notebook and jotted down her observations from the luncheon, adding a question mark beneath the man with the hat.

Brock sat nearby, scrolling through messages from the Society.

"They're still moving forward with everything," he muttered.

"Good, good," she said, pinning a new note on her board: *Motive. Who benefits?*

Brock sat on the couch, flipping through emails on his phone. He glanced up as Karen took a seat next to him.

"They voted," he said, exhaling heavily. "The Tampa Chapter wants me to pick up where Diana left off. Help oversee the final prep for the gala tomorrow night."

Karen arched an eyebrow. "You? Why not that Bethany woman? You're not even on their board."

"Who knows? Plus, you saw Bethany."

Karen nodded—he had a point there.

"Maybe they just . . . they trust me. Diana had been the lead on this, and now that she's gone—"

"They need someone trustworthy to step up."

"Exactly."

Karen tapped her chin. "That might actually be good for us. Keeps you visible and out in the open—business as usual. And while you're busy with the preparations for the gala, I'll have a little breathing room to keep digging."

"You're going back to the second crime scene, aren't you?"

"Yeah," she admitted, her voice firm. "I need to know how they tie to Diana, and more importantly, what they might have stolen. The two Exodus 20:15 notes, mine and the couple's, weren't random messages. They were pointed, purposeful. I need to figure out the connection."

"And how exactly are you going to pull that off?" Brock asked, concern etched into his face. "You're not local law enforcement, Ka. They're already wary of you poking around."

Karen smiled faintly. "I'll be careful. Besides, the way these people work, their focus has probably shifted elsewhere already. I doubt anyone's watching the suite now."

Brock exhaled loudly. "Fine. Just don't get yourself killed while I'm setting up flower arrangements, okay?"

"Deal." She kissed him on the cheek and headed out.

The late afternoon light turned golden as Karen approached the neighboring building. Her path was deliberate, her pace casual, blending in with the resort guests milling about the property. She carried a towel over her shoulder, giving the impression of a woman out for a quiet walk rather than to investigate a murder.

The ground-floor suite was situated in the far corner of the building. Karen noted how secluded it was, tucked away from the main traffic of the resort. It was the perfect spot for someone to come and go unnoticed, with a convenient patio entrance leading straight to the beach.

The police tape was still up, fluttering slightly in the afternoon breeze, but the suite itself appeared unguarded. Karen walked up to the front door, glancing around to make sure no one was watching. With practiced calm, she tried the handle.

Locked. *Damn it.*

She looked around. The walkway behind her was empty, save for the occasional rustle of palm leaves swaying in the wind, and an empty tray of food left outside a suite. She walked to the tray, and picked up the ketchup-stained knife, wiping it off on the discarded napkin. Then she placed it in her back pocket and quickly moved on.

Satisfied that no one was watching, she stepped off the narrow path and went around the side of the building toward the back. The sandy trail here was even quieter, lined with hedges that offered just enough cover.

The patio entrance came into view—a sliding glass door framed by sheer curtains, reminding her of the homes along Clearwater Beach. Karen crouched near the edge of the patio, peeking through the glass. The room appeared empty, sunlight pooling on the pristine tile floors. The resort staff had done a thorough job cleaning up after the police, leaving the room eerily pristine.

Glancing left and right one last time, Karen approached the door, took out the knife and applied gentle pressure to the lock, while lifting it upward with practiced precision. After a moment, she heard the faint click of the latch releasing.

"Still got it," she muttered.

She eased into the room and carefully shut it behind her. Taking a moment to let her eyes adjust to the dim interior, she noted the faint scent of industrial cleaner, masking any other trace of what had occurred here.

Karen's senses stayed sharp as she scanned the suite. She was no stranger to crime scenes, but something about this place felt wrong—like the silence itself was hiding something.

The room had been reset with fresh white linens on the bed, new towels hanging in the bathroom, decorative shells back in their neat arrangement on the sitting room table. The veneer of normalcy was paper thin, though. Karen had seen enough crime scenes to know that even the best cleanup couldn't erase everything.

She paused near the bed, kneeling to inspect the area around the frame. A faint indentation near the corner caught her eye—like someone had pressed down hard on the mattress. She snapped a quick photo on her phone, then ran her hand along the base of the bed, checking for anything that may have been overlooked. She came up empty.

Standing again, she moved toward the sitting area. A crumpled piece of paper sticking out from under the couch caught her attention. Karen crouched and pulled it free. It was a torn resort map, wrinkled and smudged. Two buildings had been circled in dark ink—the suite she was standing in now and the main restaurant . . .

Where Diana St. James had died.

Karen frowned, smoothing the paper carefully. Two crime scenes. Both marked. Why?

She folded the map and slipped it into her bag, her gaze shifting to the glass patio doors she'd jimmied open. Starting from the nearby bathroom, a thin line of sand trailed faintly onto the tile, leading to the base of the curtains. It was subtle—almost unnoticeable—but Karen's gut told her it didn't belong there.

She crossed to the sliding doors, crouching by the frame. Reaching just beneath the curtain, her fingers brushed against something warm and metallic. She froze, then carefully pulled the item out.

A heart-shaped pendant attached to a silver necklace.

The clasp was broken, and the pendant smeared faintly with something dark. Her pulse quickened as she examined the stain. Blood? Whose necklace was this—one of the victims? She felt like she'd seen it before but couldn't put her finger on it. Regardless, it couldn't have been here long—the cleaners would've found it.

Karen grabbed the plastic bag from a nearby ice bucket, carefully placing the necklace and the torn map inside—an improvised evidence bag. She tucked it securely into her purse, reminding herself to borrow proper supplies from one of the resort restaurants later.

A chill crept up her spine as a realization sank in. Whoever left this here may have simply been sloppy. Or maybe—it was deliberate.

The faint sound of gravel crunching outside sent her heart racing. Karen ducked low, instinctively backing away from the curtains and sliding glass door, toward the shadows of the nearby wall. She held her breath as two men in resort uniforms appeared just outside the patio, chatting in Spanish.

Her mind raced. Maintenance workers? Staff? Their tone was casual, but she wasn't taking any chances.

Karen stayed hidden, peeking carefully around the edge of the curtain as they lingered on the patio. One of them glanced toward the door and frowned, nudging the other and pointing at the latch Karen had forced open.

Shit.

The two men exchanged a few words, then turned away, continuing down the gravel path.

Karen let out a shaky breath, letting a good minute pass before moving. She left the room, ensuring there was no trace of her visit, and closed the sliding door behind her. She stepped onto the patio, checking her surroundings before slipping back around the building and returning her borrowed knife to the tray of food.

Her purse was heavier now, the necklace and torn map tucked carefully inside. As she circled back to her suite, Karen's mind spun. The map with the circled buildings . . . the necklace smeared with blood . . . more pieces to the puzzle.

Her phone buzzed in her pocket, snapping her out of her thoughts. Karen pulled it out and glanced at the screen.

Another text.

Nice try, Detective. But you're still two steps behind.

Attached was a photo—of her, jimmying sliding doors.

Karen's blood ran cold. She looked around, eyes narrowing against the darkening corridor.

CHAPTER 32

The door to the Skaryds' suite clicked softly behind Karen as she stepped inside, her pulse still racing. She locked it firmly, and did some calming breathwork for a few minutes to regain her focus. The texts were scaring the hell out of her, but even more than that—they made her blazing angry. She scanned the suite and the bathroom, then the balcony. No obvious surveillance devices, but those wouldn't be out in the open anyway. She checked the vents and light switches to be doubly sure. Nothing stood out. Everything was exactly as it should be. But that didn't mean someone wasn't still watching her—somehow. She shut the balcony curtains, wondering if it really mattered at all.

Then she moved quickly to the closet, threw the pillows to the side, and pulled out the board. The pins and threads were untouched, the players from Diana St. James to the deceased couple still anchored in place.

But Karen couldn't shake the unease twisting in her gut as she stared at the board. Whoever was watching her had managed to stay one step ahead, leaving her with breadcrumbs while they controlled the narrative.

Sliding into the chair at the table, she pulled the torn resort map and necklace still in the makeshift evidence bag from her purse. Her fingers brushed over the silver necklace with its blood-streaked heart pendant, then she picked it up and pinned it beneath a yellow marker on the board, labeled *Unknown Origin*. The map—two crime scenes circled—went directly below Diana's photo.

"They are connected," Karen muttered, her eyes narrowing at the red strings already crisscrossing the board. "And someone wanted me to find this map and necklace."

The questions kept piling up. What had the couple stolen? Who did the necklace belong to? The map felt deliberate, a breadcrumb left either by the killer or someone who wanted her to see the pattern. Either way, someone was manipulating the game, and Karen didn't like her lack of control.

Her phone buzzed again—a text from T: *Nothing from the lab. They're still processing samples. Anything else you need?*

Karen tapped out a quick reply: *Sending more evidence. A silver heart pendant—blood smear on it. See if you can get me DNA. I know it could take a few weeks.*

He texted back: *Can do. I'll see if they can put a rush on it.* Her thumb hesitated as she typed the last part: *Someone's watching me. Keep digging on Volkov.*

The knot in her chest tightened as she sent the message. T would know how to play this—he'd keep things discreet. Right now, she needed him to work the evidence while she continued her investigation at the resort.

Karen stepped back from the table, crossing her arms as she studied the board. The pieces were still too scattered. The necklace. The map. The Exodus verses left at both crime scenes.

"You shall not bear false witness. You shall not steal," Karen muttered to herself.

Her mind ticked through the possibilities. Doe 1 and Doe 2's presence in the suite still didn't make sense. Were they there by design, or had they stumbled into something they shouldn't have? Had they taken something—drugs, money—or were they simply victims of circumstance?

The distant sound of a keycard unlocking the door jolted Karen from her thoughts. She quickly shoved the board back into the closet, propping it up with the pillows again as Brock entered, looking both exhausted and irritated.

His once-crisp shirt was rumpled, a fine sheen of sweat across his forehead. He dropped a thick folder onto the dining table with a groan.

"Long day?" Karen asked, forcing a casual tone.

"You have no idea," he grumbled, collapsing onto the couch. "They had me sorting through centerpieces, wrangling vendors, and finalizing the guest list with Bethany. That woman—God help me—whining nonstop about Mario."

"Mario?" Karen's brow furrowed as she perched on the arm of the couch.

"The server from the night Diana died. Bethany swears he poisoned her." Brock leaned his head back against the cushion, rubbing his temples. "She's been telling anyone who'll listen that the local cops aren't doing enough and that Mario just 'happened' to disappear after the incident. I swear, Ka, she spent half the afternoon holding court like some sort of grieving queen."

Karen filed that away. "Mario's still missing, huh?"

"Yeah. The staff claims he just stopped showing up for work. Bethany thinks he skipped town to avoid being arrested." Brock rolled his eyes. "At this point, I think she's just looking for someone to blame."

Karen said nothing, but the information gnawed at her. Mario was at the scene when Diana collapsed. If he'd disappeared, it could mean two things—he was guilty, or someone had silenced him.

She pulled out her notebook, jotting down Mario's name beneath Diana's photo. "Bethany feels certain it's him?"

"As sure as someone who doesn't know a damn thing about actual investigations," Brock muttered. "But it does make you wonder, doesn't it? He was there, and he did serve their drinks and dessert."

Karen tapped her pen against the notebook, her gaze distant. "It *is* a lead I haven't pursued yet. I'll dig into it."

Brock sighed, sinking deeper into the couch. "You're relentless, you know that? Well, don't let Bethany corner you. She's relentless."

Karen allowed a slight smile. "Noted."

"You think we're gonna figure this out before the gala?" Brock asked.

Karen didn't answer immediately. She stared at the board, feeling the void of the missing pieces deep in her gut. Finally, she said, "We have to."

A sharp knock at the suite door made both of them freeze. Karen's hand instinctively went to her hip, where her sidearm would normally sit. She exchanged a glance with Brock, who pushed himself up slowly.

"You expectin' anyone?" he asked.

Karen shook her head.

The knock came again, louder this time.

Karen stepped toward the door, pulse quickening as she peered through the peephole. She saw nothing, so she unlatched the lock and swung the door open. Taped to the outside of the door was a small white envelope, fluttering faintly in the breeze. She grabbed the envelope and glanced down the hallway.

Empty.

She held the envelope up, her hands steady as she opened it. Inside was a single piece of paper, neatly folded.

Scrawled across it in black ink were five chilling words:

You're getting too close, Detective.

It was like this perp was inside her brain, knowing all, seeing all.

She couldn't help but feel like time was running out. For her and her husband.

CHAPTER 33

"What is it this time?" Brock asked, his voice edged with exhaustion. Karen handed him the note. His jaw clenched as he read the message aloud, "You're getting too close, Detective." He gave the note back to her, as if it burned him to hold it. "This is getting out of hand, Ka. They're playing games with you, with us."

Karen tucked the note into her purse, her expression hardening. "They're trying to rattle me, but it won't work."

"Well, it's working on me."

"Honey, listen," she said quietly. "The closer we get, the more desperate they become. That's how it works."

"Whatever," he said, before glancing at his watch with a groan. "I need to go get ready."

"For—?"

"There's this stupid cocktail hour thing at 5:30, and I can't miss it," he said. "It's at some place called La Brisa Azul."

"I remember reading about it in the resort directory."

"Yeah. Supposedly it's one of the fancier places on the property. A Caribbean-Spanish fusion theme—tapas, rum cocktails, the works. All the muckety-mucks from the Rosarian Society will be there, and I gotta represent Tampa now, of course."

Karen nodded, understanding the necessity of maintaining appearances. "Go shower. I'll get changed, and we'll head down together. I just need to stop by the front desk first. Gotta send another package to T."

By 5:30, Karen and Brock were strolling into La Brisa Azul, a stunning open-air restaurant that overlooked the resort's infinity pool and the ocean beyond. The warm golden hues of the sunset bathed the blue-and-white tilework on the walls with a soft glow.

Woven pendant lights hung from the ceiling, swaying gently in the breeze, while tropical plants framed the dining area, giving the space an intimate yet lively atmosphere.

The aroma of freshly grilled seafood mingled with the sharp scent of citrus from the signature cocktails being passed around by waitstaff. A string quartet played a lively arrangement of Latin jazz in the background, setting a cheerful yet sophisticated tone.

The room was already buzzing with conversation. Members of the Rosarian Society from across the globe mingled, their name badges glinting under the soft lighting. Karen immediately recognized a few faces from previous events—tall, distinguished Brady from London. Effervescent Lila from Sydney, Australia. And the ever-meticulous Hiroshi from Tokyo.

Each held a drink in one hand and spoke with animated gestures about hybrid strains, perfect soil pH, and the next big trend in floriculture.

Brock, dressed in a linen button-up and khakis, fit in seamlessly. Karen, in a breezy sundress and understated jewelry, stayed close by his side, scanning the room as they moved.

"Hey there, Brock," a voice boomed from across the room. Brady waved a champagne flute, his silver hair catching the light. "Glad you could make it. Tough shoes to fill, stepping in for Diana."

Brock forced a polite smile and exchanged pleasantries, while Karen tuned into the conversation around her. Bethany was nearby, her voice sharp as she lamented to a small group about the local police.

"They're useless," she was saying, her cheeks flushed from a bit too much wine. "I'm telling you, it's that server—Mario. Poisoned her, I'm sure of it. And now he's vanished! What more proof do they need?"

Karen caught Brock's eye and gave him a slight nod, signaling her intent to move away. He returned it, his face a mixture of weariness and determination as he dove into another conversation about centerpiece arrangements.

Karen took a cocktail from a passing server's tray and wandered toward the edge of the crowd, keeping her demeanor relaxed. Her attention fell on Jose, the ever-smiling staff member who had taken care of them at the pool and beach. He was standing near the bar, chatting with a colleague, his dark eyes scanning the room with the ease of someone used to observing without being noticed. Karen approached him with a warm smile.

"Jose, hello," she said, her tone light. "You're everywhere."

His expression brightened. "Señora Karen! Enjoying the evening?"

She nodded. "Beautiful venue. You must be proud to work in such a stunning place."

Jose chuckled. "Sí, it's very beautiful. But tonight, I am only here to make sure everyone has what they need."

Karen lowered her voice slightly, her smile never wavering. "Actually, there's something I could use your help with. It's about Diana St. James."

Jose's eyes flickered, his smile faltering for the briefest moment. He glanced around the room before leaning in slightly. "This is not the best place to talk," he murmured. "Too many ears."

I hate when people say that.

"Can we chat later, then?"

Jose hesitated, then gave a small nod. "I will find you."

Before Karen could say more, the string quartet shifted to a livelier tune, and the chatter in the room swelled. She took a sip of her fizzy cocktail, which tickled her nose. Her gaze drifted back to Brock, who was now deep in conversation with a group of international rosarians.

Just as she began to relax, Karen's phone buzzed in her purse. She pulled it out discreetly, her pulse quickening when she saw the message:

You shouldn't have come here.

She glanced up quickly and spun in a circle, her eyes narrowing against the festive glow of the restaurant. Whoever had sent the message was blending in with the crowd . . . watching her, right here, right now.

CHAPTER 34

Karen glanced toward Jose, whose gaze briefly met hers. His expression was serious now, and he gave her the faintest nod before turning back to his colleague to circulate the party.

Her eyes swept the room again. The cocktail hour was in full swing, with conversations humming beneath the light strains of the quartet. Brock had moved to another group of rosarians, his easy charm masking the weariness Karen knew he felt.

Screw it, she thought, deciding to seize the moment.

Jose lingered at a nearby table, so Karen slipped through the crowd, sidled up next to him, and placed a hand lightly on his arm.

"Jose," she said, her voice just loud enough to be heard over the music. "Can we talk now? It won't take long."

He hesitated, glancing around before nodding. "Follow me, señora."

He led her toward a quieter corner of the restaurant, near a small side exit partially obscured by potted palms. The music and chatter faded into the background as Jose turned to face her, his friendly demeanor replaced by a cautious intensity.

"You are policía, yes?" he asked, his voice low.

Karen nodded. "Detective from Clearwater, Florida, here on vacation."

Jose's dark eyes softened slightly, and he nodded. "I thought so. You ask questions like someone who knows how."

"What can you tell me about Mario?" Karen asked, keeping her tone steady but urgent.

Jose's gaze dropped to the floor, his shoulders tightening. "Mario is un hombre bueno."

"A good man," Karen said.

"Sí. He got me this job, you know? A few years back. He vouched for me."

"So why did he disappear?"

Jose looked up sharply, his voice firm. "He is scared. He didn't do anything wrong, but he knows how it looks. La señora died, and everyone points to him because he served her. He ran because he thinks nadie—no one will believe him."

Karen considered this. "Where did he go?"

"No sé—I don't know," Jose admitted, his voice breaking slightly. "After she died, I lent him my scooter, and that was the last time I saw him."

"Does he have a cell? Have you tried calling him?"

"Sí, pero, it goes straight to voicemail, like he's turned off his phone."

"And you believe he's innocent?"

Jose hesitated, then nodded. "Sí. Mario is not perfect, but he is not a killer."

Karen let the words settle before shifting the topic. "What about Senator Ortiz? What can you tell me about him?"

Jose's expression darkened. "Not much. He is private. Always polite, but distant. When he stays here, he keeps to himself. But this time—"

"Yes?"

He hesitated, his voice dropping further. She had to lean closer to hear him. "This time, the staff noticed him with you and your husband. We all wondered, *Who are they? Why is the senator speaking to them?*"

Karen filed that away, her thoughts spinning. She pressed on. "What about the man in the Panama hat? Have you seen him before?"

Jose opened his mouth to respond, but before he could, another staff member approached, their expression apologetic but firm. "Jose, necesitamos tu ayuda."

Karen didn't need a translation bible to know he was needed elsewhere.

Jose shot an apologetic look. "Lo siento, señora. I have to go."

Karen nodded, though she knew the frustration was evident in her expression. "Thanks, Jose. If you think of anything else, come and find me."

"I will," he promised before disappearing into the bustling crowd.

Karen lingered in the quiet corner for a moment, her mind churning. Mario's fear, the senator's strange behavior, and the elusive man in the Panama hat—every piece felt connected, but the full picture remained maddeningly out of reach.

She stepped back into the main restaurant, and her eyes landed on the May-December couple she'd noticed earlier, the woman's wrist adorned with a glittering bracelet that caught the light with every gesture.

Karen surmised it was a recent purchase from La Marina Casa de Campo—an indulgence that stood out. At the woman's feet, her chihuahua lounged contentedly, its collar glinting with the same stones as the bracelet.

Karen's gaze narrowed. Matching jewelry for both the woman and her dog? That wasn't just indulgence—it was a statement.

Or a cry for help.

Chloe and Cal caught her eye next. They were seated for dinner, and Chloe was engrossed in her phone as always, snapping selfies and chatting animatedly with someone on the other end. She wore a fitted coral dress, her blonde hair fell in loose waves over her shoulders, and her sun-kissed skin glowed under the soft lighting. Admittedly, she was stunning.

Cal, on the other hand, sat quietly in a crisp white shirt and navy slacks, his hair tousled but in a neat way. He seemed detached, his gaze fixed on the table in front of him, his hands clasped loosely in his lap.

Karen studied him for a moment. There was something unsettling about the stillness in his posture, the way his presence seemed to fade into the background while Chloe's vivacious energy took center stage.

Karen's phone buzzed, pulling her attention away.

She glanced at the screen, her heart pounding when she saw the message:

You're wasting time, Detective.

Karen's eyes narrowed into slits as she surveyed the room. *Where are you, asshole? And who are you?* She'd grown tired of this stupid game, of someone watching her every moving and taunting her.

The string quartet struck up another tune, and Karen slipped her phone back into her purse. She sucked in a deep, fortifying breath. She wasn't going to let this person dictate the rules of the game.

As the evening wore on, the festive atmosphere felt increasingly surreal. Karen's mind was already piecing together her next steps. When Brock approached, his expression a mix of exhaustion and frustration, her attention snapped back to the present.

"Ready to go?" he asked, his voice low.

Karen nodded, though her gaze lingered on the crowd. "Only if you are."

But she could have stayed until the last person left, if only to sniff out her stalker.

CHAPTER 35

The following morning, the outdoor breakfast patio buzzed with soft conversation as resort staff moved efficiently between tables. Karen stirred her coffee absently, her thoughts miles away. The events of the past few days weighed heavily on her. Each new piece of information deepened the mystery rather than clarifying it.

While she pondered, she watched her husband, who was leaning back in his chair and scrolling through his phone. His plate of food was mostly untouched—totally unlike him—though the mango slices were nearly gone. His lips were moving . . .

"Ka?" Brock's voice broke her reverie. He set his phone down, his brow furrowing. "Ya with me? I said, check this out."

"Sorry," Karen said, forcing a smile. "Just daydreaming."

"Yeah, well, dream about this," he said, his voice tinged with frustration. "Another event just got added to my plate. Some leadership roundtable nonsense. Something to do with hybrid collaborations."

Karen frowned, her mind shifting gears. "Another meeting? What happened to just attending the gala?"

Brock sighed. "Apparently, Diana's responsibilities didn't evaporate with her. It's happening at eleven o'clock this morning, so I'm stuck with Bethany and the rest of the Tampa Bay Chapter."

Before Karen could respond, a familiar figure approached. Wolfram's presence commanded attention, his navy blazer sharply pressed and a briefcase in hand. He carried himself with calm authority, though Karen noticed his subtle glance around the patio, as if assessing the audience.

"Good morning, Mr. and Mrs. Skaryd," he greeted, his tone polite but measured. "I trust you slept well?"

"Hey, Wolfram. It's Brock and Karen, remember?" Brock said, gesturing to the empty chair at their table. "Care to join us?"

"Thank you, but I won't impose." Wolfram set his briefcase on the chair. "I'm here on behalf of Senator Ortiz. He's extended an invitation for you both to join him for lunch aboard his yacht today. Noon at the marina."

Karen arched a brow. "A yacht lunch? Any particular reason for the invitation?"

Wolfram smiled faintly. "The senator would like your perspectives. He's considering a land development project in Florida and would appreciate input from residents like yourselves. He's exploring potential locations—South Florida, the Panhandle, Northern Florida, and the Tampa Bay area."

Karen exchanged a glance with Brock. "That's . . . unexpected."

"The senator values local insight," Wolfram said smoothly. "And your connections to the Tampa Bay area, especially as a law enforcement officer, make your opinions particularly relevant."

Brock leaned back, letting out a low whistle. "I'd love to help, but I'm tied up with a leadership roundtable thing."

Wolfram's brows lifted in surprise. "Leadership roundtable?"

"Yeah." Brock's frustration had crept into his tone. "Diana, you know, the lady that died? These are her old responsibilities, and I'm pinch-hitting."

"I see," Wolfram said, his gaze shifting to Karen. "Mrs. Skaryd, I mean, Karen, would you be willing to attend by yourself? The senator values sharp minds."

Karen hesitated, studying Wolfram's face. There was more to this invitation than land development.

"I suppose I could make time," she said carefully. "Brock?"

He waved his hand dismissively. "Go, have some fun. I'll do what I have to do over here."

"Okay, then—"

"Excellent." Wolfram picked up his briefcase. "The senator will be pleased. Noon sharp at the marina. I'll inform him you'll be attending—alone."

"Wait," Karen said, stopping him before he left the table. "One more thing. Are you aware of any updates on the murder investigations? Diana, the couple in that other suite?"

Wolfram opened his mouth to speak, but he paused instead, his expression unreadable. Then, "The local authorities are still gathering information. As you know, these matters take time."

"What about Brock?" Karen pressed. "Still a suspect?"

Wolfram's lips pressed into a thin line. "I'm sure if there were developments, you'd be informed."

Karen nodded slowly, her tone turning sharper. "Seems like things have gone awfully quiet for such important and unique cases."

Wolfram's gaze held hers, calm but unyielding. "Perhaps quiet is exactly what's needed to get results."

Karen leaned back, letting the silence stretch before offering a thin smile. "I guess I'll see you at noon."

Wolfram gave a curt nod and departed, his hulking figure weaving through the breakfast crowd.

Brock leaned forward. "You sure about this? Lunch with Ortiz, without me?"

"You said it was fine."

"Yeah, but—"

"If anything, it's an opportunity. If he's tied to Diana or the couple, I might learn something."

"Or walk into something," Brock countered.

Karen's phone buzzed on the table. She glanced down at the screen, her stomach tightening when she read the message:

You're asking the wrong questions.

Her head shot up as her eyes darted around the room. Nothing seemed out of place, no one seemed to be watching her, yet the unease settled deeper in her chest.

"What now?" Brock asked.

"Nothing." Karen slipped her phone into her bag. "Just T."

Whoever was behind the messages was always one step ahead, and Karen knew she couldn't afford to fall further behind.

CHAPTER 36

Karen adjusted her sunglasses and smoothed the hem of her lightweight sundress—white with soft coral accents. It was practical, chosen to keep cool in the Caribbean sun. As she approached the gleaming *Libertad* moored at the marina, her sandals clicked softly against the planks. She exhaled, steeling herself for whatever lay ahead.

Brock's parting words echoed in her ears. He had offered to skip his rosarian commitment to join her, but she refused. "This isn't my first rodeo," she had said firmly.

His worried expression lingered in her mind, but she pushed it aside. There was no room for distraction now. Camilla greeted her at the gangway, a picture of poise in a navy jumpsuit—her calm presence at odds with the sharp glint in her observant eyes. "Señora Karen, welcome," Camilla said with a warm smile, extending a hand to help her aboard. "The senator is delighted you could join us."

"Thank you." Karen stepped onto the polished deck. The faint scent of saltwater mingled with citrusy cleaning products as the sunlight glinted off the brass fittings.

"The senator sends his apologies for not being able to greet you when you arrived," Camilla continued, gesturing toward a shaded dining area. "He is wrapping up an overseas call. He'll be with you shortly, though."

Karen's lips curved into a polite smile. "I understand. Busy man."

As they approached the neatly set table, Karen noted the three place settings. Her stomach tightened. *Three?*

Before she could question it, movement caught her eye. Luz, the cheerful manicurist from her last visit, stood chatting with a staff member at the far end of the deck. Luz's smile widened when she spotted Karen.

"Señora Karen!" Luz called, waving enthusiastically as she walked over. "You never finished your manicure! Come, I'll make it perfect now."

Karen chuckled despite herself. "I will have to take a raincheck for another time."

"Sooner is better than later," she teased, wagging a finger. Then she turned and continued her conversation with her coworker.

Moments later, Camilla arrived with a vibrant drink, its orange and red hues swirling like a sunset. "A tropical hibiscus spritz," she said, setting it down. "Perfect to prepare your palate for lunch."

Karen lifted the glass cautiously, her detective instincts on high alert. She took a measured sip. The drink was crisp and refreshing, leaving no trace of anything amiss. Still, she kept her guard up, noticing Wolfram exiting from the interior cabin. He leaned casually against the railing.

Their gazes locked, and Wolfram gave her a faint nod. It was meant to reassure, but Karen felt no comfort in it.

"Do you always keep such a watchful eye on the senator's guests?" she asked, her tone light but pointed.

"It's my job," Wolfram said smoothly. "To ensure comfort and safety."

"Comfort and safety, huh?" Karen echoed. "That's thoughtful. Does it include knowing if the senator's guests are being watched? Or receiving cryptic messages?"

Wolfram's jaw tightened ever so slightly. "I'm afraid I don't know what you mean."

Karen leaned forward, her voice dropping. "You know exactly what I mean. Diana St. James, the young couple, and now me. It's all connected. And somehow, you're in the middle of it."

Before Wolfram could respond, the sound of footsteps interrupted them. Karen turned just as Senator Ortiz emerged from the cabin, his polished demeanor radiating authority.

"Mi amiga Karen," Ortiz said warmly, spreading his arms in greeting. "Thank you for joining me."

She rose, forcing a pleasant smile. "Thank you for the invitation, Juan Carlos."

But her focus shifted as another figure stepped onto the deck behind him. The man's sharp features, piercing blue eyes, and commanding presence were impossible to forget.

Karen's breath caught.

Trailing beside the man was a striking silver-furred Saarloos Wolfdog, its lean, muscular frame moving with a predatory grace. The dog's amber eyes locked onto Karen briefly before settling beside its handler, radiating silent menace.

"Allow me to introduce my associate," the senator said, his voice smooth as ice. "Señor Gregor Volkov."

Karen extended her hand to Volkov, masking her unease with a tight smile. "Pleasure to meet you."

Volkov's grip was firm, his demeanor stoic. "The pleasure is mine," he said, his accented voice low and even.

Karen's mind raced as she sat back down, every impulse screaming that this wasn't about land development. The meticulous place settings, the senator's calculated entrance, Volkov's presence—it all pointed to a far more dangerous game.

For no reason obvious to Karen, the dog let out a low, rumbling growl as Volkov took his seat across from Karen. Senator Ortiz smiled pleasantly, oblivious—or perhaps entirely aware—of the storm brewing beneath the surface of this supposedly lighthearted luncheon.

Karen's fingers tightened around her glass as she met Volkov's piercing gaze.

And she knew—this was only the beginning.

They were the hunters, and she was their prey.

CHAPTER 37

The Saarloos Wolfdog growled again, and Karen found herself wanting to scoot her chair as far away from the dog as possible.

"She's protective," Volkov said with a small smile. "But well trained. Like all my dogs."

Trained for what? Karen forced a return smile, leaning back slightly as she sipped her hibiscus spritz. "She's beautiful. What's her name?"

"Zhivka. It means 'viper.' Fitting, don't you think?"

Karen nodded politely. The calculated precision of his words, the controlled power behind his every move—this was no ordinary businessman. Volkov radiated dominance, and she imagined that Senator Ortiz was merely a pawn in his game.

Juan Carlos gestured toward the pristine marina view. "Karen, I hope we have made you feel at home. We are interested in your perspective on a project."

"Yes, Wolfram mentioned something about a land development project in Florida. It is a big state. I guess it all depends on what you're looking for."

The senator launched into an explanation of his vision—charitable initiatives, community outreach, and economic development. But Karen wasn't buying it. Every polished word reeked of a rehearsed pitch designed to mask darker motives.

Her extensive experience in both federal and local law enforcement had given her an intimate understanding of Florida's underbelly, where its sprawling coastline and countless hidden inlets made it a notorious hub for illicit and illegal ports of entry.

Volkov remained silent while the senator spoke, not once injecting a comment. Instead, his fingers idly stroked Zhivka's fur. Only when Ortiz had finished his monologue did Volkov speak.

"Florida is an untapped market," he said. "Strategic positioning, access to resources, and of course, the right partnerships. It is why we value insights from individuals like yourself, Karen."

"Law enforcement offers a unique perspective," Juan Carlos added, smiling warmly. "Who better to understand the needs of a community than someone who's served it? That's why we'd like to offer you a partnership in our project."

Karen felt the weight of their combined stares. This was more than a pitch. They wanted her to have skin in their game.

"It's certainly a unique approach," she said, her voice steady despite the rising tension. "But I'm curious, what exactly would these partnerships entail?"

Volkov's gaze sharpened. "Trust. Loyalty. Mutual benefit."

Karen leaned forward slightly. "And what happens when trust is broken?"

The faintest flicker of amusement crossed Volkov's face. He gestured to Zhivka. "Dogs are wild by nature. They require a firm hand, discipline. When they challenge authority or forget their place—" He stopped, letting the implication settle.

"You remind them?" Karen asked.

Volkov didn't blink. "Yes. Swiftly. Publicly. It keeps the rest in line."

Her stomach immediately twisted, and it was all she could do not to wrap her arms around herself. But she kept her expression neutral. The senator shifted uncomfortably as Volkov's dominance held firm.

"And people?" she asked, clearly pushing the envelope. "Do they get the same treatment?"

Volkov's smile was cold. "People are not so different from dogs."

Before Karen could respond, the sharp clatter of heels echoed across the deck. She turned to see a tall man in a crisp, white linen suit stepping onto the yacht, flanked by a shorter woman with chestnut-brown hair pulled into a tight ponytail.

"Inspector General Rafael Montenegro," the man introduced himself, his authoritative voice cutting through the tension. "And this is Detective Maria Alvarez."

The senator stood abruptly, his polished demeanor slipping. "Inspector, what brings you here?"

Montenegro's sharp dark eyes scanned the table before settling on Karen. "Señora Skaryd, we need to speak with you. Ahora."

Karen's heart raced. "Is something wrong?"

"It concerns the ongoing investigation into the recent deaths at the resort," he said, his tone leaving no room for argument. "Por favor, come with us."

Alvarez stepped forward and gestured for Karen to follow. Karen rose slowly, casting a glance at Ortiz and Volkov. Ortiz looked flustered, his hands fidgeting with the edge of the tablecloth. Volkov, in contrast, leaned back in his chair, his expression giving nothing away as to his thoughts.

"Fine. I'll go with you," Karen said, her voice steady despite the storm brewing around her. She grabbed her purse, her fingers brushing against her cell phone.

As Alvarez led her toward the gangway, Karen cast a final glance over her shoulder. Volkov's cold gaze met hers, his hand resting on Zhivka's head.

"We'll continue this conversation," he said smoothly.

Karen's pulse quickened as she stepped off the yacht, Montenegro walking beside her. The yacht's polished deck faded behind her, replaced by the gritty reality of the investigation that had followed her to paradise.

"What's this about?" she asked Montenegro as they reached the dock.

He didn't answer immediately. Instead, he exchanged a glance with Alvarez, who nodded. Montenegro's expression was grim when he finally spoke.

"It's about Diana St. James and the couple from the neighboring suite. It appears someone has been tampering with my crime scenes."

CHAPTER 38

Karen sat stiffly in the back of Montenegro's unmarked car, the humid Caribbean air seeping in through a barely cracked window. The stale tang of old tobacco mixed with cracked vinyl, and she wrinkled her nose against the smell.

Montenegro's grip on the steering wheel was tight, his eyes locked on the road ahead. In the passenger seat, Detective Alvarez scribbled in a worn leather pad, glancing up occasionally at the rearview mirror to catch Karen's reflection.

The police radio crackled, filling the silence. A garbled voice rattled off a string of Spanish. Karen caught most of it—an ongoing domestic dispute, a robbery near Bávaro Beach, and officers responding to a drunken tourist causing trouble outside a store.

Montenegro's eyes flicked toward the radio, but his hand remained fixed on the wheel. Karen shifted slightly. "Busy day," she commented, hoping to break the silence.

Montenegro didn't respond.

Another call burst through the static.

"Sounds like it's all happening at once," she added.

Montenegro's gaze didn't move from the road ahead.

"I guess stolen mangos aren't high on your list."

Still, silence.

Karen crossed her arms, glancing out the window as the luxury of the marina faded into narrow, bustling streets lined with pastel-colored buildings. Vendors leaned against fruit carts, calling out to passersby. Groups of kids kicked a soccer ball across dusty pavement. The vibrant chaos outside felt distant, like watching life through glass.

A sharp voice cracked over the radio. A homicide at a local beach.

Karen's head snapped toward Montenegro. His eyes flicked to the rearview mirror, locking with hers briefly before returning to the road.

"You're not sending anyone to the scene?" Karen asked, leaning forward slightly.

"Not my problem."

"So, dead bodies on the beach aren't, but ones at resorts—" Karen countered.

Montenegro's grip on the wheel tightened, but he didn't answer.

The station came into view—a squat, weathered structure with streaked stucco walls and rusting bars on the windows. A tattered Dominican flag drooped above the entrance, barely stirring in the heavy breeze. Stray dogs lounged near the doorway, shaded by the rusted remains of an old patrol car.

Inside, the oppressive heat settled over Karen like a second skin. The air was thick with sweat, cheap disinfectant, and stale coffee. Officers shuffled past, some eyeing her with curiosity. The walls peeled in places, and the overhead lights flickered.

Karen's heels clicked against the cracked tile floor as Montenegro led her through the bullpen. Conversations dropped to murmurs as she passed rows of battered desks piled with paperwork. Alvarez followed silently, like a shadow glued to Montenegro's side.

They stopped outside a door marked *Interrogatorio*. Montenegro pushed it open without a word, gesturing for Karen to step inside.

The interrogation room was small and dimly lit by a single bulb that cast harsh shadows across the battered metal table and two chairs. A one-way mirror stretched along one wall.

She crossed the room and sat down, smoothing the hem of her dress as Montenegro loomed over her. Alvarez slipped into the corner, her arms folding across her chest.

Montenegro tossed a folder onto the table, the slap of paper slicing through the silence.

"Señora Skaryd," he began, voice low, "your fingerprints were found at both crime scenes. Care to explain?"

Karen didn't blink.

"At Diana's scene? I was having lunch. You know this. At the second—" she leaned forward slightly, "—you invited me in."

"Convenient. But I think you're meddling, and I don't appreciate it."

Karen's gaze didn't falter. "Meddling? You allowed me into that room. I was observing."

Montenegro scoffed. "Observing? This isn't Florida. Your jurisdiction ended when you landed on my island. This is my case. I don't need you sticking your nose in."

"I was trying to help," she said. "Two people are dead. I assumed that mattered to you."

Montenegro's palm slammed the table, sending her purse toppling to the floor.

"I don't need your help," he snapped. "This is my investigation. I don't share it—especially with tourists playing detective."

"With all due respect, Inspector," Karen said, holding his gaze, "I'm not playing. I've been trained by some of the best law enforcement agencies on the planet."

"That's the problem," Montenegro hissed. "You think you know what you're doing. But here? You are out of your depth."

"So, you're more interested in guarding your turf than finding the truth?"

Montenegro straightened, pacing slowly. "This isn't a game, señora. If you keep poking around, I will arrest you. Do you know what our jails are like?"

Karen blew out a loud sigh, then, "Enlighten me?"

He stopped pacing, leaning over her shoulder with a menacing whisper. "Our jails aren't like your cushy ones back home. They're rough. Brutal. And if word gets out you're a cop? I cannot guarantee your safety."

Karen arched a brow. "Is that a threat?"

"A warning."

Her phone buzzed in her purse. Alvarez stepped forward, but Montenegro waved her off.

"May I?" Karen asked, and Montenegro nodded. She picked her purse off the floor and pulled out her phone.

Her stomach tightened as she read the message.

You're digging in the wrong places.

She lifted her gaze to Montenegro.

"Problema?" he asked, his voice dripped with mock concern.

Karen forced a tight smile. "My husband. Wondering where I am."

Montenegro chuckled. "Tell him not to wait up."

"Another warning?"

"Call it what you want. But if you don't back off, you'll see how serious I am."

Karen leaned back, tension coiled in her chest, though her face betrayed nothing. Years of FBI training—and her father's wisdom—kept her composed.

"Are we done, Inspector?" she asked evenly.

"For now," he said, stepping back. "But don't test me. Next time, there won't be a warning."

Karen rose, smoothing her dress as she held Montenegro's gaze. "I'll keep that in mind. Now, how about you drive me back to the resort?"

He leaned back against the table, arms crossed, a slow sneer tugging at the corner of his mouth. "Señora, we're the police, not Uber."

She shrugged. "Good to know. And here I was planning on leaving you a glowing review." She slipped her bag over her shoulder and made for the door.

"Don't get lost on the way back to the Utopia, señora. Would hate for you to wind up somewhere—unsafe."

Karen paused at the door, casting a glance over her shoulder. "Funny, I was about to say the same to you."

CHAPTER 39

Through the dirty taxi window, Karen could see the resort's lights flickering up ahead. The cab smelled faintly of coconut air freshener, masking something more metallic beneath. Her fingers brushed against the text still glowing on her phone screen.

You're digging in the wrong places.

She didn't know whether to feel threatened or protected.

The taxi slowed at the entrance to the Utopia, and Karen slipped a few bills to the driver. "Gracias," she muttered, then exited the cab and entered the lobby. The contrast was immediate—the crisp, air-conditioned breeze and soft Latin jazz filtering throughout the area felt worlds away from the station's stale air and overall depressing atmosphere. .

By the time she reached her suite, she felt exhaustion settling deep in her bones. She unlocked the door, stepping inside to find Brock on the couch, a drink in hand and his iPad perched precariously on his knees. His face lit up at seeing her, then quickly moved to a look of concern.

"Are you okay? How was lunch?" he asked, setting the glass down and standing.

Karen tossed her purse onto the chair and ran a hand through her hair.

"Lunch was . . . fine." She sighed. "But it wasn't Juan Carlos we needed to worry about. It was his guest."

Brock frowned. "Guest?"

"Gregor Volkov," Karen said, her tone flat.

Brock's entire body stiffened. "Volkov? As in the Volkov?"

"The one and only. He about as charming as a viper before it strikes. He brought his wolf-dog too—named Zhivka. It could have played an extra in *Game of Thrones*."

"So, shit's starting to get real," Brock said.

"Apparently. And let me tell you, that lunch had nothing to do with real estate research. Whatever they're planning . . . it's big. And they're either trying to pull me in or—"

He cut in: "You should have called me."

"Calling you wouldn't have changed the situation. And there's more."

Brock groaned and sank back into the couch cushions. "More?"

"Yeah, Montenegro showed up out of nowhere and practically dragged me to the station."

"What? What'd he want?"

Karen dropping onto the couch beside him. "Apparently, my fingerprints at the restaurant and the second crime scene were an issue. He accused me of meddling, but I think it was more to distract me."

"From what?"

Karen tapped the side of her phone, lifting the screen. "From the person who keeps sending me these." She passed him the message.

Brock read the latest message aloud. "'You're digging in the wrong places.' What?"

She nodded. "I think whoever this is knew Volkov was on the yacht and used Montenegro to get me off the boat."

"So, you think someone's trying to . . . *protect* you?"

"I don't know," she said with a shrug, scrunching her shoulders for a few seconds before letting them fall. "All I know is Montenegro used the yacht luncheon as an opportunity to remind me of my place, despite the fact that he's not pulling the strings. Of course, I don't think Montenegro's bright enough to figure that out."

"What, that he's being played?"

"Like a fiddle, in my opinion. Either way, though, I'm still on Volkov's game board, feeling like the little Scottie dog or race car piece," Karen leaned forward, elbows on her knees. "I just can't figure out why he's involved in Diana's murder. Was Diana onto something that put her in his crosshairs? And what about that couple found in the building next door—how do they fit into all of this?"

"That's a good question, babe."

She nodded, "Regardless, I have a feeling this is bigger than those murders. Guys like Volkov don't get involved unless there's serious money or influence on the line."

Brock lips pursed, tension lining his jaw. "Well, while you were playing cat-and-mouse, I was stuck listening to two hours of hybrid collaborations, which I do find interesting but still—I damn-near fell asleep twice."

Karen smiled faintly. "Sounds riveting."

"Yeah, that's what it was. So, what's our next move?"

Karen was about to respond when her phone buzzed again. She glanced down at the screen.

T: *Need to talk. The first set of labs are in.*

Karen's heart skipped. She exchanged a quick look with Brock.

"It's T," she said, pushing up from the couch. "He's received the first set of labs."

"Get what you need. I'll pour another drink."

Karen stepped onto the balcony, the humidity enveloping her as she called Terrell. Something about the way the clouds gathered in the distance felt heavy—perhaps a storm she couldn't yet see.

T picked up and before she could utter a word, he said, "Karen, you ain't gonna like the news."

CHAPTER 40

Karen leaned against the balcony railing—the phone pressed to her ear as T's voice cut through the distant hum of ocean waves.

"You still there?" T asked, his tone sharper than usual. "I said, you ain't gonna—"

"Let me guess," she interjected. "The tissue residue came back positive?"

T exhaled into the receiver. "Yeah. A poison called Nerium oleander."

Karen straightened. "Nerium oleander?" She glanced over her shoulder, and Brock had apparently heard her words. He stood frozen in place, his glass was halfway to his lips and one eyebrow arched.

"Oleander?" he said. "That stuff's everywhere down here."

Karen held the phone slightly away from her ear. "Seriously?"

Brock nodded toward the path leading from their suite. "I've seen them lining the walkways around the resort. People probably think they're roses. Idiots." He shook his head, muttering under his breath. "You'd think they'd notice the difference, but no— 'Oh look, honey. Fancy tropical roses.'"

Karen smirked despite the weight of the conversation. "Glad to know the rose expert disapproves."

"Disapprove? Ya got that right. I've had to tell five people they were one bad decision away from meeting their maker." Brock finally sipped from his drink. "All parts of an oleander, including the leaves, can be poisonous if ingested or even if, say, you touch it, then it gets in your eyes or an open sore."

"And the resort doesn't mention this? Post a sign?"

Brock scoffed. "Actually, there is one. It caught my eye the first day we were here, an engraved plaque at the end of one of the walkways. Talks about the plant and offers a subtle warning about its toxicity."

Karen snorted but quickly sobered. "T, you hear what Brock is saying?"

"Yeah. Sounds like he should lead one of those nature walks," T joked. "But he's not wrong. From what I've just read, these oleanders are fairly common down there—and deadly when ingested. It says here oleander can cause dizziness and muscle weakness, even in small doses. Larger amounts? Coma and death are big possibilities, usually between four to twenty-four hours. Sound familiar?"

"Yeah." She breathed, staring out over the horizon. "That would also mean she'd ingested it sometime before the dinner, although . . . I suppose if the dose was huge enough, it could have happened immediately." She looked at Brock, who nodded in agreement.

"Someone sure knew what they were doing," T said. "This is a killer plant."

Karen's eyes narrowed. "And it's easily accessible."

"It's practically landscaping filler," Brock added. "Trust me, it's around."

"There you have it. Conveniently deadly and easy to hide in plain sight," T said, his chair creaking loud enough for her to hear it.

She rubbed her forehead. "Great. Resort by day, murder garden by night."

"That's not the only thing, though," T said.

Great, more "good" news.

"What else?"

"It's Woody. He's on my ass for running tests off the books. Keeps reminding me I've got open homicides piling up. Says I'm wasting time playing Sherlock for you."

Karen's lips tugged into a faint smile. "Tell Woody I'll send him a fruit basket."

"You'll need more than that if he hears this next part . . ." His tone had shifted, a foreshadowing.

Karen felt the dread creep through her body. "Go on."

"It's about the Aaliyah Andrews case."

"What about it?"

"Her name popped up while I was digging into Volkov."

She gasped. "What? How?"

"Aaliyah—she fits a profile. Age, background, lack of strong family ties. She was exactly the type of girl Volkov's network targets for trafficking. I'm starting to think she wasn't just in the wrong place at the wrong time."

Karen's stomach twisted. "You're saying Aaliyah might have been a mark?"

"Maybe. I can't say for sure yet. But the deeper I dig into Volkov's operations, the more these kinds of cases seem to surface. I found notes buried under shell companies tied to him. Travel logs, transfers to accounts I know for a fact are used to move people, not just money."

Karen rubbed her temple, processing the news. "And Aaliyah's name was buried in all that?"

"It was flagged. Not under her real name but aliases she'd been using on social media. Someone was watching her, Karen."

"Jesus," she murmured.

"We were so focused on Sasso—

"We missed the bigger picture."

"Yeah, and Volkov may not have killed her, but he sure as hell could've had plans for her."

Karen felt her pulse thrumming in her ears. "And you explained all this to Woody, and he still wants you to drop this? Even with the new information?"

"Like yesterday. Or at least 'til you get home. He feels if I keep working this Aaliyah/Sasso case alone, things could unravel fast, and I'll be drowning in paperwork for months."

"T, look, you don't need to keep looking into my case down here. I know how tight your time is."

"And leave you hanging? No way, Ka. We're partners."

Karen's throat tightened, and she forced a quiet laugh. "Thanks, T. Just be careful. If Volkov's network is that wide, someone will notice you sniffing around."

"Yeah, I know. But I'll work on it when I can, and I'll try to stay under Woody's radar. Based on everything I'm reading about Volkov, the guy's not the type to let cops snoop around his business."

Karen swallowed hard, turning slightly to catch Brock's watchful gaze. "I know."

CHAPTER 41

As dinnertime drew near, the Skaryds strolled down the resort's stone pathway. The soft glow of lanterns lined the walkways, casting shadows over neatly trimmed hedges and flower beds—oleanders in plain view.

Sandals dangling from her fingers, Karen eyeballed the oleander bushes as she pondered her conversation with Terrell. She wasn't looking for trouble, just answers, and she was determined to get them. Brock stayed close beside her, scanning the foliage with an expert's eyes. The Dominican rum and coke he'd made in the room sloshed gently in the glass—he'd refused to rush drinking the cocktail, insisting that he bring it with him.

"So," Brock said, squinting toward a hedge, "T really thinks someone's used oleander to kill Diana?"

"Wouldn't be the first time poison's been used to, say, tie up loose ends."

Brock leaned over to eyeball one of the pale pink flowers in a nearby bush. "These are all over the place. You'd think the resort's landscaper was trying to take out half the guests."

Karen smirked. "Well, maybe they are."

Brock raised a brow. "Nice. Nothing says 'paradise' like a side of cardiac arrest."

He chuckled, then tossed back the rest of his drink. Karen's expression remained serious as she studied the oleander flower.

"They are pretty," she said.

"Like I've heard people say, these are 'beautiful tropical roses,'" Brock said jokingly, shaking his head.

Karen glanced toward the poolside bar, watching happy tourists, oblivious to the silent threat woven into the landscape. "It's easy to hide danger when people aren't paying attention."

"Guess that's the trick, huh? Disguise death with a little . . . *scenery*."

Karen put her arm in his, and they resumed their stroll. "I'm going to talk to one of the landscapers tomorrow."

"And say what?" Brock asked. "Hey, buddy, I'm curious—how often do you lace the property with toxic flowers?"

"I'll figure it out." Karen's phone buzzed, and she pulled it from her purse and read the message:

Stay away from the garden.

"Jesus," she said, turning in a circle in hopes of catching her stalker.

"I'm guessing that ain't T."

She showed him the message and said, "No. It's not."

And I'm really getting tired of this shit.

They arrived at the Brisa del Mar, a restaurant requiring no reservations. It was tucked along the far side of the resort, partially hidden by a curtain of palm trees and flowering vines. The faint hum of a live guitarist trickled into the air from inside the restaurant, the sounds blending with the rhythmic crashing of waves.

Brock and Karen entered, greeted by the rich scent of grilled seafood and warm bread. The place exuded effortless charm—chic, but relaxed. Wicker pendant lights dangled over polished wooden tables, reflecting off of the sleek marble floors.

The staff, dressed in linen shirts carrying the resort's logo, weaved between tables with trays laden with tropical cocktails and steaming dishes.

Karen's eyes drifted to the blackboard near the entrance, where the specials were written in a looping script: mahi-mahi with plantain puree and grilled langoustines with a tamarind glaze.

"This'll do," Brock said, sliding his hand lightly over the back of one of the chairs.

As they settled at a table beneath a broad, woven fan lazily stirring the air, the hostess placed a small plate of fried tostones onto the table—the restaurant's version of breadsticks and oil. The delicious starter was sprinkled with sea salt and served with creamy avocado dip.

"God, I love Latin food," Brock noted, snatching one from the plate.

Karen lifted the menu but found herself more interested in the crowd. The Rosarian Society was out in full force. A few familiar faces passed by their table, tossing waves and pleasantries Brock's way.

A silver-haired woman in a silk blouse paused at their table, her gold bangles clinking softly. "You ready for the gala, Brock?"

"Getting there," Brock said, flashing his easy smile. "You know how it is. Still wrangling final touches."

"I'm gonna step out and check in with T," she whispered to Brock as a new group of rosarians approached.

He waved her off as he stood to greet the newcomers. "Okay, babe. I'll hold down the fort."

Karen headed toward the terrace, letting the sea breeze cool the tension creeping along her neck. T had nothing new to report—just the usual digging, more dead ends than not.

When she returned, Brock was halfway through another cocktail, though he seemed to be savoring each ounce. Across the restaurant, the May-December couple caught her attention. They sat by the railing, sharing a platter of grilled shrimp and papaya salad while Sable the chihuahua, dressed in a rhinestone-studded collar, perched contentedly on the woman's lap.

She wore a flowing white sundress with colorful drop earrings, her wrists adorned with equally colorful bangles that jingled softly whenever she reached for her glass of rosé. Her partner, tanned and impeccably groomed, reclined in a linen shirt and loafers, lazily twirling his fork.

As casual as they seemed, however, Karen couldn't help the suspicion that flared in the pit of her gut. Something about them still didn't sit right.

Brock followed her gaze. "You think they dress the dog too?"

Karen smirked. "Wouldn't surprise me."

She settled back in her chair when the waiter arrived with to take their dinner order, but she couldn't get the May-December pair out of her mind.

CHAPTER 42

Karen twirled her fork through a plate of grilled snapper, the fish resting atop coconut-infused rice, garnished with lime and fresh cilantro. A side of maduros—sweet plantains caramelized to perfection—balanced the flavors, while Brock's plate boasted a generous serving of slow-roasted pork shoulder marinated in citrus and garlic.

"Jesus, Ka . . . You gotta try this," Brock said, nudging his plate toward her.

Karen took a bite, savoring the tangy-sweet contrast. "Not bad," she admitted, nodding in approval.

"Not bad?" Brock scoffed. "This is like heaven on a plate."

Their paradise dinner, however, was anything but—they were constantly uninterrupted by Society members wanting to chitchat with Brock. A few offered enthusiastic invitations to join them later at El Cielo, the resort's beachfront bar, where the Rosarian Society made a habit of "holding court" until the wee hours.

"You're coming tonight, right, Brock?" The tall, distinguished Brady from London grinned as he leaned heavily on the back of Brock's chair. "We need your expert opinion on this new rum they're pouring tonight. Purely for research."

Brock laughed, raising his glass. "Wouldn't miss it."

Brady winked at Karen. "You too, copper."

Ha-ha-ha, not funny . . . But she put on a smile. "I'll be there. Someone needs to keep him out of trouble."

By the time the Skaryds finished their meal, the sun had dipped below the horizon. Karen looped her arm through Brock's as they strolled toward the bar. Its open-air setup sprawled along the beachfront, string lights stretching from palm to palm, illuminating the sand in warm, golden pools.

"You up for this?" Brock asked, squeezing her hand.

"Sure. A few cocktails won't kill me. Besides, we're on vacation, right?"

Brock arched a brow. "After everything, I think that's still up for debate."

They settled at the bar with their rosarian buddies. Brock dove headfirst into flights of rum samples, while Karen sipped slowly on a mojito, more content to observe than indulge.

Across the room, she spotted the newlyweds, Chloe and Cal. Chloe posed dramatically, snapping selfies with two other guests who looked close in age to the newlyweds, while Cal sat at the edge of the group, nursing a glass of wine, and scrolling through his phone.

"He looks *so* thrilled," Karen murmured.

Brock followed her gaze, shaking his head. "He's living the dream."

Karen's phone buzzed. She glanced at the screen, expecting exactly what she got. Another text:

Enjoy the night, Detective. Have a drink on me.

Karen's eyes lifted immediately, scanning the crowd. At the far end of the bar, the man in the Panama hat slipped quietly toward the exit, his face hidden beneath the brim.

Brock noticed her change in posture. "What's the matter?"

Karen stood, setting her glass down. "I need some air."

She followed the hat out the exit, but when she stepped outside, the man had seemingly disappeared in thin air. She stood there, debating.

She could hear her husband's laughter over the crowded noise.

On the one hand, she longed to be with him and just enjoy their vacation. No care in the world.

On the other hand, she wanted to keep walking into the night and find this man. Question him.

She turned around and made her way back to Brock.

The morning sun had barely crept over the horizon when Karen stepped into the resort's garden. Dew clung to the leaves, and the air carried the faint scent of hibiscus and sea salt.

Brock stayed behind, nursing a well-earned hangover. While he'd opted for room service and the safety of air-conditioning, Karen wasn't ready to sit idle.

She spotted a groundskeeper near the fountain, his straw hat pulled low as he trimmed the hedges. Karen approached slowly, offering a polite smile.

"Buenos días," she greeted. "Mind if I ask you something?"

The man straightened, wiping his hands on his pants. "Si, señora?"

Karen gestured toward a nearby oleander bloom. "I've noticed these everywhere. Who chose to plant them?"

The man's eyes flicked to the flower, and for the briefest moment, Karen caught hesitation in his expression. "Ah, well, management. They are sturdy bushes and colorful, very popular for landscaping. You like them, yes?"

"No mention about how poisonous it is?" she asked.

The groundskeeper's smile faltered. "Es . . . uh, not my concern, señora. I only plant what they tell me."

Karen studied his face. He wasn't lying—but he wasn't telling the full truth either.

"Does Senator Ortiz spend time in the garden?"

The groundskeeper stiffened slightly but shook his head. "No. He tends to stay near la marina."

"Well, thanks for your time."

As she walked away, the phone buzzed again in her pocket. She pulled it out, reading the new message:

He's watching you.

Karen glanced over her shoulder. The groundskeeper had resumed his hedge trimming efforts, his back to her.

CHAPTER 43

Karen stepped quietly into the suite, letting the door close softly behind her. The curtains were drawn just enough to let the late morning light spill across the room in golden slants. Brock lay sprawled on the couch, one arm slung over his eyes, a glass of water and two Tylenol sitting untouched on the coffee table.

"You look good," Karen joked as she slid off her sandals.

Brock groaned without lifting his arm. "Thanks, babe. Love you too."

Karen set her bag down, crossing the room to sit in the chair beside him. "I think someone had a little too much fun last night."

"Just a bit," Brock grunted. He peeked out from under his arm, squinting at her like she was the sun itself. "Haven't drank like that in years."

"Ya think?" She snorted, leaning back in her chair, watching him with amusement.

Brock slowly sat up, rubbing his temples. "While you were out playing detective, I decided we needed a break."

"Oh?" Karen arched a brow.

Brock pulled a printed card from the side table and handed it to her. "Couple's spa package. Two hours. This afternoon."

Karen glanced at the reservation card. Heaven's Cove Spa – Lovers' Retreat Package. Full body massages and hot stone therapy, champagne, and access to a private plunge pool.

She lifted the card, hiding a smile. "Romantic."

"Figured you deserved something after putting up with my nonsense last night. I still can't believe I tried keeping up with Brady. That guy could drink a horse under the table."

"If you snore during the massage, I'm recording it," Karen joked.

"Deal."

While Brock went to the bathroom to clean himself up, Karen took some time to update the murder board. She added the latest tidbits: *Diana St. James missing an earring, Doe 1 and Doe 2, and male victim's missing thumb ring, tan line visible.*

On the resort map showing where the bodies had been found, she noted the oleander poison used on Diana and question-marked when the deadly dose had been ingested. She also wrote "staged overdose" next to the suite where the couple had been found.

She stepped back to study the growing pattern of missing items—trophies, she suspected—each connection tightening the noose around an unseen killer.

What am I missing?

The spa session proved every bit as indulgent as promised. The pair emerged rejuvenated, the tension in Karen's shoulders replaced by a pleasant heaviness that tugged her toward sleep. Unfortunately, the evening's plans left no time for rest.

The Rosarian Society had organized a sunset catamaran cruise across the water to Boca Chica, a nearby coastal town renowned for its artisan markets, colorful buildings, and energetic vibe.

Karen and Brock settled in for the ride, and the catamaran eased away from the marina. The wind carried the faint scent of salt and sunscreen as the crew bustled about, preparing drinks for the passengers.

One crew member stood out. Bare-chested, tanned, and with the kind of swagger that Karen recognized instantly—the boat captain, Marco. A caricature of a thirtysomething Latino—oozing both machismo and charm.

The man flirted shamelessly with nearly every woman on board, his gleaming smile and flashing eyes lingering just long to entice. When he poured Karen a drink, he leaned in closer than necessary, his hand lightly grazing hers.

"If you need anything, señora, anything at all, just ask for Marco," he said, his voice low and suggestive.

Karen smiled, raising her glass. "I'm sure I'll manage."

Marco grinned, undeterred. "Ah, but why manage alone when you could have company?" His eyes flicked to Brock, who was deep in conversation with Brady and two other rosarians.

Karen chuckled softly. If she were younger and less married, she might have entertained the idea. Marco was handsome in a reckless, *cheesy romance novel* sort of way, but Karen had no interest in sampling his wares.

Her loyalty to Brock—and the knowledge of this guy's obvious endgame—kept her firmly on her side of the railing. Instead, she gravitated toward Brady's wife, Margaret, a silver-haired Brit with a sharp wit and an easy laugh. Like Karen, Margaret had little interest in roses but accompanied her husband out of love and habit.

"Brock and Brady could talk for hours about pruning," Margaret said, sipping a rum punch. "I let him indulge as long as I get a vacation out of it."

Karen laughed. "Same here. Keeps him happy, and I get a tan."

Margaret smiled. "Married thirty-two years next month. Brady and I have two boys—Arthur and George—and our daughter, Penelope, is an artist. Sculptor, actually. Makes the most bizarre things but . . . what can you do? She's brilliant."

Karen felt a tug in her chest. Margaret's talk of her children had Karen missing her own. She slipped her phone from her pocket and sent a quick check-in text to her kids and their grandfather. The replies were short but sweet—everyone was fine, going about their daily routines.

"Kids, okay?" Margaret asked, noticing Karen's softened expression.

"Yeah. Just busy." She pocketed her phone. "Sometimes I forget they have their own lives now."

Margaret gave her a knowing look. "It happens to all of us."

By the time the catamaran docked at Boca Chica, twilight had settled over the narrow streets. String lights zigzagged above, illuminating cobblestones worn smooth by time.

Brock pulled Karen's hand through his arm as they walked along the promenade. Karen viewed it as a downscaled version of La Marina Casa de Campo. More Hampton Bay compared to East Hampton, or Indian Rocks Beach compared to Clearwater Beach.

Like many tourist traps, souvenir shops lined up either side of the street, filled with local crafts, jewelry, and hand-painted ceramics.

"Let me guess," Karen said, eyeing a table full of carved wooden roses. "You're gonna buy one of these."

Brock shrugged. "Maybe."

They passed a small open-air café where tourists sipped on strong espresso beneath vine-laden trellises. Karen slowed, her gaze drifting to a figure weaving through the tables.

Wolfram.

CHAPTER 44

He moved with purpose, his gaze flicking left and right as if searching for someone—or avoiding them.

Karen gently tugged on Brock's arm. "Go on ahead. I'll catch up. I want to see what this café has on the menu."

Brock looked at his watch. "Don't be long. We're meeting up with everybody for apps and drinks in a few minutes."

Karen trailed Wolfram from a safe distance as he left the café area and started walking down a side street, away from Brock.

Her law enforcement training kicked in naturally—keeping a measured pace, never locking eyes, blending with groups of tourists. She lingered at a nearby souvenir stall, watching him through the reflection of a polished silver tray.

Wolfram stopped abruptly near an alleyway, stepping out of sight. Karen drifted forward, glancing at the narrow passage just in time to see him shaking hands with someone.

Detective Alvarez.

Karen's pulse quickened.

Alvarez's body language was relaxed yet defensive. Her left arm hung loosely at her side, while her right thumb was hooked into a belt loop. While her posture gave off a casual vibe, her eyes were sharp, constantly assessing her surroundings.

Wolfram's hand rested lightly on her shoulder, fingers flexing as if he were kneading her muscles in reassurance that they were on the same team. Whatever they were doing, the two were in it together.

Karen stepped under canopy of a jewelry vendor, pretending to browse as she watched.

Their exchange was brief—an envelope slipping discreetly from Alvarez's hand to Wolfram's pocket.

Cooperation between a pair with a history—professional, and possibly romantic too.

Whatever was in that envelope was important. Without a doubt in her mind.

After Alvarez turned and left, Karen debated following Wolfram some more, but he had already blended into the crowd, vanishing into the maze of stalls.

Karen's phone buzzed. The text:

Enjoy the island, Detective.

Karen's breath hitched. She turned, scanning the faces in the crowd.

No sign of Wolfram.

No sign of Alvarez.

Just tourists, wandering, buying, eating ...

Her hand tightened around the phone.

Having lost her prey, Karen decided to track down, and rejoin her husband. She'd barely made it ten feet when a firm hand closed around her arm, pulling her into a recessed doorway.

"You're not as stealthy as you think," Wolfram murmured, releasing his grip. His dark eyes locked onto hers, the faintest smile tugging at his lips.

Karen glared at him. "I wasn't exactly trying."

"Sure, you weren't," he said, leaning casually against the wall and crossing his forearms over his chest.

Karen took a step back, giving herself space. "Why were you meeting with Alvarez? Is she your inside source?"

Wolfram's smile faded, replaced by something more guarded. "She's helping me out. That's all."

"Helping you how? I've heard you mention your 'contacts' more than once. Alvarez is one of them, isn't she?"

He hesitated, as if weighing how much to reveal. Finally, he exhaled. "Sí, I mentored her when she joined the force. Back when I was still with local law enforcement."

Karen's brow arched. "So, she's helping you because . . ."

"Loyalty," Wolfram admitted, glancing down the alley as if expecting someone to interrupt. "We worked together, as you know."

"And that's it? No other reason?"

"If you are asking if we have a romantic history, that's none of your business."

Karen nodded.

"Let's just say," he added, "we come from the same area."

"So, she views you as an older brother-type from the old neighborhood?"

Wolfram chuckled at the thought, "Sí y no. Mira, we both grew up in La Romana. Poor, like a lot of kids in that town. I figured a badge was my ticket out—earn a living, gain respect, stability. Turns out, respect didn't exactly pay the bills."

Karen crossed her arms. She'd heard the same story before—different faces, same desperation.

"So, you left?" she asked.

"More like, changed teams. When you wear the badge long enough, you start to see the cracks. Temptations, traps. Someone offered me a better deal."

Karen studied him carefully. "And now you're playing babysitter for a corrupt senator and trying to . . . what? Recruit Alvarez to join your side?"

"No. She's more valuable where she is," Wolfram said, his eyes flicking back and forth, sharp and unreadable.

"Does she know this? That she's merely a pawn in your game?"

"Call it what you will, pero do not judge what you do not understand," he hissed.

Karen didn't respond, but her silence spoke volumes.

Wolfram pushed off the wall. "I need to get back. Ortiz doesn't like me disappearing for too long."

Karen took a step forward. "What's really going on here, Wolfram?"

He paused at the alley entrance and glanced back at her. "Haven't you already figured that out? I guess you are not as good a detective as you think."

Before she could reply, Wolfram melted into the crowd, leaving Karen standing alone in the fading light.

Her phone buzzed in her pocket, and she dropped her head back, blowing out a long sigh. "It never ends," then she glanced down at the screen.

A picture of her, chatting with Wolfram.

The text: *Still watching, Detective.*

Whoever was following her was close but so very elusive. Whether friend or foe, this person was flat-out taunting her, and that pissed her off more than anything else.

CHAPTER 45

The rhythmic hum of conversation and the faint clang of glasses welcomed Karen as she approached the stand-up bar nestled beneath a string of soft lantern lights. The crowd of Rosarians mingled casually, their laughter drifting over the warm night air.

Brock's broad frame stood at the edge of the bar, elbow propped against the counter, a chilled glass of white wine within hand's reach. His eyes lit up the moment he spotted her weaving through the crowd.

"There's my wandering wife," he greeted, leaning in to kiss her cheek. He held the glass out to her. "For you, my queen."

Karen took it gratefully, the condensation cooling her palm. "Thanks. What are you drinking?"

Brock lifted his own glass—something amber and, she imagined, potent. "Hair of the dog."

Karen chuckled. "Trying to undo last night's damage?"

"Something like that. Where'd you get off to? I thought you were just checking out a menu." He popped an eyebrow.

He knows.

"You got me," she said, nudging his arm. "Later," she added, locking eyes with him to signal this wasn't the time for explanations.

Nodding, Brock didn't press. Instead, he slid his arm around her waist, pulling her gently against his side. "Fine. But I expect the full story when we get back to the room."

The light chatter around them lulled Karen into temporary ease. A platter of crisp tostones and chicharrón made its rounds, followed by bite-sized empanadas filled with spiced beef and plantains. Brock snagged two, handing one to Karen.

"You can't come to the Dominican Republic and not eat your weight in food," he teased.

Karen took a bite, savoring the crunch. "I'm not complaining."

Their peaceful indulgence was cut short when Karen's eyes drifted past the bar.

At the far end, partially hidden in the flicker of low lantern light, Wolfram stood by the entrance, his posture tense and rigid.

And he wasn't alone.

The man in the Panama hat stood close to him, speaking low, his hand subtly gesturing.

Karen leaned subtly against Brock, angling herself just enough to catch more of the interaction without drawing attention. She tugged on his shirt, and when he looked at her, she gestured toward the entrance.

"Isn't that Wolfram?" Brock asked, seeing the direction of her gaze.

Karen nodded. "And he's not alone."

Even from a distance, Karen could see the flash of annoyance in Wolfram's eyes, the tight clench of his jaw. Whatever Panama Hat Man was saying, Wolfram didn't like it. His shoulders squared, but his lips never moved as he listened.

"He doesn't look thrilled," Brock noted, sipping his drink slowly. "What do you think's going on?"

Karen watched carefully as the Panama Hat Man stepped in closer to Wolfram, as if lowering his voice. Wolfram shifted his stance, leaning away slightly, his head tilting in a subtle but unmistakable show of defiance.

Karen's lips tightened. *Instructions.*

This wasn't just a casual meeting. The man was giving orders, and Wolfram was not on board with them.

"I don't like this, Ka."

"Neither do I," she said. "But whoever that guy is, it looks like he's reminding Wolfram who's in charge."

The conversation ended when Wolfram straightened, his mouth a hard line, and walked out, disappearing into the night without so much as a backward glance.

The man in the Panama Hat lingered for a moment, watching Wolfram's retreat with an almost amused expression before adjusting his sleeves and strolling casually out the exit.

"Whatever that was," Brock said, tipping his glass toward the departing figure, "it didn't look like friendly small talk."

"No, it didn't."

She turned back toward the bar just as Marco, the catamaran's captain, slid into view.

Bare-chested beneath his loose linen shirt, sleeves rolled high on his forearms, Marco casually brushed against one of the rosarian wives, leaning in too close, flashing that signature rogue smile.

Karen's lips pressed into a thin line. "Still at it," she muttered.

Brock followed her gaze, smirking as he sipped his drink. "Nothing a good pipe cutter and blowtorch can't fix."

A pair of crew members nearby snickered, their hushed conversation barely masking Marco's name.

"Ese pendejo never quits," one of them said. "Swears he's going to bag another one tonight."

"Marco's slept with so many married women this past month, I'm surprised his bicho still works," the other said with a low chuckle. "At this point, we should rename the boat, *El Adúltero*."

Brock shook his head and turned away. "That guy's gonna screw with the wrong husband one of these days,"

"Odds are he's been caught with his pants down at least once," Karen added dryly.

Marco's gaze briefly caught hers from across the bar. He grinned, lifting his glass in a wordless toast.

Karen arched a brow but returned the gesture out of politeness. The captain oozed confidence, but Karen had dealt with his kind before—men who charmed their way into trouble without realizing when they'd crossed the line.

After another round of drinks and laughter with the rosarians, the boat crew signaled it was time to head back. Passengers gathered on the dock along the catamaran, and the crew prepared to sail under the soft glow of stars.

As they made their way down the gangplank, Karen's eyes caught a shadow moving along the dock.

The man in the Panama hat.

CHAPTER 46

The rhythmic lull of the waves rocked the catamaran and its passengers as it drifted back toward the resort. Karen stood at the bow, sipping on a bottle of water, watching the distant glow of the Utopia shimmer against the dark coastline.

Brock stood nearby, listening to Brady recount his latest misadventure. Marco remained on deck, laughing loudly with a group of rosarian wives who seemed all too eager for his attention. Karen caught the occasional flicker of lingering gazes, playful taps on his arm, and the subtle lean-ins as the boat captain effortlessly worked the crowd.

"That man's a walking HR violation," Karen muttered under her breath.

Brock glanced at her, then followed her line of sight. "He's definitely got that whole rogue-pirate thing down to a science."

Karen smirked. "He's practically giving them a personal tour, leaning hard into their vacation fantasies."

They watched as Marco spun one of the women—Brady's wife, Margaret—under his arm in a playful dance near the railing. Margaret laughed, shaking her head. Brock gave Brady a wide-eyed look, and Brady threw up his hands in mock surrender.

Brock turned back to his wife. "You think Margaret's really buying into his bullshit?"

"Her? Nah. She's humoring him. It's harmless."

When the boat docked at the resort, Brock helped Karen onto the gangplank, his arm steady beneath hers. The marina buzzed with low conversation and the sound of waves lapping against hulls, but Karen's eyes were fixed on the farthest end of the pier.

Aboard the *Libertad*, under the glow of deck lights, Senator Ortiz and Volkov sat with the May-December couple. The woman's laugh, high and lilting, floated across the water as Ortiz poured champagne into her flute.

That's new, Karen thought.

Volkov leaned back casually, cigar smoke curling from his lips as the older gentleman gestured animatedly toward the horizon, clearly deep into whatever expensive alcohol Ortiz had provided.

"Ka?" Brock nudged her, sensing her distraction. "You, okay?"

Karen nodded, eyes lingering on the yacht a moment longer. "Yeah. Hey, listen, why don't you go on ahead? I'm just gonna grab another bottle of water."

Brock followed her line of sight, then shot her skeptical look. "Another bottle of water, huh? Got it. Just don't stay too long, Detective—you're on vacation. Besides, the bed is less comfortable without you in it. Hey—" he took hold of her hand "—you want me to come with?"

She gently touched his face and smiled. "You're tired. I can see it in your eyes. Go, and I'll be there soon." Reluctantly, he disappeared up the stone path leading toward their suite. Her attention snapped back to the pier just in time to see Wolfram walking toward the senator's boat.

He moved with the confidence of someone who belonged, crossing the dock like he owned it. But as he boarded the *Libertad*, Juan Carlos stepped forward.

Karen ducked behind a stack of life vests and coiled ropes, close enough, she hoped, to hear fragments of conversation.

Unfortunately, Juan Carlos' voice was too low for her to catch a single word, but Wolfram's stiff posture gave away his displeasure. His hand hovered near his belt, fingers twitching. A brief exchange followed, sharp and tense. Juan Carlos gestured toward the resort.

"Handle it," Juan Carlos's voice cut through the night, clear enough to make Karen straighten.

Wolfram's lips barely moved in response, but she caught the tension that rippled through his shoulders as he nodded curtly.

Karen lingered a moment longer, watching the *Libertad* bob gently as Volkov toasted the May-December couple. During that toast, she finally learned their names: Gerald and Lila Devereaux—*thank you, Volkov, for your big mouth.* Wolfram stood off to the side, an unmoving silhouette.

Something was brewing.

And she didn't want to get caught in the crossfire, literally or figuratively. She slunk out of sight and made it back to the suite just past midnight, careful not to wake Brock. His soft snores echoed from the bedroom—one arm slung lazily over her pillow.

Moving quietly, Karen pulled her makeshift murder board from the closet and placed it carefully onto the kitchen counter. While she had a deep appreciation for the technology behind the murder boards at home, this one—made of cork, shreds of paper notes, strings, pins, and tape—was the board she felt most proud of.

Karen grabbed a pen, jotting down fresh observations.

Wolfram met Alvarez – an envelope passed.

Wolfram met with the man in the Panama hat – given orders?

Wolfram was confronted by Juan Carlos aboard the Libertad.

May-December couple entertained by Ortiz and Volkov.

She tacked those to the timeline section.

Below that was the map of the resort, where the critical events had happened. She marked the marina as her latest addition.

Karen tapped the pen against her chin as she studied the missing items—Diana's earring and Doe 1's ring. Trophies, to be sure. She'd seen it before—killers collecting mementos from their victims, keepsakes from each twisted conquest.

She studied the board. Then . . .

"Check this out," she said to herself.

With each victim, the killer took something—the jewelry.

With each victim, the killer also left something behind—a message.

Her eyes shifted to the verse left at the last scene.

Exodus 20:15 – You shall not steal.

Interesting that the killer had stolen, despite his admonishment.

A pattern was forming, but not all the pieces were clear. Not yet. Not enough to lead her to a resolution.

But she'd keep building her case. The answer would come.

CHAPTER 47

A call from Terrell jolted her to attention. She fumbled the phone, trying to answer it. Finally, hit the button and said, "Tell me you have something."

"I always have something," T said, the faint rustling of papers audible in the background. "I ran the image you sent of our guy in the Panama Hat."

"And . . .?

"We got a hit. His name's Thibo Laurent, goes by Bo."

Karen sat up straighter. "Bo? This is great, T."

"Yeah, it is. And check this out—he's not just any tourist. He's a cop, like us. An inspector. His official title: Senior Criminal Intelligence Officer with Interpol's Human Trafficking and Migrant Smuggling Unit."

Karen let out a low whistle.

He continued. "Still, I'm wondering why he's in Punta Cana—at the Utopia, no less? He's connected somehow. Maybe it's for good, and he needs to stay undercover, or whatever. Or maybe it's for bad, because we know damn well that there are plenty of bad cops out there. But I'm telling you, Ka . . . this isn't some random vacation. You hearing me?"

Karen nodded, though he couldn't see it. "It's starting to make sense . . . well, a little bit. I saw him last night giving orders to Wolfram, who didn't look so happy."

"Orders? Interesting. You think this Wolfram guy's running errands for Interpol?"

"Not sure." She rubbed the back of her neck. "But this is great information. I'll keep digging. Let me know if anything else pops."

"You got it. Watch your six."

"Always."

Karen set the phone down, staring once more at the board. Bo Laurent. She scrawled his name beneath Wolfram's and circled it.

Interpol.

Her pen lingered over the board, tapping absently beside the names. A knock at the door startled her. Karen stood, tucking the board back into the closet before answering.

Jose greeted her with a small smile, then bowed his head as he handed her a small, folded note. "For you, señora."

Karen took the paper cautiously. "Who left this?"

Jose glanced toward the elevator at the end of the hall. "I'm not sure, señora. It was left at the front desk. They asked me to bring it to you."

Karen's breath caught. "Thank you, Jose."

He gave a polite nod and walked away.

She closed the door, leaning against it as she unfolded the note. One line stared back at her:

Exodus 20:4

Her stomach twisted.

Another warning.

The killer was preparing to strike again.

And someone at the resort was about to die.

She hopped onto her phone and googled the verse.

"You shall not make for yourself an idol ..."

Wealth.

Excess.

The May-December couple.

It had to be.

Her mind flashed to all her encounters with that couple—the woman's glittering jewelry, the bedazzled chihuahua, and last night, the way Ortiz and Volkov had entertained them like royalty aboard the *Libertad*.

She had to warn them.

Karen's eyes flicked to the balcony. Brock sat outside, legs stretched across the chaise, coffee in one hand and his iPad balanced on his lap. When they had awoken that morning, still snuggled under the covers, she shared what she had seen at the marina the night before. He had been understanding of her need to spend some time with her notes and the board, and agreed to give her that space. The man was a keeper, and she felt a wave of gratitude fill her as she watched her husband, amazed at his ability to live in the moment, seize the calm and relaxation—despite the weirdness she always brought to the table.

She stepped out and leaned against the railing. "Hey, honey."

He glanced up, holding his hand above his face to block the sun. "Finished playing with your murder board?"

"T called with some new information about the man in the hat." She paused. He waited. "Oh, and I got another note just now."

He wiggled his fingers—the *spill it* gesture.

She gave him the rundown. "So, something's afoot, and I think I can stop it. I need to track down that May-December couple who were on Ortiz's boat last night. Oh, I happened to overhear their names. Gerald and Lila Devereaux."

"Sounds like things are moving along," he said. "Ka—just call Montenegro."

"It'll take too long. Plus, it's not enough to go on, really," she argued. "My instincts, mostly, and I highly doubt he'll give two shits about my instinct. I just need to warn this couple. That's all."

Brock sighed, setting his iPad aside. "Ka, listen. I get it. But you're here on vacation and out of your jurisdiction. You need to let the locals handle it. They will listen. You're not the only one who can solve cases."

"I know." She dragged out the last word. "But my gut says they're in trouble. I can't sit on this while I wait for time with Montenegro."

Brock studied her for a long moment, then threw his hands in the air. "God, I love you when your passion is aflame."

She kissed his cheek and squeezed him tight.

"But!" he said, holding up a hand. "Just a warning. And be quick about it. We have the gala tonight, and you promised to be my plus-one."

"I'll be there," Karen said, offering him a soft smile. "I'll make it quick."

Brock chuckled lightly. "You never make anything quick."

Karen grabbed her bag, tucking the note into her pocket as she headed for the door.

Finding the May-December couple would not be difficult. A quick inquiry at the concierge desk with a vague reference to the *Libertad* led her to the guest registry. Gerald and Lila Devereaux. Villa 14.

Karen strolled along the cobblestone pathways leading to the private villas, the lush greenery casting dappled shadows across the walk. The closer she drew to Villa 14, the quieter it became.

She slowed at the gate, hesitating just as the faintest sound of footsteps approached from behind.

Karen turned, and there he was.

The man in the Panama hat.

Bo Laurent.

"Detective Skaryd," he greeted, his Belgian accent curling over the words. "We need to talk."

CHAPTER 48

Karen froze, the path ahead momentarily forgotten as her eyes locked on Bo Laurent. His calm demeanor did little to mask the intensity behind his sharp blue eyes. He had a commanding, take-charge energy. The brim of his hat tilted slightly, shielding part of his face.

"Detective Skaryd," he repeated, "we need to talk."

Her instincts screamed for her to either step forward or retreat, but her body refused to obey. "You know who I am," she said evenly, though her heart was pounding.

Bo offered a small smile. "Of course. Former FBI, now homicide detective with Clearwater Police Department. Married to a plumber, two kids. Your father, a decorated lieutenant with Suffolk County Police. Impressive pedigree."

Karen tightened her grip on her bag. "You've done your homework."

"Necessary precautions. You've been looking into things you shouldn't."

She stepped forward, closing the gap between them. "I don't have time for games, Inspector Laurent."

He arched a brow.

"You're not the only one with access to information. Now, there's a killer on the loose, and I think the Devereauxs are the next targets. So, unless you're here to help, I suggest you step aside."

Bo held his ground, his expression hardening. "You're not listening.

This isn't your jurisdiction. This investigation—this entire operation—is mine."

Karen's jaw clenched. "Yours? I didn't realize Interpol sent officers to Punta Cana to stalk American tourists and hand out cryptic warnings."

"Careful, Detective," Bo said, his voice dropping to a dangerous calm. "You have no idea what you're walking into. This isn't just a few murders at a resort. It's part of something much larger."

Karen's pulse quickened, but she refused to let him see her falter. "Then why haven't you stopped it? What's your connection to Wolfram, to Ortiz, to Volkov?"

Bo's lips pressed into a thin line. "That's classified."

"Convenient," Karen shot back. "And what about the text messages? Or even the Bible verses—those are from you too, aren't they? Trying to scare me off?"

Bo hesitated, just long enough for Karen to know she had hit on something—finally. "Bible verses, no. Text messages, oui," he admitted, his tone softening. "For your own good. You're putting yourself—and your fellow cops—at risk."

Karen narrowed her eyes. "You mean Terrell."

Bo exhaled sharply, his patience visibly wearing thin. "Yes. Tell Detective Danielson to stop digging. The people we're dealing with have eyes and ears everywhere. If he keeps pushing, it won't end well for him—or for you."

Karen took a step closer, her anger flaring. "Is that a threat?"

"C'est reality. You're good, Detective, but you're not untouchable. These people don't care about jurisdiction or badges. They play a different game entirely."

The air between them crackled with tension, a professional standoff that neither seemed willing to break.

Karen inhaled deeply, forcing herself to stay calm. "Inspector, I don't have time for this. If the Devereauxs are in danger, I need to warn them."

"No," Bo said sharply. "You need to let *me* handle it."

"And what's your plan exactly? Wait for another body to turn up?"

"I will keep them safe, Detective." His jaw flexed, a tell that she'd hit a nerve. "But if you continue to interfere, you'll only make things worse,"

Karen stepped past him toward the villa. "We can argue about this later. You can join me now or leave me the hell alone. Either way, I'm not letting them die over some turf war."

Bo grabbed her arm, his grip firm but not aggressively so. "Detective .. . Karen," he said, "with your history as a law enforcement professional, you *must* know, we cannot be seen together. If my cover is blown, this entire operation is compromised."

Just like Terrell had said—Bo was working undercover.

Karen pulled her arm free, her glare unwavering. "Maybe you should've thought of that before meeting me here, face to face."

"I felt it was necessary. Had to be done. I had to make sure you understood the stakes. This isn't about just you."

Karen stared at him for a long moment, gritting her teeth. He had a point, but it wasn't the whole point. "You've got your job, and I've got mine. Stay out of my way, and I'll stay out of yours."

Bo's eyes flickered with something unreadable—regret, perhaps. Without another word, he turned and disappeared into the shadows of the foliage, leaving Karen standing alone on the path.

She exhaled slowly. The weight of his warning settled heavily on her, but she couldn't let it deter her.

Not now.

Turning back toward Villa 14, Karen quickened her pace. The Devereauxs' lives—and perhaps her own—depended on what she did next.

CHAPTER 49

The door of the Devereauxs' bungalow was slightly ajar. A chill that had nothing to do with the Caribbean breeze ran down her spine. She pushed gently, the door creaking open with an almost theatrical groan.

"Mr. Devereaux? Mrs. Devereaux?" Her voice cut through the silence, but no reply came.

Karen stepped inside cautiously, her hand hovering near her hip out of habit out of habit. She longed to feel the familiar weight of her Glock 19 service weapon, which she'd nicknamed Lion-O, after her favorite cartoon character. But it was thousands of miles away, locked away in her Clearwater home, probably missing her too.

The bungalow was pristine, a picture of wealth and indulgence— marble floors, handwoven rugs, gilded accents. But the air was suffused with the kind of stillness she had encountered too often in her line of work.

Death had a way of settling into a room.

She was too late.

A faint sound—scratching, high-pitched barking—filtered through the stillness. Karen's head turned toward one of the closed doors at the far end of the bungalow.

Sable the dog.

Her heart quickened. Why was the chihuahua locked away?

She took slow steps into the room, her head on a swivel. The scent of perfume. The barking of the dog a sharp contrast to the underlying quiet. Loud. Nails on a chalkboard.

The sliding door to the expansive patio was open, the curtains fluttering in the gentle breeze.

She stepped through the opening.

The deck stretched out beyond the glass doors, overlooking an infinity pool and the calm expanse of Caribbean Sea. That's where she found them.

Lila Devereaux reclined in one of the deck chairs, still in her outfit from the previous evening, the fabric draped elegantly over her legs . . . as if she had simply fallen asleep in the moonlight.

Her neck—sharply misaligned.

Snapped at the base.

Gerald sat beside her, rigid. A glass with small amount of what she guessed was a dark liquor still in his hand, which rested on his lap.

Same condition—neck spun around like a top.

The shards from Lila's champagne flute lay in glittering fragments next to her chair.

Karen's breath hitched, her eyes narrowing at the small ivory card resting on the table between them.

A handwritten note.

Exodus 20:4 – You shall not make for yourself an idol.

"So much for keeping them safe, Laurent." She whispered to herself, as she bent down inspecting the victim's remains.

Lila's jewelry was meticulously arranged around her—bracelets lined up in a neat row, a ruby pendant draped over the back of the chair, and even the chihuahua's matching jeweled collar had been purposefully laid out beside the card.

She examined it further.

A ruby was missing from the collar.

Another trophy.

Karen swallowed against the rising bile in her throat.

Someone had taken their time.

She stepped closer, crouching by Gerald's side. Her fingers brushed his wrist, though she already knew the truth.

Cold.

Stiff.

Sable's barking had grown faint as she zeroed in on the tragedy before her, but it broke through the horror, startling her. The poor thing was now scratching madly at the closet door.

Karen rose, moving swiftly across the room. She unlatched the door, and the tiny tan and white long-haired chihuahua burst out, paws skittering across the marble and toward the patio. It darted toward Lila, circling her chair and pawing at her limp hand.

Karen followed, bent down, and scooped the trembling animal into her arms. It whimpered against her chest, vibrating with fear.

"Shhh," she whispered, stroking its soft fur.

The small comfort she offered the dog did little to ease the gnawing pit in her stomach.

She needed to report this.

Karen pulled out her phone, her thumb hovering over Montenegro's number.

Bo's voice echoed in her mind: "You're not in your jurisdiction. Stay out of this."

Her jaw tightened. If this was connected to Bo's operation, alerting Montenegro could throw everything into chaos.

But she couldn't just walk away.

The faint creak of the front door made her spin sharply, her heart leaping to her throat.

Her hand instinctively hovered near her hip—useless.

A figure filled the doorway of the patio—the Devereauxs' butler dressed in a pristine white jacket and dark trousers. His face was a mask of utter horror, his eyes wide and disbelieving—flicking from Karen, to Sable trembling in her arms, to the broken figures of Lila and Gerald in their deck chairs.

The silver breakfast tray he carried, laden with what looked like an assortment of fresh fruit and mimosas, tilted precariously in his shaking hands.

"Dios mío." The words escaped in a whisper.

Karen took a step forward, lifting the dog slightly. "I knocked, but no one answered."

The butler dropped the tray. Glass shattered, sending broken stems skittering across the floor.

He stumbled back, nearly tripping over the threshold in his rush to put distance between himself and Karen.

She extended her hand. "Wait. Listen—"

Without saying another word, he bolted, rubber soles slapping hard against the stone pathway as he disappeared down the garden-lined trail.

"Wait. Come back!" Karen called after him, moving toward the door before realizing how that would look.

She froze, watching helplessly as the butler fled toward the main part of the resort.

The chihuahua whimpered in her arms, nuzzling into her neck.

Karen exhaled slowly.

Great, now I'm a suspect.

CHAPTER 50

Karen placed the trembling chihuahua inside the bathroom with its water and food dish, shutting the door gently. She tried to ignore Sable's small whimpers, stepping back into the main living area of the Devereauxs' bungalow.

Her phone buzzed.

She tossed in her earpiece and answered immediately. "T, I don't have time. I'm standing in the middle of another murder scene."

"What the—? Another one?"

"The Devereauxs. Villa 14. They're both dead, T. Different MO— broken necks. The wife's jewelry laid out like a display, including the dog's. A ruby stone missing from the dog's collar. Champagne flute shattered at the women's feet. Husband sitting upright, glass still in hand. Staged by a pro." The words rushed out of her.

She hurried over to the bodies and snapped close-ups of everything, then stood back and took a few more from a wide angle.

"Take notes," she instructed. "Ivory card between them on the table. Same handwriting as the last one. Exodus 20:4. 'You shall not make for yourself an idol.'"

T's keyboard clattered faintly on the other end. "Jesus, Ka."

"It gets worse."

"Worse?"

"The butler," Karen said, trying hard to speak clearly and calmly through her labored breaths. "He found me here—thinks I did it. Bolted like his life depended on it. He'll be calling Montenegro any minute."

"That's not good."

"No shit."

"So, now, you're a suspect," T muttered.

"Yep," Karen said, snapping a few more pictures. "Which is why I need you to look into the Devereauxs—everything. Background, business dealings, connections to Volkov or Ortiz. I need leverage before Montenegro pulls me in."

"What about Woody? Want me to loop him in?"

Karen pulled in a long breath, then let it out. Did she want her boss involved right now? "No. Not yet. Just get me something I can work with."

"Fine," T said, his tone shifting. "But listen—there's a reason I called. This thing is worse than a spider's web. Every lead I chase connects to something else. The deeper I go—"

"The bigger it looks."

"Exactly. It ain't just that senator or Volkov. We're talking high-level people—politicians, CEOs. It's ugly."

Karen stopped at the edge of the deck, staring out at the horizon. "How ugly?"

"Like Epstein Island ugly. And all these names floating around? They don't like exposure. From what I've been able to gather so far, this Laurent's been chasing this human trafficking thing for years, but they're slicker than owl shit, as the saying goes. Based on these files, someone keeps shutting him down whenever he gets close, it seems."

Her grip on the phone tightened. "Which means they've probably got people inside Interpol."

"That'd be my guess."

"T . . . I ran into Laurent. Right here in front of the Devereauxs' villa. He told me to back off."

"Shit, Ka—" T cursed. "Glad you told me."

"Yeah, imagine my surprise. He knows who I am, T. My jacket, my family. Everything. Said he's been the one texting me—told me it was to protect me."

T went silent for a beat.

"And you believe him?"

"I believe he's telling me just enough to keep me guessing. But if he's protecting anyone, it's himself."

"Great. So now you've got Interpol breathing down your neck, and you're the prime suspect in a double homicide."

Karen's lips curved grimly. "I always wanted a vacation full of excitement."

"Yeah, well . . . bad idea."

"I'm heading back to my room," she said. "I've got some pictures headed your way. Text me if you find anything."

"You got it. And Ka—Montenegro isn't gonna go easy on you. If you need me to fly down, for backup—"

"I know you've got me. Thanks, T."

Karen ended the call, slipping her phone into her pocket as she stepped out of the bungalow.

By the time Karen returned to the suite, Brock was pacing on the balcony, his expression creased with worry.

"What happened?" he asked, setting aside his iPad.

Karen dropped onto the sofa with a sigh. "You remember that May-December couple?"

"How can I forget? You were worried they were next in line." He drew his finger across his neck to symbolize a cut throat.

"You have no idea how close to accurate you are. Yes. They're dead."

Brock sat up straighter. "Jesus. How?"

"Broken necks, staged scene, Bible verse," she recounted. "It gets worse."

"Worse?"

"The butler found me there, and when he saw the bodies . . . well, he thinks I'm the murderer."

Brock rushed to embrace her. "What are we gonna do?

"Prepare."

He stepped back, holding her at arm's length. "Are we in danger?"

Karen hesitated before answering. "I won't let it get that far."

"You need to get in front of this, Ka. Clear things up. Reach out to Montenegro. Let him handle this. We ain't in Clearwater."

"I know." Karen rubbed her temples. "I'll calling him now."

Before she could, a sharp knock rattled the door.

Karen exchanged a glance with Brock before walking over to answer the door. Through the peephole, Inspector Montenegro stood in the hallway, his dark eyes heavy with suspicion.

"It's Montenegro," she informed Brock before opening the door.

"Detective Skaryd," he said, his tone unusually formal. "You need to come with me."

She lifted her chin and met his gaze steadily. "What's this about?"

"You're under investigation for the deaths of Gerald and Lila Devereaux. I'd recommend a lawyer."

Brock stepped forward, his voice tense. "Is this really necessary? Can you at least question her right here, at least initially?"

Montenegro grunted as if he found Brock's suggestion amusing. "No. And don't worry, Señor Skaryd—she will be, how do you say . . . *Mirandized,* if needed."

Brock stepped aside, his head low and shaking.

Karen calmly grabbed her bag.

As Montenegro led her toward the elevator, her mind raced.

The web was closing in, and she had no intention of being caught in it.

CHAPTER 51

Karen's pulse was steady—during this vacation alone, she'd learned to control it—but she could feel the heaviness of what was to come. Montenegro guided her toward the elevator, his pace was slow and deliberate, as if savoring the moment.

"I warned you, Detective," Montenegro he without looking at her, "that your curiosity would get you in trouble."

Karen stayed silent, watching the elevator doors slide open with a soft chime.

He gestured for her to step inside first, and she did.

When the doors closed and they began to descend to the lobby, she said, "I didn't kill them."

Montenegro smirked—hands clasped behind his back. "That's not for me to decide. The local judge will handle that."

Karen arched a brow. "Seriously? No discussions, nothing?"

Montenegro's eyes flicked toward her. "A couple found dead in their private villa, no signs of forced entry. And who's standing over the bodies when the butler arrives?"

"Circumstantial at best. You and I both know I didn't do it."

"I also know you're former FBI," Montenegro said. "You would know how to kill quietly, without leaving a trace. Broken necks—clean, efficient. Sounds like something a trained agent could do."

Has everybody accessed my jacket?

"You can try painting me as the suspect," she said, her tone measured. "But you're missing one thing—motive. Why would I kill a couple I barely knew?"

Montenegro's eyes narrowed slightly. "You tell me. Maybe a disagreement over some trinket, and it got out of hand. Maybe the Devereauxs saw something they shouldn't have, and you wanted to make sure they kept their mouths shut. Or maybe you didn't like the way la señora Devereaux flaunted her wealth." He shrugged. "Who knows? Could be so many reasons."

Karen let out a humorless laugh. "Really? That's what you're going with?"

"Judges here are strict. They don't need the same airtight cases you're used to in the States. Sometimes circumstantial evidence is enough to keep someone in a holding cell for a very long time."

The elevator slid open on the ground floor.

Karen stepped out, Montenegro at her side. The lobby was quiet, but a few guests, including Selfie Chloe and her hubby Cal were there. Staff members glanced at her, then quickly looked away. Chloe actually snapped a damn picture. *Whispers travel faster than footsteps*, she thought.

"Come on," Montenegro said. "I'll walk you to the car. You'll be processed and questioned at the station."

Karen exhaled slowly. "Will I really need a lawyer?"

"Yes," Montenegro said. "And unless you've got someone in mind, I suggest contacting the US Embassy. They can recommend local counsel."

Karen's mind spun. Getting a lawyer in the Dominican Republic wasn't like finding one back home. Embassy officials often operated within the polite confines of diplomatic channels, and this wasn't the kind of double murder they could simply make disappear with a phone call or a favor. "Montenegro, please listen" she said as they exited through the glass doors into the blazing sunlight. "This isn't what you think."

He opened the passenger door of his black SUV. "I don't think anything. I follow the evidence."

Karen slid into the seat. He closed the door and rounded the car to get behind the wheel.

"And the butler?" she pressed. "Have you questioned him yet?"

Montenegro adjusted his seatbelt. "He's nervous. Scared. And I'd say he's got a right to be. He was there when you were discovered with the bodies, after all."

Karen's grip tightened around her bag. "That may be true, but there is a good reason for it."

Montenegro pulled onto the main road leading away from the resort. The palm-lined streets blurred past as they drove in silence.

Finally, he glanced at her. "Let's hope you're right. For your sake."

Twenty minutes later, they arrived at the station, taking the same interrogation room as before. The humid air barely circulated from the creaky ceiling fan overhead. Karen sat at the metal table with arms crossed as she waited.

Her phone buzzed in her purse. She rushed to pull it out and check the screen. A phone call from Terrell.

She answered quickly. "Holy shit, I'm glad you called. I'm sitting in an interrogation room. Where are we on the Devereauxs?"

"Digging," T said. "So far, nothing screams *cartel* or *deep criminal ties*. But I did find something weird—Gerald made a series of offshore transactions last year. Big money. Moved millions from various shell companies to a number of Ortiz's ventures."

The hair on her neck stood on end.

"So, the Devereauxs were dirty?"

"Looks like it. But the kicker? The shell companies he used to move the cash lead right back to Volkov's network."

Karen's stomach twisted. "Of course they do."

"Listen, I'm good with flying down there. You could use—"

"No."

A sharp knock interrupted the silence, and she disconnected the call and placed the phone in her bag. Montenegro entered, none the wiser.

Or so she thought.

"I'll take that, Detective." He held out his hand and wiggled his fingers.

Karen hesitated, then surrendered the device. Montenegro slipped it into an evidence bag. "Standard procedure."

She rolled her eyes and muttered, "Good grief."

Montenegro gave a thin smile. "Oh! Some good news for you. Your attorney is here."

Karen tensed as Montenegro stepped aside, revealing a man in a sharp navy suit with dark, slicked-back hair and a leather briefcase.

"Detective Skaryd," the man greeted, extending his hand. "I'm Joaquin De La Cruz. I'll be representing you."

Karen shook his hand firmly, eyeing him with scrutiny.

"Señor De La Cruz," she said slowly, "I appreciate the quick response, but who requested your counsel?"

CHAPTER 52

Karen's grip lingered in De La Cruz's handshake longer than necessary, searching his face for any tell—any flicker of recognition or deceit. But his expression remained impassive, polished like someone used to keeping secrets for a living.

"I'll ask again, who requested your counsel?" Karen demanded.

"That's the question of the hour," De La Cruz said smoothly, removing his hand from her grip. "I was contacted this morning by an associate who felt you could use competent representation."

Karen's eyes narrowed. "Who's this associate?"

De La Cruz opened his leather briefcase, producing a sleek black notepad. "I'm afraid confidentiality prevents me from disclosing that information. For now, let's focus on keeping you out of a cell."

Karen crossed her arms and leaned back in the metal chair. The interrogation room's overhead fan rattled uselessly.

"That's convenient," she said, her tone sharp. "And how exactly did you know where to find me? I wasn't here long enough for my husband to call the embassy. Hell, I've only just moments ago walked through the door."

De La Cruz's dark eyes flicked up from his notepad, holding her gaze with unsettling ease. "The question you should be asking is why someone went to such lengths to ensure you had legal counsel. Whoever it was— they're invested in keeping you protected."

Terrell?

No. He didn't know.

Had Brock somehow—

No. Even if the staff had mentioned it to him, he'd want to talk to me first. That left . . .

Bo.

It had to be him.

But why?

Before she could press further, Montenegro reentered the room with a file tucked beneath his arm. He took a seat at the table.

"You two bonding?" Montenegro asked, voice low and gruff.

"Just getting acquainted," De La Cruz said coolly.

Montenegro let the file hit the table with a heavy thud, his gaze pinning Karen like a nail to a board. "Let's get started."

Karen leaned back, folding her arms. "Aren't you forgetting something? Or do you just skip the part where I'm supposed to be Mirandized like you told my husband?"

A faint grin tugged at the corner of Montenegro's mouth. "There's no need, at the moment." You're not under arrest—yet."

Karen arched a brow. "I'm free to go, then?"

Montenegro shook his head slowly. "Not exactly. At the moment, you are *still* a suspect. So, no—you are not free to go."

Karen slapped the table with a *whack*. "Seriously?"

Montenegro leaned forward, folding his hands over the file. "Here's the problem, Detective. A trained officer—former FBI—walks into a scene where two wealthy tourists are found dead. No sign of forced entry. No defensive wounds. Just two snapped necks, clean and efficient. That sound familiar?"

Karen narrowed her eyes. "You think I staged it too? You know how insane that sounds?"

Montenegro shrugged, but his eyes betrayed nothing. "People kill for very small things, barely any reason at all, sometimes. So, no . . . not insane at all."

"Come on," Karen shot back. "You know I had no connection to them. What's my motive, Inspector? That they took my cabana at the pool . . . stole my dinner reservation . . . what?"

Montenegro's lips quirked in a faint smile. "Like I said before, maybe they saw something they shouldn't have. Maybe you were paid to clean up loose ends."

"That is such a reach."

"Doesn't need to be tight," Montenegro said, his voice dropping an octave. "As I also mentioned, our judges aren't as forgiving as back in the States. It's not about reasonable doubt. It's about evidence that points the right way."

Karen exhaled slowly and leaned back, closed her eyes to regain composure.

De La Cruz finally spoke up, his tone measured. "With respect, Inspector, that theory lacks weight. My client didn't flee the country, and she's cooperating fully."

Montenegro's eyes flicked toward him, and for a moment, Karen could see the unspoken tension simmering beneath the surface.

"She was caught standing over the bodies," Montenegro said.

De La Cruz's gaze didn't waver. "By a butler who panicked. I doubt his testimony will hold up against her record. Perhaps we should step back and allow this woman to explain herself, which apparently you have not yet done."

Montenegro's sneer faded. "We'll see about that."

Karen's eyes snapped open and her glare landed on the inspector. "I get it, man—you're under pressure to close this fast. But you're looking in the wrong direction. The Devereauxs were involved with Volkov and Ortiz. Offshore accounts. Shell companies. *That's* the thread you need to pull."

Montenegro's expression hardened. "You have proof?"

"I'm working on it," Karen said.

Montenegro arched a brow. "You mean with the help of your colleague back in Florida? Detective Danielson, I believe? Sí, I'm well aware of your little network."

Of course you are.

Karen didn't blink. "Then you know I'm not making this up. Volkov isn't just here for pleasure. And the Devereauxs were part of it."

"And yet, here you sit in my station."

Karen met his gaze head-on. "Because you're jumping to conclusions without hearing everything I have to say."

De La Cruz nodded. "Exactly my point, Inspector."

Montenegro exhaled sharply. "No. It's because you were found at the scene, a place you had no business entering. That's what the evidence says. There's nothing tying Señor Volkov to their deaths."

"At least not yet."

Montenegro straightened, smoothing the front of his shirt. "That's not how this works. Need I remind you, every time we meet, that you are not a detective here?"

De La Cruz opened his mouth, perhaps to protest, but Montenegro was already on his feet, file in hand. "And señora—don't leave town."

Karen's eyes narrowed. "Need I remind you that I'm here on vacation, and we're scheduled to leave in a few days."

Montenegro didn't turn around. "You may need to change your plans."

He paused at the doorway, tossing one final jab over his shoulder. "Oh, and let's not forget—your husband is still a suspect in la señora Saint James' death. That makes one murder for each of you. ¡Bravo! Who knows, maybe we can tie you to the deaths of Scott and Heather Saunders, the young couple found dead in the vacant suite—right next to your building, in fact. It would certainly make my life easier."

Both Karen and De La Cruz winced.

"Maybe the courts will let you share a cell," were his parting words.

The door clicked shut behind him, leaving Karen alone with her attorney, the weight of his words pressing around her like a vise.

CHAPTER 53

The silence lingered between Karen and De La Cruz long after Montenegro's footsteps faded down the hall. At least, she now had a name for victims Doe 1 and 2.

De La Cruz broke the quiet, his tone light but steady. "Well, that was . . . charming."

Karen exhaled sharply, pulling herself from her thoughts. "Yeah, Montenegro's got a gift for making people feel welcome."

De La Cruz slid his notepad back into his briefcase, snapping the clasps shut. "Let me drive you back to the resort. We can grab a cup of Joe, as they say in the States, and discuss your case. Details and strategy."

She stood, running a hand through her hair. "Fine, but first, I want my phone back."

She pushed open the door to the hallway, heading toward the front desk where Montenegro stood talking with another officer.

Montenegro barely glanced at her. "Señora Skaryd."

Karen folded her arms. "I'm here to retrieve my phone."

"Ah. That is now evidence."

"It's my personal property, and I'm not being arrested."

"Watch your tone, señora. The phone is part of an ongoing investigation," Montenegro stated. "You will get it back when I'm finished with it. Maybe."

De La Cruz tried to nudge her forward, hand on her elbow, but she stood steadfast, her fists clenched at her side. "My phone has nothing to do with the Devereauxs' deaths."

Montenegro leaned in closer, lowering his voice. "Anything connected to you right now has *everything* to do with those deaths."

De La Cruz cleared his throat, smoothly stepping between them. "Inspector, I trust my client will be allowed to leave without further issues?"

Montenegro flicked his fingers. "Go."

Outside, De La Cruz's car was parked a short distance from the station—a sleek, black Mercedes Benz C-Class that looked far too clean for the Dominican streets. He unlocked the door with a click, gesturing for Karen to get in.

As they drove away, she watched the station shrink in the rearview mirror.

She spoke first. "So, who hired you?"

De La Cruz smiled, keeping his eyes on the road. "I'm afraid I can't answer that. I really can't."

Karen dropped her head back against the headrest. "You can't or you won't?"

"Sí."

Karen scoffed. "I'm your client. Don't I have the right to know?"

De La Cruz didn't flinch. "Attorney-client confidentiality works both ways. Whoever hired me believed your safety and legal protection were paramount."

"Bo Laurent," she pressed, watching his reaction carefully. "Is it him?"

De La Cruz's grip on the wheel didn't tighten, but his posture shifted ever so slightly. "I can neither confirm—"

"Nor deny," Karen shook her head. "Right. I've heard it before. Hell, I've said it myself."

"Detective," De La Cruz said, glancing at her, "I suggest you spend less time worrying about who hired me and more time focusing on keeping yourself out of trouble."

"I've been doing that since I set foot here," Karen said. "Sort of."

Silence stretched between them for a moment.

"Look, I understand the frustration," De La Cruz said with a softer tone. "But whoever reached out has resources and influence. That counts for something."

Karen's mind whirled. Bo had been watching her. Texting her. Warning her. Could he have pulled strings this fast? And if so, what's his endgame?

"Let's stop at Plaza Lama," De La Cruz said, slowing the car. "You can pick up a temporary phone. It's not your usual device, but at least you'll stay connected."

Karen gave a curt nod. "Fine. But I'm not letting this go."

"I wouldn't expect you to."

By the time they reached the Utopia, the sun hung low in the sky, casting long shadows across the resort's pristine paths. The staff's usual warm smiles faded as Karen walked through the lobby, murmurs trailing behind her like whispers in the wind.

Word had spread.

She could feel the stares, the suspicion following her every step.

De La Cruz noticed it too. "It seems the news travels fast here."

"I'm not surprised. Small place," Karen muttered.

They settled at a corner table in the resort's café, tucked away from prying eyes—at least as much as possible. De La Cruz ordered two coffees as Karen pulled out the temporary phone.

"Give me a second," she said, dialing Brock's number.

He answered on the second ring.

"It's me."

"Ka?" His voice was laced with concern. "Whose phone are you using? Where the hell are ya?"

"I'm back at the resort," she said, keeping her tone even. "Come down to the café. I'll fill you in."

"You, okay?"

"Fine. Just come down. Oh, and I have an attorney."

"What? How?"

"His name's De La Cruz. We'll explain when you get here."

"Who hired him?"

"That's the question of the day."

"I'll be right down."

Karen ended the call, setting the phone down on the table with a soft clink.

Minutes later, the café's door opened, the bell jingling softly as Brock entered. His gaze locked on Karen immediately, striding toward their table.

Before he could sit, De La Cruz stood, extending his hand. "Joaquin De La Cruz. I'm representing your wife."

Brock shook it, but his eyes stayed on Karen. "How did he end up here, Ka?"

"That," she said, "is what we're about to figure out."

CHAPTER 54

The waitress set down two steaming cups of coffee in front of Karen and De La Cruz. Her eyes flicked to Brock as he slid into the chair beside Karen, his arm brushing lightly against hers.

"Anything for you, sir?" the server asked.

Brock glanced at the untouched coffee in front of Karen, grinning. "You got anything stronger than coffee?"

De La Cruz chuckled softly, lifting his cup. "Añejo rum, perhaps? Or a Brugal 1888. Smooth and aged."

Karen shook her head. "He's joking. Another coffee's fine."

The waitress nodded, stepping away as Brock leaned back. "I wasn't completely joking," he muttered.

Karen arched a brow. "I know. But let's hold off on the day drinking until we're both cleared of murder."

Brock snorted, folding his arms. "Fair point."

De La Cruz sipped his coffee, then set the cup down. "Now that we're settled, let's get down to brass tacks, as they say in the States." His eyes locked on Karen. "Tell me everything—start to finish."

Karen hesitated, her hand tightening around her cup as he turned on his handheld recorder. She wasn't sure she trusted him. But there was something steady about De La Cruz, something grounded.

"You want a full debrief?" she asked.

De La Cruz nodded, pausing the recorder. "Detective, I can't defend you if you keep me in the dark. Consider this a briefing. Just the facts."

Karen exhaled, stealing a glance at Brock. His quiet nod urged her on.

"Three deaths," she started, her voice low and steady. "First was Diana St. James—poisoned at the resort restaurant. Oleander."

De La Cruz raised a brow. "Biblical verse left at the scene, correct?"

"Exodus 20:16. 'You shall not bear false witness.'"

He nodded. "Go on."

"Next was the young couple, building next door. Pills and booze staged by the bed. Looked like an overdose, but it was too neat."

"Another verse?"

Karen's fingers tapped lightly on the table. "Exodus 20:15. 'You shall not steal.'"

De La Cruz kept his expression unreadable.

"And the Devereauxs," Karen continued, leaning in. "Villa 14. Both with broken necks. No sign of forced entry. The jewelry was staged—ritualistic."

"The verse?"

"Exodus 20:4. 'You shall not make for yourself an idol.'"

De La Cruz tapped his finger thoughtfully on the table. "So . . . poison, a staged overdose, and now broken necks. It feels like escalation."

"There's more. I haven't mentioned the trophies. Something is missing from each scene."

De La Cruz's eyes narrowed. "Interesting. Please explain."

Karen shifted in her seat, mentally retracing her steps.

"Diana—first victim. Her jewelry was intact, but . . ." She paused. "One of her earrings was missing. Not lost. Taken."

De La Cruz's gaze sharpened, "By the staff? A waiter or waitress?"

"Possible. To be honest, it was the last thing on my mind. I barely noticed it until later."

"And the Saunderses?"

"The man had a thumb ring. There was a tan line where it should've been."

"And the Devereauxs?" the lawyer asked.

Karen's eyes darkened. "The dog. Not the dog itself, but the collar. One of the gems was missing. A ruby. It wasn't lost. Someone removed it."

De La Cruz stopped the recording. "An earring, a ring, and a gem."

"And it's no coincidence," Karen said. "It's a pattern. The killer's collecting trophies—personal items from each victim."

"Like antlers off a deer," Brock said.

She glanced at him, nodding. "Exactly."

De La Cruz sat back, swirling the remnants of his coffee. "Three scenes, three missing objects—all tied to biblical scripture."

Karen's fingers drummed once more. "That's what's bothering me. This isn't just ritualistic; it's also personal. The trophies—they mean something."

"Religious?" Brock asked, his brow furrowed.

"I don't know," she said, then addressed the lawyer specifically. "We've been calling him Moses, because of the Bible verses."

"Moses, huh?"

Karen shrugged. "It fits. But I'm starting to think he wants it to look that way."

De La Cruz leaned forward, clasping his hands. "Detective, you understand how this looks, right? The missing items. The staged scenes. And you—at the center of it."

Karen met his gaze, her voice flat. "I didn't kill them."

Brock's hand rested briefly on her arm. "We know that."

"I believe you," De La Cruz assured her. "But the court? That's a different matter."

"Look, I've seen this all before. Killers who take trophies don't stop. Each item represents a success. A reminder. They're building a collection."

"Which means..." De La Cruz prompted.

"He's not done."

CHAPTER 55

Brock shifted uneasily. "You think we're targets?"

"I'm not ruling it out," she said.

"Then we must move quickly, Detective," De La Cruz said. "The longer this drags on—"

Karen finished the sentence. "The worse it looks, I know." Karen leaned back, folding her arms across her chest.

Brock chimed in, "Well, if Moses ain't finished . . ."

"Then neither am I," she concluded.

"You mean *we*, señora." De La Cruz smiled, and she welcomed the support.

Brock's phone buzzed faintly against the table, and his eyes flicked to the screen. "T? Why's he calling me?"

"He probably tried my phone first."

"It's her partner back home," Brock explained to De La Cruz as Brock handed Karen his cell.

"Hey, T. What's up?"

"Oh, thank God. I've been trying you for over an hour."

"Give me a sec." She stood abruptly, tucking the phone against her chest. "Please excuse me. I need to take this."

De La Cruz rose as well, offering a small nod of understanding. "I'll give you a moment. I'll be by the entrance."

As he walked away, Brock caught Karen's arm gently.

"Ka . . . you think this killer is watching us?"

Her gaze darted toward the café window, scanning the distant resort grounds.

"I don't think," she said quietly. "I know."

She stepped away from the table, moved toward the far corner of the café, then pressed the phone to her ear, lowering her voice.

"Hey, T. I'm back. Listen, my cell's been confiscated—long story. I grabbed a burner. I'll text you the number."

"Ka, I've got you on speaker," T informed her.

This could only mean one thing. He wasn't alone.

A second voice, deep and gravelly, cut in, confirming her suspicion. "Skaryd, what the hell have you gotten yourself into?"

Shit.

"Greetings from the Utopia, Lieutenant."

"Not funny." Woody David's voice filled the line. "I'm sitting here in my damn office, fielding calls from DC, the embassy, and my boss, Captain Numbnuts. You know, the one who loves to bust my stones? And guess what, Detective? Every single one of them is asking about you. So, I'll ask again—what the hell is going on?"

Karen rubbed the bridge of her nose, pinching hard between her eyes. "Look, Wood—LT, I didn't expect this to blow up like it has. I just . . . stumbled into something."

"You don't stumble into international incidents, Karen," Woody snapped. "You trip over a curb—you don't trip into Interpol cases!"

"To be fair, I didn't know it this was an Interpol case at first," she shot back.

"Well, whoopsie-fuckin-do, Detective."

She kept her voice measured but tense. "Boss, listen. It started with Diana's death, then some young couple, and now the Devereauxs. I had no idea it would unravel this far."

T sighed on the other end. "She's not wrong, LT. It's all tied together. I've been digging, and guess what? The Devereauxs weren't exactly tourists on vacation."

Karen straightened. "Go on, tell him."

T's voice shifted into his usual work mode, calm but clipped. "Okay, let's start with Diana St. James. Her ex-husband, Nathaniel is on the board of that organization called the Horizon Initiative, which you know, Karen."

"Yeah. The one tying him to Ortiz."

"That's the one. Well, Gerald Devereaux is on the same board. Hell, the dude's name pops up all over their filings."

Karen's grip on the phone tightened. "You're telling me Diana's ex and Gerald were playing for the same team?"

"More like running the damn league," T said. "Gerald's signature is on major funding transfers. Offshore accounts. The kind of paper trail that doesn't just scream 'shady,' it belts it out in full surround sound."

Woody cut back in. "I'll tell you what this sounds like—human trafficking."

Karen's stomach twisted. "Yeah, boss. We're thinking the same thing. On the surface, it's all clean. Philanthropy, housing projects, scholarships for displaced families. But if you dig deeper—"

"You find missing persons," Woody finished.

"Exactly," T confirmed. "Diana was married to Nathaniel for years. Maybe she caught wind of what was happening and confronted him. From what I've read about this lady, she wasn't exactly, uh . . . subtle."

Karen nodded, pacing near the edge of the café. She could practically see Diana, digging where she shouldn't.

"Diana had no problem stirring the pot," Karen agreed. "She was vocal about everything. It tracks."

"But that doesn't explain the Devereauxs," Woody countered. "Why break their necks?"

"Maybe they were the latest loose ends," Karen said.

T's voice darkened. "If that's the case, Ka, you're standing right in the middle of it. And I'm not sure they're done cutting strings."

Woody sighed, the sound grating. "Listen, Karen. I'm gonna cover your ass for now, but you need to tread lightly. Whatever this is, it's bigger than you—and it's not just ticking people off locally. I've got big suits breathing down my neck. And if this keeps up, you're going to find yourself up shit's creek."

"Understood, LT. So we're clear, I didn't go looking for this. But now that I'm in it, I can't just walk away."

"Figured as much," Woody muttered. "Look, I'll keep Captain Numbnuts and DC off your back for as long as I can. But if they want answers, you're explaining this mess yourself."

"I'll handle the fallout when I get back."

"You damn well will," Woody growled. "Watch your goddamn six. These aren't small fish you're tangling with."

"I always do, boss."

The line clicked, and Karen lowered the phone, leaning against the café wall.

Brock's gaze met hers across the room, concern etched into the creases of his face.

"Bad?" he asked as she slid back into her seat.

Karen offered a tight smile. "Nothing I can't handle. Apparently, I've pissed off half of Washington."

Brock snorted. "At least you're consistent."

CHAPTER 56

De La Cruz returned to the table, eyes flicking between Karen and Brock as he sat down, his expression unreadable but sharp.

"Interesting call?" he asked, setting his coffee cup down carefully.

Karen took a slow sip from her own, the coffee lukewarm and bitter now. "Let's just say there's more layers to this thing than my abuela's Tres Leches cake."

De La Cruz's brow lifted in quiet amusement. "Care to elaborate?"

Karen leaned in, lowering her voice. "The Horizon Initiative. Ever hear of it?"

His gaze darkened, showing a flicker of recognition. "Sí. They operate in the Caribbean, known for housing projects and charity work."

"On paper," Karen said. "But behind the scenes, it looks more like a front. Diana St. James's ex, Nathaniel, sits on the board. So does—rather, did—Gerald Devereaux."

De La Cruz nodded slowly, steepling his fingers beneath his chin. "Rumors have circled about this organization. But no solid evidence. Nothing anyone could act on, at least."

"Well," Karen said grimly, "*someone's* acting on it now, and it's not the good guys. And it appears they're tying up loose ends."

Brock, arms crossed, frowned. "And we're standing dead center in this goddamn web."

"For now," Karen said, locking eyes with him.

"Detective, if what you're saying is true, you understand the risk, sí?" De La Cruz asked.

"I don't need a lawyer to explain the risks. Yes, I understand completely."

"What's our next move?" Brock asked, rubbing his hands together.

De La Cruz raised an eyebrow. "Our?"

"She ain't doin' this alone."

Karen's lips twitched at the corner, but the weight of the situation crushed any hint of humor.

De La Cruz exhaled softly. "Fair enough."

Before they could continue, the café door creaked open, and Bethany's unmistakable voice carried across the room.

Her shrill sliced through the room like a rusty blade, loud and invasive. Karen's shoulders stiffened before she even looked up.

"Brock," Bethany's voice rang out, high-pitched and too eager.

Karen didn't need to glance at her husband to know he was already suppressing a groan.

"I've been looking for you!" Bethany hurried over, heels clicking too loudly on the tile. She zeroed in like a heat-seeking missile, practically buzzing with gossip. Her gaze flicked to Karen, then lingered on De La Cruz.

"Oh . . . *hello*," she said, drawing the word out with obvious curiosity. Her eyes sharpened, registering De La Cruz as someone new—and interesting.

De La Cruz bowed his head slightly in greeting. "Señora."

Bethany's smile thinned before snapping back toward Brock. She leaned in, lowering her voice as if sharing national secrets.

"They arrested him," she whispered, eyes glittering.

Brock frowned. "Who?"

Her voice dropped further, but she couldn't contain her excitement, "The server—Mario. The one who brought Diana her dessert. I told you he did it. I just knew it!"

Karen's grip on her coffee cup tightened.

"Montenegro made the arrest?" she asked.

"Oh, yes." Bethany puffed up, clearly proud of herself for sharing exclusive news. "I've been calling that police station since the morning after Diana passed. I just learned they brought Mario in late last night. Guess it's official, then."

Karen forced a neutral expression, but inside, alarms blared.

Brock crossed his arms. "You really think he did it?"

Bethany blinked, as if the question itself was absurd. "Well, who else could it be? C'mon, Brock."

Before Karen could steer the conversation away, Bethany's focus narrowed in on her.

"And how are things going for you?" she asked, that pointed edge creeping into her voice. "I heard they took you in today."

Brock shifted in his chair. Karen could sense his body tensing at Bethany's not-so-subtle jab.

"Routine questioning," Karen said evenly, forcing a polite smile. "Nothing more. Inspector Montenegro likes to be, shall we say, *thorough*."

"Thorough, huh? Funny, I heard it was more than that," Bethany said. "People are talking, you know. And you were at that villa when they . . . well, you know." Her eyes widened with performative innocence, but the hunger for scandal was clear beneath it.

Karen felt a strong desire to throat-punch this woman, but . . . well, that wasn't her style. Brock's voice was low and firm. "Bethany, maybe it's best if you go on about your day. We're busy here."

"Oh, I'm just saying," she said, tilting her head toward Karen. "I mean, three deaths in one resort—and you being at the center of two? Some people might call that suspicious. You know how people like to gossip."

De La Cruz's eyes flicked toward Karen, his expression calm but watchful.

"Bethany," Karen responded smoothly, "I assure you, I have zero involvement in any of this, aside from trying to save Diana, as you know. The police are simply being cautious, that's all."

Brock tossed in his two cents. "Exactly. Standard police procedure, right, babe?"

Karen nodded as Bethany's lips curved, but the glint in the woman's eyes only grew brighter.

"I'm just looking out for you," she said sweetly, brushing imaginary lint from her blouse. "It'd be awful if you or Brock ended up tangled in something down here, in this backward country." She reached out a hand to De La Cruz and added, "Oh, no offense."

He smiled, unfazed. "None taken, señora."

"Anyway, from what I hear, things don't work like they do back home. You, of all people, know how the authorities are."

"Yes, I do," Karen said sharply.

Bethany blinked, momentarily thrown off by the steel behind Karen's words.

The moment hung heavy between them until Brock shifted forward, shoulders squared. "Appreciate the concern, Bethany. We've got this covered."

Bethany hesitated, clearly debating whether to push further.

Finally, she exhaled with exaggerated drama. "Fine. Just thought I'd pass along the news."

Karen's eyes followed her as she drifted to the café counter, greeting other Rosarian members with an animated recounting of Mario's arrest.

De La Cruz leaned in, lowering his voice. "Persistent, isn't she?"

Karen's gaze didn't waver. "She's a special one, all right. People like Bethany keep pushing till they cause real damage or get into trouble."

Brock nodded. "That lady's a walking nightmare, just like Diana was, may she rest in peace."

De La Cruz adjusted his cuffs, the polished veneer returning to his face. "Then we ensure there's nothing for her to latch on to."

"Right, and tonight, Ka and I will attend the gala, smile, drink champagne, and give 'em nothing."

Karen grinned, wagging her eyebrows. "Just blend in with the sharks."

"Exactly." De La Cruz's eyes glimmered with quiet approval.

Brock drained the last of his coffee. "So, what happens to this kid, Mario?"

"If things down here are anything like the nonsense I deal with back home," Karen said, "Montenegro's probably under pressure. His bosses need a scapegoat, and Mario's it."

"Sí, and they won't care if he's innocent. They will simply tie him up with a bow and call it justicia—justice." De La Cruz's expression darkened. "While the real killer continues unchecked."

CHAPTER 57

Karen and Brock returned to their suite, the hum of the resort muffled by the heavy door swinging shut. She leaned against it, arms crossed, eyes narrowed in thought.

"Think she's gonna be a problem?" Brock asked, tugging off his flip-flops by the balcony door. His T-shirt clung to him like a second skin from the heat, and he wiped the sweat from the back of his neck with it.

"Not if we make it easier for her," Karen said, peeling off her flats.

"Easier? Babe, Bethany is all about the drama. She could find dirt at a church bake sale."

Karen smiled faintly as she pulled her hair up into a ponytail. "All the more reason to keep her guessing. Tonight, we act completely normal. Go to the gala, mingle, and keep our eyes open."

"Yeah, because nothing says normal like attending a fancy gala while half the resort thinks you killed someone."

"Since when do you care what anyone thinks?"

Brock grinned. "I don't. But I do care about keeping you out of jail."

Karen slid off her sundress and pulled out a fresh tank top and shorts. "Then help me play it cool."

"Oh, I'm all about playing it cool." Brock wrapped his arms loosely around her waist from behind.

His voice dropped to a low murmur, lips brushing against the back of her neck.

Karen laughed softly, leaning back into him. "You're impossible."

"You love it," Brock teased, his grip tightening as he pressed a kiss behind her ear.

"Yeah, I do."

She turned to face him. His T-shirt was soft beneath her hands as she tugged him closer.

"Shower first?" she asked with a sly smile.

Brock gave a playful groan and followed her into the bathroom, peeling off his shirt as she turned on the shower.

Later, Brock lounged on the bed in board shorts, flipping through channels on the resort TV while Karen stood at the bathroom sink, brushing out her damp hair.

Her phone sat nearby on the counter. She checked it—there was still no response from the kids or her father. She texted them all earlier to make sure all was well.

"Any word from the kids?" Brock asked.

Karen's thumb hovered over the call button. "Nothing."

"They probably don't recognize the number, that's all. I'm sure things are fine."

"You're right," she said, though she wasn't so sure. "Besides, between T and my dad keeping their eyes on them—"

"Exactly."

"I'll try them again in another hour."

Brock pulled her close to him. "I'm sure things are fine, Ka. If anything was wrong—"

"They'd reach out. I know. I just . . . with everything going on—"

"You feel like things are out of your control."

"You married a control freak, what can I say?"

He kissed the top of her head. "C'mon. Let's pick something to wear for tonight's thing. We've got to blend in with the fancy crowd."

CHAPTER 58

By the time they made their way to the gala, the sun had dipped below the horizon, casting the resort in deep hues of orange and purple.

Brock wore his blue-and-white-striped Brooks Brothers button-down and khaki slacks, the kind he'd wear to a churchyard barbecue, while Karen pulled on a simple but sleek sundress—nothing flashy, but it suited the occasion just fine.

"You think I'm fancy enough?" Brock asked as they walked toward the event space.

Karen glanced at his Sperry boat shoes, "You're lucky I didn't make you wear actual shoes."

Brock grinned. "These are formal somewhere, I'm sure."

Her phone buzzed as they crossed the sand, the glow of the gala tent growing closer. She fished it out of her crossbody bag, glancing at the screen. *T. Finally.*

She slowed her steps, nudging Brock gently. "Go ahead without me. It's T."

Brock hesitated but nodded. "Don't be long."

Karen watched him continue toward the event before answering. "T. I was starting to think you'd gone dark."

His voice crackled through the speaker, low and urgent. "I've been digging. You're not gonna like what I found."

"I'll add it to the list. Just give me the *Reader's Digest* version."

"You remember Nathaniel St. James, Diana's ex?"

"Yeah. Tied to the Horizon Initiative with Gerald Devereaux, blah blah blah. What about him?"

"Turns out, Gerald wasn't just some silent board member. He was knee-deep. I dug up recent transfers. We've got big money moving through places in the DR and Mexico. Diana might've found out and started blabbing, which is why she ended up dead. Just a guess."

"Maybe not too far off. And the Devereauxs?"

"That's the kicker. Gerald's wife wasn't just collateral. Her fingerprints were all over this too. Both were targets, Ka. Loose ends. And guess whose name keeps popping up?"

Karen's footsteps slowed. "Volkov."

Her eyes locked on the distant marina where the *Libertad* bobbed quietly in the water.

"Bingo. Devereaux, Nathaniel, even that senator guy . . . all just pawns," T said. "Looks like you were right. Volkov's pulling all the strings."

"That all tracks, but why the murders? What's the endgame? Killing Diana, the young couple, the Devereauxs—it feels like overkill."

"That's the part I'm still piecing together," T admitted. "From what I can tell, Diana got too close to the financials. The young couple? Wrong place, wrong time. And the Devereauxs . . . maybe they pissed him off."

"Volkov's making a statement," Karen said, her gaze drifting toward the glowing tent filled with guests oblivious to the danger lurking all around them. "But why now?"

"Who knows, Ka? Maybe he's burning everything down to the roots, like a wildfire clearing the forest—the only way for this guy to start over with a different crew. And if you keep poking around . . ."

"Yeah, I know. Brock and I might be next."

"By the looks of things, Volkov's got ties to mercenary outfits, so stick together and stay sharp."

Before Karen could respond, movement caught her eye.

A figure, silhouetted against the moonlight, strode briskly along the beach and toward the marina.

Her pulse quickened. *Wolfram?*

"I gotta go, T," she said.

"What's up?"

"Wolfram. He's heading toward the *Libertad*. And he's in a hurry."

"Ka, stay cool. Don't do anything crazy."

"Who, me?"

"Yes, you. Why do you think I'm saying it?"

She hung up and slipped her phone back into her bag as she eyeballed the grand yacht and Wolfram from her position. Deciding her next move.

Brock's laughter floated from the tent, mixing with the low hum of chatter. Karen hesitated for a long moment.

She could see him from where she stood, and he, her. "Ka?" he called out to her, waving. He was seated at their table, his arm draped lazily over the back of an empty chair. Brady and Margaret were seated at the same table, chuckling at some off-hand joke. Brady's drink was half-empty, his face flush from one too many rum punches, Karen guessed.

She forced a smile, waving back to her husband.

Wolfram could wait.

Duty called.

Karen stepped into the warmth of the tent, greeted by the soft glow of string lights and the floral-scented air.

The gala was in full swing, tables draped in white linen, each adorned with intricate rose centerpieces. She grabbed a program from the nearest table and slid into the empty seat beside Brock.

"Missed you." Brock grinned, nudging her arm. "How's T?"

"Same," she said, keeping her voice light. "I'll update you later."

He sipped his drink, lowering his voice. "Anything we need to worry about?"

Karen shook her head. "Not tonight."

She flipped open the program, and scanned the list of award categories, rolling her eyes at the overly grandiose names.

Best New Hybrid in the Southeastern United States

Most Vibrant Rose of the Caribbean Region

Best Use of Rare Soil Techniques

Best Hybrid Tea Named After a Loved One

Brady leaned over, tilting his glass toward Brock. "Here's to surviving this circus. And to whatever poor soul wins the 'Best Hybrid Tea Named After a Loved One' category."

"That's your category," she teased, nudging Brock.

"Hey, I had to enter that one." Brock shrugged. "My ma would haunt me otherwise."

The description of Brock's entry—Angel Rose, a large coral-orange bloom with a rich fruity fragrance—was printed proudly beneath his name.

"She'd be proud," Karen said softly, tapping the page.

"She'll be pissed if I lose," Brock quipped, flashing a smile.

Brady chuckled. "Diana's Peace Rose is still in the running, right?"

Brock's expression faltered slightly. "Yeah. Hard to beat the dead for sympathy votes."

Karen's gaze shifted across the room, landing on the memorial photos of Diana scattered along the edges of the tent.

"She's still running the show," Brock muttered.

"Even from the grave," Karen agreed.

From a nearby table, the shrill voice of Bethany carried just loud enough to make Karen's eye twitch.

"I just can't believe she's gone," Bethany lamented dramatically, dabbing at the corner of her eyes with a tissue.

Karen didn't need to turn around to know she was performing for the table.

"She was one of my dearest friends," Bethany went on, voice thick with exaggerated grief. "Poor Diana. And to think . . . killed by a waiter."

Brock rolled his eyes—hard. "You'd think she lost a sister the way she's playing this up."

Brady snorted into his drink. "Bethany's never met a situation she couldn't milk for attention."

Onstage, the evening's MC, Geoffrey Whitcomb, cleared his throat and approached the podium.

"Ladies and gentlemen," Geoffrey began, adjusting the microphone, "thank you for joining us tonight. As president of the British Rosarian Society, I'm honored to be here celebrating your accomplishments and your dedication to the cultivation of beauty."

Margaret leaned over to Karen, whispering, "It's like listening to a documentary on watching paint dry."

Karen chuckled, but her attention was drawn toward the distant marina.

Her curiosity gnawed at her.

"I'm going to find the restroom," Karen said, pushing back her chair.

Margaret perked up. "I'll come with you."

"Oh, you don't have to."

"I insist," Margaret said, already standing.

Karen forced a smile. "Okay, then."

As they stepped out into the warm night air, Margaret linked her arm with Karen's.

"You've been quiet tonight," Margaret said softly. "I know things have been unpleasant. Brady and I are here if you and Brock need anything."

Karen's defenses eased slightly. "Thank you. That means a lot."

She shared what she could with Margaret as they made their way to the restroom. It felt good to have moral support from a friend in a foreign land. As they made their way back to the tent, Karen took off her earring, letting it slip into her palm.

"Damn it. I think I lost an earring," she lied.

Margaret frowned. "Want me to help look?"

"No need," Karen said casually. "I probably dropped it in the bathroom. I'll go back and check. You go on ahead. I'll catch up."

As Margaret disappeared back into the tent, Karen waited a moment before veering away, her footsteps light and quick as she made her way down the beach—toward the *Libertad*.

CHAPTER 59

The breeze tugged at her dress as she stepped closer to the dock, watching as Wolfram walked up the steep gangplank to the *Libertad*.

Karen slowed her pace, scanning the area cautiously. The faint hum of the gala drifted from the distant tent, but where she stood, it was quiet.

Too quiet.

Karen adjusted the strap of her bag and took another step forward, her gaze fixed on the *Libertad*.

She didn't sense the footsteps behind her and bolted, spinning around when she heard, "Detective."

Bo Laurent stepped from the shadows, his hands raised in a defensive posture.

Karen's pulse hammered in her ears.

"You need to stop," he said quietly, his dark eyes narrowing.

Karen forced herself to relax. "And you really need to announce yourself sooner than when you're right on top of my ass."

Bo smiled faintly but stayed where he was, even as she stepped back a few steps.

"What's going on over there?" she asked, nodding toward the yacht.

"That's my question," Bo said. "I told you to stop digging. You've now crossed into something you can't control."

"Oh, really? Funny. Last I checked, I wasn't the one sneaking around in the dark."

"And what would you call this?" Bo countered, stepping closer, his voice lowering. "Walk away, Detective Skaryd. Now."

She squared her shoulders, standing her ground. "Why? Because I'm too close to whatever you and your operatives are covering up?"

"No," he said. "You should back off because you're about to get yourself—and your family—killed. Don't believe me?"

Karen's posture stiffened as he handed her a plain manila folder.

"What's this?" she asked.

"Proof."

Karen's fingers brushed his as she took the folder, flipping it open under the pale light of the marina's lampposts. Her breath caught.

Inside were surveillance photos—grainy but unmistakable. Her father leaving Okeefe's Tavern in Clearwater. His favorite spot for fish and chips. Ellie walking to her car after work. Richie grabbing coffee with friends near the main campus of the University of South Florida.

Karen's stomach twisted into knots, and she nearly doubled over.

"Volkov's people know exactly who you are, Detective," Bo said, sympathy in his tone. "And more importantly, they know who your family is."

Karen clenched her jaw, forcing herself to stare at the photos longer than necessary, memorizing every detail. "They've been watching them."

Bo nodded. "And they're waiting. One wrong step from you, and they'll use it as leverage. Volkov doesn't make idle threats. Trust me—I know."

Karen exhaled slowly, pressing the folder shut. Her father could handle himself—decades on the force had taught him how to spot a tail—but Ellie and Richie? They were civilians.

Kids.

This wasn't their fight.

"You should've told me sooner," she said.

"Would you have listened?"

Her instincts screamed at her to move, to act. She pulled out her cell phone.

Bo stepping forward, his body blocking her view of the *Libertad*.

"Don't," he said quietly, reading the fire in her eyes.

"You think I'm going to let this slide?"

"I already called it in," he said. "Your kids, your father—they're being watched as we speak."

Karen's pulse hammered in her ears. "By whom?"

"Local law enforcement. And some of my people. They're under surveillance. It's discreet, but no one's getting near them tonight."

Karen swallowed, her throat dry. "Not good enough. I need to call my partner. My father."

Bo held up a hand. "He's getting looped in as we speak. So is your supervisor, Lieutenant David."

Her eyes flashed with frustration. "Bo, this is my family."

"I know. I know what this feels like. But doing more only risks exposing the entire operation."

She hated the truth in his words. If Volkov got even the faintest whiff that law enforcement outside Interpol was involved, he'd disappear—again.

Still, this was her family.

Bo took a step closer, his voice steady. "I promise you, Detective, I've already secured them. Besides, Volkov's people won't do shit unless he tells them to."

Karen exhaled slowly, forcing herself to meet his gaze.

"If anything changes," Bo continued, his tone firm, "you'll be the first to know."

Karen nodded stiffly, returning her phone back to her bag, the manila folder tucked under her arm. She trusted Bo, at least as much as she could trust anyone in this tangled mess.

But the thought of her kids . . .

Please let them be safe. "So, what now?" she asked.

Bo glanced in the direction of the *Libertad*, and she followed his gaze. Wolfram's silhouette passed briefly in front of the bridge window, moving like a shadow against the faint light inside.

"Now?" Bo responded. "You go back to the gala. Pretend like nothing's wrong. Keep your head down, and let me do what I need to do."

Karen arched a brow. "You really think I can just sip champagne and be all happy-clappy while there's a fucking hitlist on my family?"

Bo's lips twitched, but it wasn't amusement. It was exhaustion, "That's exactly what I think you need to do."

"You're out of your mind."

"Look, Detective . . . Karen. If Volkov sees you panicking, if he thinks you're pulling the threads, he'll use that against you," Bo said softly. "You know how this works. If you stay calm, the family stays safe."

Her stomach twisted once again.

She hated how right he was.

Bo tilted his head. "You think Volkov doesn't want you to crack? To panic and do something stupid? He wants you to call your partner. He's counting on it."

Karen pressed her lips together, saying nothing.

"The only reason you haven't already been shut down is because Volkov's watching, assessing the threat. But that can flip on a dime."

Karen took a step back, her pulse slowing to something more manageable.

"You leave in two days, no?" Bo reminded her. "If so, that's all you need to make it through."

"And if something happens before then?"

"I'll handle it."

"The same way you took care of the Devereauxs?" she countered.

While her remark was stinging, he handled it like the seasoned professional he appeared to be, "I promise you, on the souls of my family, I will handle this."

She studied him carefully. Something in the way he'd mentioned his family. This was more than a job. This was personal to him. But as quickly as his demeanor had changed, had softened, it reverted back to the steely persona she was used to. Unreadable, a man far too comfortable navigating the spaces between shadow and light.

Finally, Karen nodded. "All right. But if I catch even a whisper of something wrong back home—"

Bo inclined his head slightly. "Understood."

Karen's eyes lingered on the yacht, anchored for the moment, but ready to be set adrift. Just like her.

"And Wolfram?" she asked, breaking the silence.

Bo nodded. "Doing his job."

"I still don't get it. How does he fit into all of this?"

"He's been embedded in Volkov's network for over a year. I placed him close to Ortiz. He is not just muscle—he is my eyes."

"You trust him?"

Bo met her gaze without hesitation. "With my life."

Karen exhaled softly, nodding.

She turned toward the path leading back to the gala. The distant hum of conversation drifted toward them, a reminder of the normal world still spinning beyond the chaos.

Before she took another step, she glanced over her shoulder.

"Bo," she said.

He paused, one foot already on the gangplank leading to the *Libertad*.

"Thank you," she murmured.

Bo's gaze softened for a fraction of a second. Before he could respond, the soft chime of his phone cut through the night air. He fished it out of his jacket pocket, the screen briefly illuminating his face as his eyes scanned the message.

Karen caught the sender's name at the top—*Wolfram*.

CHAPTER 60

Bo's expression shifted, the steely veneer cracking just slightly. Without a word, he turned toward the yacht.

"What is it?" Karen asked, stepping in line beside him.

His strides lengthened. "Wolfram needs me on the *Libertad*. Go back to your party."

"Yeah, that's not happening."

Together, they made their way across the beach, the *Libertad* looming ahead like a specter in the night. The last two times Karen had boarded, the yacht had been alive with a menacing elegance—Camilla's welcoming smile, the soft clink of champagne glasses, the hum of activity, and the threatening presence of Volkov's wolfdog.

Now, there was nothing but darkness.

The yacht's exterior lights were off, save for a faint glow filtering from one of the upper cabins. The lack of noise set her teeth on edge.

She hesitated at the base of the gangplank. "This doesn't feel right."

"Because it's not," Bo said, continuing ahead of her.

She carefully followed, the planks creaking underfoot. Her senses were on high alert as they boarded the deck, moving silently toward the cabin entrance. The silence broke with the faint creak of a door swinging open.

Wolfram emerged from the shadows—his face only partially visible in dim light from above. Taking in his hulking figure, Karen's eyes landed on his shoes . . . and stayed there.

They were darkened at the edges and shimmered slightly, indicating a wetness.

Blood?

Wolfram's face betrayed nothing, his eyes meeting Bo's as if Karen wasn't even standing there.

"They are gone," Wolfram said, stepping fully onto the deck.

"Who is gone?" Bo asked.

"Todos—everyone." Wolfram's voice was cold, detached. "Ortiz. Camilla. The crew. The other guards. It's a bloodbath back there."

"Oh, God," Karen said, wrapping her arms around her torso.

"If Ortiz hadn't sent me on that errand, I'd be with them," Wolfram added.

"What about Volkov?" she asked.

Wolfram shook his head. "Missing."

Bo slammed his fist against the edge of the boat. "Dammit."

Karen's instincts screamed at her to leave—to listen to Bo and walk away.

But she couldn't.

"I need to see it," she said, already moving toward the entrance to belowdecks.

Bo's arm shot out, catching her by the wrist. "No, you don't."

"Please I've seen it before, if not worse."

"Not like this," Wolfram warned.

"I can handle it." She pulled free of his grip.

Wolfram led the way. The faint hum of the yacht's engines provided the only noise as they walked toward the deadly scene.

The scent hit her first.

Coppery.

Pungent.

Wolfram opened a side door, stepping aside as Karen peered inside.

The salon was bathed in shadows, but the shapes were unmistakable. Four bodyguards sat slumped in their chairs, hands bound to the armrests. Their throats were slit clean, the dark stains pooling beneath their feet.

But Ortiz was the centerpiece.

His body lay sprawled across the ornate rug, arms splayed wide as if embracing the afterlife. A Havana cigar jutted grotesquely from the deep wound in his throat, smoke still curling faintly from its tip.

The rich scent of tobacco mixed with the sharp tang of blood, an eerie mockery of his refined tastes.

Karen's eyes lingered on the absurd image, bile rising in her throat. Ortiz had always been larger than life, with his slicked-back hair, expensive suits, and fancy cigars clenched between his perfect teeth. But that was before.

A large canvas hung above them, tilted slightly as if it had been disturbed. The painting—*El Sacrificio de Camila* by Ramón Oviedo—depicted a woman standing at the edge of a cliff, arms outstretched in surrender.

Across the canvas, in sharp crimson strokes, was a single phrase:

Exodus 20:13 – You shall not murder.

Karen swallowed hard, stepping back into the hall.

Her gaze locked with Wolfram's, whose expression was stone cold, unreadable.

"Jesus," she whispered.

Bo stood at the entrance. "It's a message for sure."

"Yeah," she muttered, "but who is the sender? And where is he?"

Bo's face darkened, his eyes narrowing toward the blood-soaked room. "Most likely? Out recruiting his next crew."

Karen's mind raced. Ortiz's execution—along with his bodyguards—was precise and methodical. There was nothing chaotic about it.

Volkov wasn't just sending a message.

He was resetting the board.

Karen exhaled slowly, gripping the edge of the doorway.

"I think we are done here," Bo stated, his voice low.

Karen cast one final glance at the carnage, the image searing itself into her memory.

"For now," she said quietly.

Bo nodded toward the exit. "Go back to your husband. I'll take care of this."

Karen hesitated, scanning Bo's face for answers she wouldn't find.

"You better," she murmured, brushing past him as she stepped onto the deck.

The cool night air washed over her as she left the marina. She would return to Brock and the gala, knowing full well the storm was far from over.

Volkov was out there, somewhere in the dark. Watching.

Karen exhaled slowly, pressing the manila folder Bo had given her tighter against her chest. Inside were the surveillance photos of her father and her children, Ellie and Richie. She could see their faces in her mind— her daughter's soft smile, her son's carefree laugh. But now, those memories felt fragile. Breakable.

Her heart twisted.

Brock.

She picked up the pace, breaking into a slow jog to get back to the gala. Back to her husband. She could almost picture him now—lounging at the table, chatting with Brady while Margaret laughed at one of his jokes. When he saw her coming back into the tent, he'd wink and smile . . . and pretend not to notice the weight she carried.

He had no idea. And this wasn't something she could simply tuck away.

He deserved to know.

She stepped through the opening of the tent.

The music had shifted to something livelier, the hum of conversation mingling with the clinking of glasses and faint applause. It felt worlds away from the massacre she'd just witnessed.

Margaret's sharp eyes caught her immediately. She stood near the bar, swirling a glass of rum punch.

"There you are," Margaret called out with a warm smile. "I was beginning to think you'd fallen into the ocean."

Drawing closer, Karen mustered a tight grin. "Just needed some air."

"Everything all right?" Margaret studied her face, concern flickering behind her eyes.

Before Karen could answer, Brock appeared beside Margaret, his hand already reaching for Karen's.

"There she is," Brock said, pressing a kiss to her cheek. His hand lingered on the small of her back, his touch grounding her. "You okay?"

Karen nodded, feeling the warmth of his palm spread across her skin.

"Yeah," she said, forcing her tone to steady. "I just . . . got caught up."

Brock frowned but didn't press.

"They're about to start the awards," he said, guiding her back to their table. "Figured you'd want to be here . . . you know, just in case I won."

Karen smiled despite herself. "Wouldn't miss it."

Brady raised his glass. "Better be ready to lose to my Black Pearl rose."

"Dream on," Brock shot back, grinning.

Karen eased into her seat, folding the manila folder beneath her clutch. Her gaze swept the room, but Bethany's familiar chatter from a few tables away snapped her attention.

"...and to think Karen was there," Bethany was saying, her voice pointed enough to carry. "Poor thing, caught at that bungalow. Can you imagine?"

Karen's muscles tensed.

Brock caught the shift, his eyes darkening as he followed Karen's gaze.

"She's still at it?" he muttered.

Karen exhaled, smoothing the napkin over her lap. "Let her talk."

"You sure about that?"

"It's fine. She'll move on eventually."

Brock didn't look convinced but relented.

At the front of the tent, Geoffrey Whitcomb returned to the podium, clearing his throat. The crowd fell into a hush, the stage lights casting a soft glow over his silver hair.

"Ladies and gentlemen," Geoffrey began, "thank you again for joining us tonight. It is my honor to recognize the dedication, talent, and passion each of you has poured into your work. Tonight, we celebrate not only the art of cultivation, but the bonds we've created through it."

Karen's attention drifted as Geoffrey continued. At the back of her mind, the image of the cabin inside the *Libertad* lingered. Four men—tied down and left to bleed out beneath the chilling words of Exodus 20:13. So calculated. So . . . evil.

And Volkov wasn't finished.

A soft round of applause broke out, pulling Karen from her thoughts. Geoffrey was announcing the next category—Brock's.

She squeezed his hand. "Here we go," she whispered.

As Geoffrey listed the nominees, Karen's gaze flicked to the marina through the tent's opening—she couldn't help it.

The *Libertad*'s lights had gone dark. Every single one.

It was an ending.

And a beginning.

CHAPTER 61

The applause rippled through the tent as Geoffrey Whitcomb called out the victor's name.

"And the winner for Best Hybrid Tea Named After a Loved One goes to . . . Brock Skaryd for his Angel Rose."

Karen's hands moved on autopilot, clapping as Brock grinned, rising from his chair. His brown eyes sparkled beneath the string lights, and he shot her a wink.

"Told you Ma wouldn't let me lose," he said, planting a kiss on Karen's cheek.

Brady groaned from his chair, raising his glass. "Enjoy it while it lasts. Next year, the Black Pearl is coming for you."

Brock laughed. "I'll believe it when I see it."

Karen smiled, feeling the warmth in the moment—Brock's genuine joy radiated outward, and for a brief stretch of time, the murders, the blood, and the dark silhouette of the *Libertad* faded into the background.

Margaret patted her hand. "He deserves this."

"He does," she agreed.

Brock stepped onto the small stage, shaking Geoffrey's hand as the crowd applauded. He hoisted the glass trophy above his head, a boyish grin tugging at his features.

Karen tried to focus, holding on to the simplicity of the celebration.

Brady stood, clapping harder than anyone and shouting, "Next round's on me, mate."

Brock bowed, then pointed at Brady. "You got it, mate."

Laughter filled the space, light and easy, and for the first time all night, Karen allowed herself to breathe.

Jose, the resort staffer who'd been especially helpful during their stay, weaved through the tables. His polite smile broadened as he approached, a small envelope pinched between his fingers.

"Señora Karen," he said, handing her the envelope. "For you. Congratulations to your husband, ¿sí?"

"Oh, sí, yes. Yes, thank you." She examined the envelope with her name scribbled across it. "What is this, do you know?"

Jose gave a small shrug. "It was left at the front desk."

The atmosphere shifted—from joyous to cautious. Her fingers slipped beneath the envelope's flap, pulling out the folded paper inside.

Her pulse quickened as she read the words.

Exodus 20:14 – You shall not commit adultery.

The paper trembled in her grip.

Karen's eyes darted toward the marina. The *Libertad* remained as before—dark and silent. Ominous.

Farther down the dock, though, she spotted the mast of the catamaran.

Her stomach twisted.

The boat captain.

She understood the biblical reference immediately. She'd seen the captain more than once charming tourists with his rugged smile and overly personal jokes. Karen had overheard enough staff gossip to know he had a reputation for more than just sailing.

And she remembered Bo's words and her instincts telling her that Volkov . . . he wasn't finished.

"Ka?" Brock's voice pulled her back to the moment. Trophy in hand, he was staring at her curiously. "What's going on?"

Karen forced a tight smile, hurriedly tucking the envelope and the note into her clutch.

"Nothing, babe," she said, standing to hug him. "I'm so proud of you."

When she released her husband, he was immediately inundated with well-wishers. She slowly stepped toward the opening of the tent to get a better view of the dock, noticing Bo and Wolfram moved like shadows towards the catamaran.

She had to tell Bo what just happened.

Karen leaned onto Brock's side, kissing his cheek lightly.

"Gotta step out," she whispered, holding her phone up and waving it back and forth to indicate she had a call waiting, which she did not. "Need some quiet so I can hear. I won't be long."

Brock's brow creased. "Geez, can't you put that thing on silent or something?"

"It's important. I promise I'll be back before they cut the cake."

Brock studied her for a long moment but relented with a small nod. "Go. I understand."

Regretfully, she left the tent and crossed the sand, moving quickly toward the dock. The celebration behind her faded with each step, replaced by the rhythmic lap of waves against the hull of the catamaran.

She climbed aboard cautiously, the faint creak of the fiberglass planks echoing louder than it should have.

The door to the small cabin hung ajar.

Karen's hand hovered over it, hesitation flickering for the briefest second. Then she pushed forward.

The scene inside froze her in place.

The catamaran's cabin was dark, save for a lantern casting flickering shadows against the walls, revealing Bo and Wolfram standing opposite a gruesome sight.

And there, strung up by a thick rope, hung the captain.

His lifeless body dangled from the rafters, his bare chest streaked with blood.

Around his throat-slit neck, a crude sign dangled.

Exodus 20:14.

But Karen's eyes locked on one particularly grotesque detail—his genitals had been severed and stuffed into his mouth, a horrifying mockery of the verse that condemned him.

She swallowed hard, nausea doubling her over. She clutched her stomach.

Bo turned and said nothing at first, his eyes moving slowly from Karen to the swaying corpse, his expression hard and emotionless.

Wolfram's gaze lingered on the captain's defiled body for just a moment before he blew out a long breath.

Bo tugged the sign from the body with a single rough motion. The captain's corpse lurched slightly as the rope groaned overhead.

"What now?" Karen asked in a shaky whisper.

"More clean-up," was his flat reply, to which Wolfram nodded somberly.

She took half a step back, trying hard not to breathe in the metallic tang of blood in the air. "I need to tell Brock. This guy is snipping all loose ends, and we're next on his hit list. I know it."

"Go back to the gala, Detective," Bo said. "Celebrate with your husband. Let him enjoy his evening. You can tell him tomorrow."

Her mouth opened to argue, but Bo's tone hardened.

"This isn't for you," he said.

Karen's jaw tightened, her eyes flicking between Bo and Wolfram.

But she understood.

This wasn't an investigation anymore.

This was a war—and Bo was leading the charge.

CHAPTER 62

She lingered one moment longer, memorizing the grotesque image before making her way to the creaking dock.

No matter how Bo wanted to lay it out, this was Volkov tying up loose ends, and Karen and Brock were dangling dangerously close to the edge.

The gala celebration stretched late into the evening, the air bubbling with laughter and the soft hum of music—a stark contrast to all she'd seen recently.

Brock sat at their table, his glass trophy reflecting the candlelight. He was mid-conversation with Brady, the two swapping stories and playful jabs as if there wasn't a care in the world.

Karen watched her husband, his relaxed posture, the easy smile that tugged at his lips. She wanted to freeze this moment—hold on to it before the storm inevitably pulled them both under.

Her mind kept circling back to the catamaran.

To the captain, strung up and mutilated.

She could still smell the blood from both scenes, no matter how much she tried to bury the memories.

"Ka," Brock said, nudging her gently. "You with me?"

She blinked, forcing a smile, though small. "Yeah. Just thinking."

"Don't hurt yourself," Brady teased.

Karen chuckled, but Margaret's sharp gaze lingered on her.

The woman scooted closer to her. "Just thinking, my ass," she said, tilting her head, curious. "What's going on?"

Karen hesitated. Oh, how she wanted to share. To release the tension, the fear. Let it drift away from her, leaving behind a safe and comforting space.

"I'm fine. Just tired," she said smoothly, meeting Margaret's gaze. "It's been a long trip."

Margaret's lips pursed, but thankfully, she let it go.

As the gala began to wind down, a small group from the Rosarian Society invited Brock and Karen to join them for a drink at the resort bar. It was the last night for many of them, and the energy was light, celebratory.

Karen hesitated, feeling the tug of exhaustion—the dark images still lingering behind her eyes.

But Brock's hand slipped into hers, his fingers warm and familiar.

"Come on," he said softly. "Let's enjoy tonight. You can be Detective Skaryd tomorrow."

She wanted to protest. To tell him about the slaughter on the *Libertad* and on the catamaran—about the sign hanging from the captain's neck and the grotesque mockery added to that. But the warmth in Brock's gaze grounded her, and she couldn't deny themselves this moment of pleasure. Locking her detective self away for the night, she squeezed his hand.

"Music to my ears," she said.

At the bar overlooking the Caribbean Sea, Brock and Brady slid onto barstools, immediately falling into easy conversation. Karen stood beside Margaret, each of them holding a glass of rum punch.

Margaret pressed her for clarity. "You sure you're all right?"

"I'm so proud of Brock," was Karen's non-response. She remained steadfast in her resolve to stay focused on the celebration, one of the last as their vacation wound down.

Margaret gave a knowing nod. "Sometimes the hardest thing is pretending nothing's wrong."

Karen's eyes flicked briefly toward the distant marina, barely visible beyond the edge of the resort. "You have no idea," she murmured.

As the night stretched on, Karen began to relax and even joined in the easy banter fueled by liquor and jubilation. Brock's hand rested lightly on her thigh, and her heart swelled with pride—even as more sinister things swirled outside this tight circle.

Margaret approached, looping her arm through Karen's. "I need another drink. Walk with me?"

Karen hesitated but nodded, following Margaret toward the bar.

Margaret ordered another cocktail, and as the bartender worked, she said, "I really don't want to pry, but whatever's happening—I can see it's really got to you."

"I don't want to burden you," Karen whispered, dropping her head. She suddenly felt tired, so tired.

Margaret squeezed her arm gently. "That's what friends are for, love."

Karen smiled, grateful for Margaret's kindness, but this wasn't something she could share.

Not yet.

The stroke of midnight came and went, and guests began to filter out, exchanging plans for next year's Rosarian Society gala. The destination was still undecided, but the buzz leaned toward Italy—affordable, elegant, and filled with vineyards.

Karen lingered by the bar, watching Brock laughing with Brady near the entrance. Then her eyes drifted toward the dock in the distance.

Bo was out there, cleaning up the mess Volkov had left behind.

"Ka, what's going on?"

Brock's sudden presence startled her. He'd just been over there, with Brady. And now he was here, sensing all of her tension. This couldn't wait any longer.

Rip off the bandage.

"Come sit," she whispered, guiding him toward a quiet corner of the bar.

As they sat, his gaze flicked down to her shoes, and his face crumpled in concern. She looked too.

A rust-colored stain near the toe.

"That's not just dirt, is it?" he asked quietly.

She licked her lips. "No."

"Jesus, Ka—"

She placed a hand on his. "I wasn't in danger, but I do need to tell you something. And you're not gonna like it."

CHAPTER 63

Brock nodded. "All right, I'm listening."

Karen shifted closer, lowering her voice, but this time she didn't hold back. He needed to know.

Everything.

After she'd shared the horror-filled side of that night, she finished with the kicker: "Volkov's not just after Ortiz or the Devereauxs. He's watching us, Brock. And he's watching our family."

Brock's entire body stiffened. His grip on her hand grew tighter, but his voice was dangerously controlled. "What do you mean?"

Karen glanced toward the dimly lit marina in the distance. "Bo showed me surveillance photos. My father. Richie. Ellie. Volkov's people know where they are. They've been following them."

"What?" He shot up, spinning in a circle, pulling at his hair. "Fuck that!"

"Calm down, please."

"Don't fucking tell me to calm the fuck down." His face was beet red with anger.

Karen pulled him back into his chair. "They're safe."

"Bullshit. We're checking out tonight and heading back home."

"Brock, please."

"No. No! I've had enough. Let's go."

Karen pulled at his arm. "Honey, listen. People are already in place.

Woody, T, and some local LEO's are keeping an eye on them—quietly. And Volkov's people won't make a move without receiving orders from him. Nothing's happened, and nothing will happen."

Brock's eyes locked on hers, disbelief flashing behind them.

"You mean like nothing happened to Ortiz and his crew? Or Captain Flirt?" he said, voice laced with sarcasm. "Because that turned out great for all of them, didn't it?"

Karen winced. She couldn't argue with that. The images of massacres on the two vessels would never leave her.

"I get it," Brock continued, his voice tight. "But you can't seriously expect me to feel good about this. Our kids, Ka. Our family."

"I-I know." Her voice quaked, and she took a deep breath. "I hate this too. We just need to leave it be. Carry on as usual."

"Isn't that what I've been telling you all along? To leave it be? Now look at us!"

"Please, Brock. If we panic, if we overreact—they'll see it as weakness. And act."

Brock's arms crossed over his chest, his shoulders rigid. "So, what—sit here and do nothing?"

She hated this, what she had brought into their circle. The danger, the fear. But . . . no. She hadn't asked for it. She'd been drawn to it, and she could hardly have ignored the call. "No," Karen said firmly. "We keep our heads down. We get through the next day and a half. Then we go home."

Brock shook his head, muttering under his breath.

Karen inched closer, resting her hand against his chest, feeling the steady thump of his heart beneath her palm.

"I truly believe we're okay, Brock. We have our family covered. Volkov's too busy chasing his tail right now, cleaning up his messes. He's not coming after our kids."

Brock's hands dropped to her waist, pulling her in slightly. His forehead rested lightly against hers. "I hate this," he said.

"I do too."

His arms tightened around her for a long moment, and she felt tears forming, something she rarely felt. The hard façade she wore was cracking, letting in the hurt.

Finally, Brock stepped back. "All right. We're here for the duration. But the second something feels wrong . . ."

"Yes," was all she said . . . all she needed to say.

CHAPTER 64

After long goodbyes with Brady, Margaret, and the other straggler rosarians, they finally departed the bar, hand in hand. United. Committed.

When they reached their suite, however, Karen's instincts prickled.

Something felt wrong.

The Do Not Disturb sign was missing from their doorknob.

"Hold on," she said, taking the keycard from Brock's hand.

"What now?"

"The sign—it's missing from the door. I know for sure that we placed it there when we left."

He nodded. "Yeah, we did."

Karen slid the keycard in, and the light flashed green. As the door creaked open, she swept the room with sharp eyes.

The atmosphere inside felt . . . off.

"Ka?" Brock said softly, standing behind her.

She stepped inside slowly, passed their hall closet and guest bathroom. Her gaze landed on the dinette table.

The murder board.

It had been packed away.

Hidden.

Now it sat propped against the wall, index cards pulled of the board and splayed out on the table.

Names crossed off—Devereaux, Ortiz, Camilla.

Including the name in the center.

Volkov.

Karen's breath caught.

She grabbed her husband's arm.

"What's this mean?" he asked.

Karen's eyes narrowed, "Another message."

"From who?"

"Moses."

CHAPTER 65

She needed to clear their suite, make sure they were alone.

They stepped into the kitchen, and Karen's hand trembled slightly as she slid a knife from the butcher block, the cool handle grounding her in the present. Brock stood by her side, rifling through the bottom cabinet for something heavier than the glass trophy he won—a frying pan.

"Seriously?" Karen muttered, eyeing the makeshift weapon.

Brock gave a small, tense shrug. "Better than nothin'."

They exchanged a brief glance. Karen could feel the tension rolling off him—years of unclogging drains and replacing pipes hadn't prepared him for this. But Brock wasn't the kind to back down, even when everything screamed at him to walk away.

Karen stepped in front of him, inching toward the hallway. "Stay behind me."

Brock snorted softly. "Yeah. Not happening."

"Brock, I mean it."

"So do I."

His voice was firm, unwavering. Karen didn't argue. She knew Brock—knew that stubborn streak that ran deep. He stepped in front of her, the frying pan held high in one hand, glass trophy in the other, ready for some action.

The soft hum of the ceiling fan barely masked the silence that pressed down on them as they crept deeper into the suite. Everything looked normal—the half-finished bottle of water on the coffee table, Brock's sandals by the door.

But looks could be deceiving.

Karen's eyes flicked toward the hallway leading to their bedroom. The door was closed, and a faint light spilled from beneath the door, painting thin slivers across the cool tile floor.

She grabbed Brock's shoulder and pointed. He stopped cold.

"Did we close the door and leave the light on?" she asked, stepping up next to him.

"Fuck no, we didn't." Brock shifted beside her, gripping the pan handle tightly.

"Wait here," she whispered, taking a step forward.

"The hell I will," Brock shot back, moving in stride with her.

They paused outside the door. Karen pressed her palm flat against the wood, as if she could feel movement on the other side. Maybe not "feel," but she might sense something.

But . . . nothing.

She glanced at Brock, nodded once, and twisted the knob.

Swung open the door.

At that moment, the world seemed to stop.

Volkov's body lay sprawled across their bed. His throat had been slit ear to ear, the sheets saturated with deep red, his blood bloomed beneath him like water spreading through a paper towel. His left hand dangled limply over the edge, fingers slightly curled.

His face—partially obscured by a pillow—was pale, sunken. The left eye socket gaped empty, a hollow pit of darkness.

The right eye was gone too, but in its place, nestled grotesquely within the cavity, was the ruby stone from the Devereauxs' dog collar.

Above the headboard, scrawled in red across the cream-colored wall, were the words:

You shall have no other gods before me. (Exodus 20:3)

Brock staggered back, his free hand slamming into the wall to steady himself. "Jesus Christ."

Karen's stomach twisted, but her training kept her focused. She forced herself forward, scanning the room.

"Ka," Brock's voice rasped behind her, "is that—"

"It's Volkov," she confirmed, kneeling beside the bed to check his pulse. She knew it was pointless, but habit drove her hand to his cold wrist.

Brock dragged his hand down his face, pacing a few steps back, turning away as if he could shake the image loose from his mind.

"This is insane," he muttered, his breathing shallow. "Who the hell does this?"

Karen rose to her feet, her eyes locked on the writing above the bed.

"Moses," she whispered.

Brock spun toward her. "You're telling me he was in here?"

Karen checked the closet and the bathroom. Everything was eerily still.

"He's long gone," she said, more to herself than Brock. "This wasn't about us."

Brock gestured wildly toward the bed. "Not about us? He left a fucking *body* in our fucking *bed*. How is that not about us?"

Karen exhaled, tightening her grip on the knife. "It's about Volkov."

Brock let out a hollow laugh. "Not anymore," His voice cracked. "Damn it, Karen. Our vacation has become nothing more than a freaking horror show."

"I know."

"What if he's watching us right now somehow?" His eyes darted around the room, to the window, to the bedroom door.

Karen turned to him, steadying his shaking hands with her own. "Look at me."

He did, his eyes wild with fear.

"He's not here," she said firmly. "He's not watching us. I'm going to secure the scene, then track down Bo."

Brock's head jerked back. "Seriously?"

"At this point, it's our only option," Karen said. "With Volkov's body in our suite? We can't exactly explain it away. If we leave, it'll look worse. Montenegro already thinks I'm involved in the Devereaux murders."

Brock's lips pressed into a thin line. "Great. Now people are going to think we're running a damn hit squad out of our suite."

Karen managed a faint smile, despite the situation. "Bo will handle it. He's already taking care of two other scenes, might as well add this one to his list. But first—"

She stepped toward the balcony door, checking the lock. Secure. Then the lock on the suite door. Same.

"He didn't break in," she muttered.

"Meaning?"

"Meaning Moses gained access somehow."

"That doesn't exactly make me feel better."

Karen reached for her phone, scrolling to his last text message warning her off.

"Wait," Brock said, catching her wrist.

Karen glanced up.

"Are you sure about this? Calling him instead of Montenegro?"

Karen hesitated for only a second. "First Bo, then Montenegro . . . if we have to."

Brock nodded slowly, though she could see the unease lingering in his eyes.

Karen stepped toward the doorway but glanced one last time over her shoulder at Volkov's lifeless form.

Moses had left a message.

And it was loud and clear.

We need to play nice or we're next.

CHAPTER 66

Wolfram knocked twice before Karen allowed him into her suite. To her and Brock's surprise, Jose, the ever-diligent resort staffer, trailed a step behind, his easy smile a fragile facade against the tension thick in the air.

Brock stood near the bedroom door, arms crossed tightly. His eyes glued to the body sprawled across their bed.

"Sorry it took so long," Wolfram said, scanning the main room.

"Why're you here? Where's Bo?" she asked.

"He is still down at the docks. He sent me up. We're stretched thin, but he will be here soon. Are you two okay?"

Brock let out a humorless laugh. "Oh, yeah. Never better."

"We're fine. But this isn't exactly how we pictured our vacation. The body's in there," Karen said, gesturing to the bedroom.

Wolfram nodded and got down to business without further comment.

Jose shifted uneasily by the door, his body trembling. "I will arrange for another suite," he offered, gulping hard.

Karen gave him a grateful nod. "Thank you, Jose."

He nodded as he stood there, as if waiting further instructions. Karen let him be.

Wolfram knelt beside the bed, pulling on latex gloves with a snap. "All right. Let's get this over with. We will document everything for Bo. Eventually we will have to loop in Montenegro, but not yet."

Brock's head jerked up. "I still don't understand . . . why not loop him in now?"

"Local law enforcement can't touch this until Interpol secures the scene," Karen explained, anticipating Wolfram's answer. "If Montenegro gets here too soon, the way he did with the previous scenes, his guys could compromise evidence."

Wolfram nodded, glancing over his shoulder. "Exactly. Montenegro's team are incompetent, and this is not a routine murder. Given Volkov's connections to the human trafficking investigation, Interpol takes precedence. This isn't just a murder scene—it's part of an international case."

Brock ran a hand over his face. "So, what happens now?"

"Now?" Wolfram stood, carefully taking photos with his phone, moving in precise, methodical steps. "We document everything. Nothing gets touched until Bo arrives. Same protocol we followed with the catamaran and the *Libertad*."

Karen crossed her arms. "Bo mentioned getting a team on scene."

Wolfram nodded. "Sí. One's overseeing the yacht, another at the catamaran. Both vessels are sealed, and the docks are under surveillance. This suite will be next."

Brock frowned. "Surveillance?"

"Sí. Once we leave, Interpol will post someone outside the door. It'll stay secured until Bo processes it formally." Wolfram's gaze hardened as he met Brock's eyes. "I need you both to stay clear once you leave this room. No coming back. You don't want to accidentally interfere with the process."

"What do you mean, interfere with the process? Isn't this...aren't you..." Brock stammered.

Karen stepped closer to her husband, resting her hand on his shoulder. "Honey, it's okay. Jose . . . can you take Señor Skaryd to our new suite?"

Jose's smile returned, though thinner this time. "Of course, señora. Right this way, señor."

Brock appeared too tired to argue. He blew out a long breath. "This is insane," he muttered. "It's like we're living in a damn horror movie."

Karen's lips twitched into a faint smile. "Maybe you'll write the screenplay one day."

"Yeah, right." He shook his head. "Don't take too long, okay?"

Karen kissed his cheek. "I'll be there as soon as I can."

As Brock and Jose headed toward the front door, she called out, "Jose."

He paused, glancing back. "¿Sí, señora?"

"Not a word about this to anyone. Understand?"

Jose nodded, puffing out his chest a bit. "I won't say anything. You can count on me."

The door shut behind them with a quiet hiss, leaving her alone with Wolfram. The faint hum of the ceiling fan seemed louder in the sudden quiet.

She joined Wolfram in the bedroom, her posture shifting into something more clinical. "Let's finish this up. You got enough photos?"

"Almost," Wolfram said, crouching to take another shot of the blood trail leading from the bed to the floor. "I need more angles on the incision. The throat work's too clean for a rush job. It's almost surgical. And look at this. The back of his head."

Karen stepped closer, eyes narrowing in on the corpse. "Looks like blunt-force trauma. Got an extra pair of gloves?"

Wolfram tossed her a pair without looking up.

She snapped them on with practiced ease. "Three in one night. I think our Moses is showing off."

Wolfram stood, stretching his back. "Yeah. But hauling a body up here unnoticed? That takes skill."

"Or luck." Karen countered, crouching to examine Volkov's contorted limbs. "You think he had help?"

Wolfram rubbed his chin. "Maybe. Or he's just that good. Stuffed the guy's body into a laundry cart or something. Who knows. The *Libertad* was a slaughterhouse. This is so much more . . . intricate, but still the thing of nightmares."

"Poison for Diana St. James. Pills and alcohol for the Saunderses. The Devereauxs' necks snapped. The Libertad—a massacre. And the catamaran captain—what's worse than a massacre?"

"I hear what you are saying. The captain was strung up, his, uh . . . *member* stuffed into his mouth," Wolfram shivered. "Now Volkov. It's like Moses is evolving. He went from simplicity to unchecked brutality."

Karen exhaled. "Yeah. First it was quiet, almost clean. Now it's loud, messy. He's not just a killer anymore. He's a predator. Like Volkov's wolfdog gone bad, wild and uncontrollable."

"You know what they say about tigers." Wolfram met her eyes. "Once they get a taste for human blood, they never stop with one kill."

Karen sighed. "And neither will Moses."

CHAPTER 67

Karen perched on the edge of the armchair outside the suite, the muted glow from the resort lights spilling from the balcony. Wolfram stood by the open glass doors, his back straight and hands tucked into his pockets. The faint rhythm of waves outside set an oddly calm backdrop to the carnage inside the bedroom.

Karen broke the silence first. "How did you end up involved in all this, Wolfram?"

He glanced at her, one brow lifting in faint amusement. "All this?" He gestured loosely toward the bed. "Long road. Longer story."

Karen leaned forward, elbows on her knees. "I'm not going anywhere."

Wolfram hesitated, then sighed, taking a seat on the sofa opposite her. "Started in Santo Domingo. Worked Major Crimes there for years. A lot of paperwork and none of the glamour."

"Major Crimes?" Karen's head tilted. "You were a homicide detective?"

"Among other things." His tone darkened slightly. "Drugs, arms trafficking, even human smuggling cases. You learn quick that law enforcement down here is complicado—complicated."

Karen nodded in quiet understanding, starting to put two and two together. "How'd you get involved with Bo? Interpol just came knocking one day?"

Wolfram chuckled softly. "Not exactly. It started with a bust. We intercepted a cartel shipment tied to an international syndicate Interpol had been tracking. I didn't know it at the time, but the operation had ripple effects across three continents."

Karen arched a brow. "Let me guess. They liked how you handled it."

"Something like that. A few months later, I was invited to a regional task force. Took me away from here, had me working alongside agents de España, Brazil, even Los Estados Unidos." He leaned back, his gaze distant. "That's when I met Bo. He liked the way I handled myself, so when the opportunity came to pull me into more permanent work, he made the call."

Karen smirked. "Bo has a way of getting what he wants."

"Sí, he does."

"And how did the missus feel? Is there a Señora Wolfram?"

He smiled. "There was. Divorciado—divorced. She couldn't handle the hours, or dedication. She said I was—"

"Lemme guess, too married to the job?"

He nodded. "I don't know how you do it."

"Twenty-five years and counting. I got lucky when I met Brock. He puts up with a lot. Thankfully, he's not the jealous type." Her expression grew more serious. "But going undercover isn't something you just slide into. How did you go from Major Crimes to being Ortiz's errand boy?"

Wolfram's eyes flicked to the doorway, as if checking for Brock before answering. "Had to leave the force first. Publicly, anyway. Interpol needed someone to go in undercover, with access but no ties. So, I staged my own downfall."

Karen's brows knitted together. "In disgrace?"

He shrugged. "More or less. Botched a case, let a suspect walk. Got accused of taking bribes. Enough to ruin my reputation but not land me in prison. Ortiz needed someone dirty, someone he thought he could control."

Karen leaned back, folding her arms. "Smart. Risky as hell, but smart."

"I take it you've done something similar?"

Her lips pressed into a thin line. "Leaving the FBI wasn't as dramatic. Clearwater PD was more—necessary."

Wolfram arched a brow. "Necessary? Por qué?"

Before she could answer, a sharp knock echoed from the suite's front door. Both instinctively straightened, eyes locking in silent communication.

Karen rose first. "I'll check it."

Wolfram stood, trailing a step behind. "Como dijeron en *Top Gun*, never leave your wingman."

She didn't argue. She padded toward the door, missing her service weapon tucked close to her hip. Reaching the door, she hesitated for just a moment before looking through the peephole.

Seeing who it was, she opened the door.

Jose's usual cheerful expression dimmed by cautious professionalism. "Señora, your new suite is ready. I brought the key."

Karen exhaled, offering a grateful nod. "Thank you, Jose. And Brock?"

"He asked me to tell you, not to dillydolly?"

"Dillydally," she corrected, taking the keycard "Thanks, Jose, for everything."

"Por supuesto, Señora Karen." Jose dipped his head. "And I will not speak of what I saw earlier."

"We'd appreciate that."

He let out a breath and stepped away, his footsteps echoing down the hallway.

Karen closed the door and turned to Wolfram. "What's our ETA on Bo?"

Wolfram took out his cell and sent a text. After a moment, he replied, "He's on his way up."

"Good. Good," she said, returning to her chair.

The faint hum of the ceiling fan resumed its reign over the quiet room, but the shadows lingering in the corners suggested they weren't quite alone—not really. Moses's message was clear.

He was still out there.

Ready to strike his next victim.

CHAPTER 68

Wolfram's phone buzzed, the screen lighting up with Bo's name. He glanced down at the message, relief crossing his face.

"Bo's stepping off the elevator," Wolfram said, slipping the phone back into his pocket.

Karen nodded, crossing her arms as she paced near the balcony doors. "Good. I want this wrapped up before Montenegro decides to show up uninvited."

A soft knock at the door moments later announced Bo's arrival. Wolfram opened it, stepping aside to let him in. Bo's sharp gaze swept the suite, lingering for a beat too long on the doorway to the bedroom.

"All right, let's get to it. Walk me through the scene," he said.

Karen and Wolfram launched into the debrief, detailing the timeline, the discovery of Volkov's body, and their efforts to secure the suite. They explained how they had documented everything, then established a perimeter around the bedroom, controlling access to ensure nothing was disturbed, contaminated, or removed.

"We then did our best to preserve what little pieces of evidence we could, which wasn't much, for your forensics team." Karen concluded. Bo listened, arms crossed, his expression blank as Karen finished. "I must call Montenegro. We can't keep this quiet. A bunch of bodies, two vessels, and now your suite? This isn't just one-off violence. It's organized. And it's escalating."

Karen frowned. "Who did you send to lock down the yacht and catamaran?"

Bo met her eyes. "Interpol agents from the local branch. I trust them to keep it locked until I get back down there myself."

Karen nodded, seemingly satisfied. Her phone vibrated in her hand, and she glanced down to find a message from T:

Interpol dialed us in. Woody and I are keeping an eye on the family. We've got this.

Karen's chest eased slightly. She looked at Bo. "Thank you."

"For?"

She held up her temporary cell. "My partner just texted me. My family's safe."

Bo shrugged, brushing it off. "We take care of our own. You'd do the same."

Karen hesitated for a moment. "One last thing—we need to dial in the lawyer—De La Cruz."

Bo stared at her blankly for a moment, as if he had no idea about who De La Cruz was. He then turned to Wolfram, "Keep this room secure. I'm heading back to the dock."

Wolfram stood guard at the bedroom door.

As Bo disappeared down the hallway, Karen stared at her phone, the weight of an unanswered question pressing down on her.

Karen lingered near the balcony doors, the faint shimmer of moonlight dancing across the ocean's surface. Her reflection in the glass mirrored the unease curling in her chest. Wolfram stood nearby, quietly organizing the last of the evidence logs, his movements efficient and focused.

"The way Bo looked at me, when I mentioned De La Cruz," Karen murmured, more to herself than Wolfram. "It's like he didn't know who he was."

Wolfram glanced up. "Maybe he doesn't."

"Then who's paying his bills?"

"I wonder . . ." Wolfram said, pausing for a beat. "Do you think Moses is paying for De La Cruz?"

As if he'd read her mind. "Well, if it's not Bo, then it's gotta be. The timing, the secrecy. Moses doesn't just kill people—he plays with them—manipulates them first. Why not use De La Cruz to keep tabs on me legally? It's perfect, really."

Wolfram rubbed his chin thoughtfully. "It's a stretch, but not impossible. This Moses likes to get creative. If he's watching you that closely, he might be laying groundwork for something bigger." He winced. "Hate to say it."

"But it's true. And we need to stop it. I want my name cleared. When Bo calls Montenegro, I need him to set the record straight about the Devereauxs and help the server, Mario. I'm not going to have that hanging over his head, or mine."

Wolfram crossed his arms. "Bo will step up. He knows the stakes, and he won't leave you out to dry. But Montenegro—he's a different story."

"You think he'll fight it?"

"Montenegro doesn't play well with others. He hates being told how to handle his cases. But if Bo pushes hard enough, he'll have no choice."

"The inspector knows damn well I didn't kill anyone. If he wants cooperation, he'll clear my name. Mario's too—he didn't kill Diana."

Wolfram studied her for a long moment before nodding. "I'll make sure Bo knows it, if he doesn't already."

Karen took a deep breath, the weight in her chest lightening just slightly. "Good. Because if Montenegro thinks he can pin this on me, and Diana on Mario, then he's about to realize he picked the wrong person to mess with."

"That might happen sooner than you think."

Karen followed his gaze, her heart kicking up a notch. "Why?"

Wolfram's phone buzzed again. This time, he didn't look relieved. "Bo just texted. Montenegro's down at the docks, and he's been arguing with Bo about jurisdiction. And he's heading this way next."

Karen smirked faintly. "So, basically a pissing contest. Typical."

CHAPTER 69

The minutes stretched on as Karen and Wolfram waited, the tension lingering between them like a guest who had overstayed his welcome.

Finally, Wolfram's phone vibrated again. He glanced down, then straightened. "Montenegro's on his way up. Bo says he's not happy."

"Not surprised," Karen set her water bottle down gently. "He's never happy."

A sharp knock echoed at the suite door moments later. Wolfram opened the door to reveal a scowling Montenegro standing in the hallway, Alvarez at his side. He stepped into the suite without waiting for an invitation, eyes sweeping the room before settling on Karen. His underling followed suit.

"Convenient that you are always in the middle of things," Montenegro said.

Karen refused to be baiting into an argument—for now. "Hello to you too, Inspector Montenegro."

"I should have been called immediately. This is my crime scene."

Karen's lips twitched into the faintest of smiles. "In my experience, Interpol has jurisdiction, so I called Inspector Laurent."

"You are already a suspect in another murder," he snapped at her. "I would not be so quick to play games."

Wolfram shifted but stopped when Karen gave him a subtle glance.

"One, I'm not playing games. Second, I have an alibi," she informed him flatly. "I was at the Rosarian Society gala, with my husband. And there were plenty of witnesses."

"Mira, I could care less about your gala. The only thing I care about is the body in your suite."

Karen's gaze sharpened. "Then let's go look at the evidence. You'll see, I couldn't have put him there."

Montenegro motioned for Alvarez to follow him. The junior detective hesitated for half a beat before stepping inside the bedroom. The second she crossed the threshold, the grisly sight hit her like a train, and her knees actually buckled. She caught herself on a chair and managed to remain upright.

For all of three seconds.

With a muffled curse, she spun on her heel and darted toward the en suite bathroom. The door clicked shut behind her.

Montenegro rolled his eyes. "Coño."

Wolfram hesitated for a moment, then headed to the bathroom. "I will check on her."

Karen's eyes tracked him as he rapped lightly on the bathroom door.

"You okay, Maria?" he asked softly.

After a pause, Alvarez could be heard through the door saying, "Necesito un minuto."

"Take your time." Wolfram said, before informing the others, "Needs a minute."

Karen's eyes lingered on Wolfram as he stood outside the bathroom, one hand lightly brushing the doorframe. His concern was subtle but noticeable to anyone paying attention.

Karen was. Montenegro was too.

Fortunately, they were interrupted by another knock echoing from the suite's entrance. Karen answered the front door, and Bo entered, walking to the bedroom.

He scanned the room, then greeted the inspector. "So we meet again."

Montenegro scowled. "As I already told you at the docks, this is my case."

"Sorry, Inspector." Bo spread his feet apart and crossed his arms. "Interpol jurisdiction. And I'm the lead investigator assigned to this mess."

Montenegro squared his shoulders in turn. "With the resources I have to cover multiple crime scenes, I cannot let you lock me out of this."

Bo's expression didn't shift. "Then let's not play games. You'll get access, but not at the cost of compromising evidence."

"I don't need your permission to conduct my investigation."

"You do if you want to keep this case from collapsing under procedural errors," Bo countered. His tone was calm, but there was no mistaking the steel beneath it.

A tense silence filled the room before Montenegro finally exhaled sharply. "Fine. I'll make some calls. But this isn't over."

He turned toward the bathroom, rapping on the door. "Alvarez, we are leaving."

After a long pause, the door opened. Alvarez stepped out, her features pale.

"See you 'round, Inspector," Karen hollered as the inspector and Alvarez walked through the suite to the front door. When he turned to shoot her a final glare, she wiggled her fingers in a wave. The inspector growled something; Alvarez had her arms around her torso, saying nothing.

When the door clicked shut behind them, Bo let out a breath. "You always like to stir the pot?"

Karen shrugged. "It's a gift."

Another knock on the door. It was Jose, holding a small, sealed envelope featuring the resort's logo.

"For you, señora." He handed her the note.

"Thanks, Jose. Any idea who left it?"

"Sorry, señora. No."

Bo stepped up. "Who's it from?"

Karen turned the envelope over in her hands, dread pooling in her gut. "I guess we'll find out."

CHAPTER 70

Karen's fingers hovered over the envelope flap. She had half a mind to rip it open, but Bo placed a hand on her arm.

"Take it slow," he advised. "This person knows how to get under your skin. Don't let him win."

Karen exhaled, carefully peeling the seal back. Inside, a small card slipped into her palm. The handwriting was painfully familiar:

Enjoying my gifts, Detective?

Her jaw tightened, the words swimming in her vision. Bo leaned over her shoulder, reading the note.

"He's taunting you," Bo said.

Karen stuck the note back in the envelope, then slapped it into Bo's open palm. "Here. Process it. "Process it. I doubt you'll find anything, but maybe we'll get lucky. Saliva, fingerprints, something."

Bo dropped the note into a plastic evidence bag he'd pulled from his jacket pocket. "We'll run it through everything we have. If he has slipped up even a little bit, we'll catch it."

Karen held doubts. "He hasn't so far."

"True," Bo admitted. "But it only takes one mistake. And the more he plays this game, the more likely it is."

"I hope you're right."

Bo glanced at her, his eyes showing concern—for her. "Detective . . .

Karen, you should turn in. Go find your husband in the new suite. Worry about all this tomorrow."

"I can't just walk away."

"You'll be no good to anyone exhausted. Your husband needs you. Take the night, clear your head. We'll regroup in the morning."

Karen finally relented, knowing she had nothing else to give in this moment. "Fine. But I'm supposed to be leaving the day after tomorrow. I need this wrapped up, and I need your help clearing my name for the Devereaux murders . . . and clearing Brock's name too."

"You know I'll do what I can."

She grabbed her bag and exited the suite. The hallway was dim with just small glimmers from the recessed lighting. An officer stood at attention just outside the door to her left. He nodded as she walked to the elevators.

Three floors down, she entered her new suite—smaller, darker, and lacking the sweeping ocean view she'd grown accustomed to.

Inside, Brock was pacing on the balcony, the breeze coming through the open doors and rustling the curtains. At the sound of her entering, he rushed over to her, his expression etched with worry.

"Jesus, Ka. I was starting to think I'd have to come looking for you."

Karen set her bag down by the door, walking to him. "I'm fine. Montenegro stopped by—threw his usual fit, but Bo handled it."

Brock's arms tightened around her, his breath slow against her temple. "I hate this," he admitted. "Like we're stuck in a nightmare or something."

"I know. We'll be gone soon."

Brock pulled back slightly, his eyes searching hers. "Listen, I haven't called the kids. I don't want to panic them, but it's killing me not to warn them."

"We can call my father. Check in, keep things light. I'm sure by now he knows officers are watching his house, their movements. They'll be safe."

"Well, he hasn't called to question it, so . . ."

"He wouldn't. He knows to wait to hear from us. It's time."

Ignoring her husband, she took his phone—her father would at least recognize the number—and dialed for a video call. Brock hovered behind her.

It rang twice before her father answered. His face appeared on the screen, gray-haired and sharp-eyed, even in the dim light of his family room.

"Karen," he said flatly.

Shit, he called me Karen. He always calls me Ka.

The look on his face and his tone of voice carried the weight of suspicion. "What's going on? Why are there local LEOs stationed outside my front door?"

Karen's heart dropped, her grip tightening on the phone. Brock stiffened beside her.

"Dad," Karen started, but the words tangled in her throat, "there have been a few developments, as you might guess."

Her father leaned closer to the camera, voice low. "Well, whatever it is, young lady, you need to tell me. Now."

CHAPTER 71

Karen clutched Brock's phone tightly, her father's stern gaze burning through the screen.

"Dad, I was going to call you sooner," she began, her voice tight, "but things escalated quickly."

His eyes narrowed. "Clearly. Start talking."

"There have been some incidents."

"What kind of incidents, Karen Marisol?"

Marisol.

Damn, he added my middle name—my goose is cooked.

While Brock shifted beside her, clearly uncomfortable, Karen pressed on. "There have been multiple homicides—all connected. One from the rosarian society, two separate couples, a retired senator from the island and his crew, and last, someone we all thought was the ringleader, a guy named Gregor Volkov."

"Sounds Russian."

"Ukrainian, actually."

"Same difference. Doesn't explain the people sitting outside my house."

"I'm getting to that."

"Get there quicker."

"There's someone else. Someone we're calling Moses"

Her father's brows lifted slightly. "Moses?"

Karen licked her lips and pushed on. "He's been leaving messages at each scene tied to the biblical commandments. He's methodical and brutal, but he's not just after random people. There's some organization and purpose to it. And the whole thing may include human trafficking, Dad. Might even connect to a case T and I had been working on back home, one we'd closed. Interpol's involved on this one."

Her father leaned back in his chair, rubbing his temple. "Interpol, huh? This is a nasty pile of incidents, as you call them."

She forced a faint smile. "Bo Laurent is running the investigation for Interpol. You'd like him. He's sharp. But Montenegro—local law enforcement—isn't so thrilled about Bo's involvement. You would not like him."

Her father's lips pressed into a thin line. "Let me guess. Pissing contest. Don't play well with others in the sandbox."

"Bingo."

"I worked with a guy like that back in '92. Gallagher out of the Third Precinct in Brentwood. A real hack. Always looking for someone to pin the blame on."

"Yeah, well, Montenegro suspects me."

Her dad sat up straighter. "Of what?"

"The Devereauxs' murders, one of the couples I'd mentioned who'd been murdered. I was basically in the wrong place, wrong time. I found their bodies. Butler walked in. He assumed the worst. Things got messier from there."

He let out a slow breath, the weight of his years in law enforcement surfacing in his eyes. "Damn it, Karen. You should've called me the second things started getting ugly. I could've provided coverage, sent a few favors your way."

"I know. I thought I could handle it."

"Clearly you couldn't," he snapped.

She swallowed hard. "Dad, I need you to stay vigilant. Keep an eye on Richie and Ellie. Don't let them suspect anything, unless it's absolutely necessary. T and Woody are watching them too."

"I know how to run a case, young lady. Now, is there anything else I need to know?"

Karen hesitated, then, "Ah . . . yeah. There's one more thing."

"Go on."

"I have a lawyer—De La Cruz. Someone paid for him, but I don't know who. I thought it was Bo, but he denied it. I don't like not knowing who's pulling strings."

"Dammit," he said, gripping the side of his chair. It's gotta be Moses, then."

"That's what I think too."

A few beats of silence, then her father wagged a finger at her. "You need to get out of there, Karen. Come home."

"Not without clearing my name," she said. "We're supposed to leave the day after tomorrow. This gives me a day and a half to see this through."

He dropped his hand, shaking his head. "I knew that's what you were going to say. But I want you or Brock to call me with updates."

"We will."

"And Ka," he added, his voice lowering, "if this Moses bastard tries to get close to our family—"

Her eyes flickered with the same resolve. "I'll take him down first."

Her father nodded, apparently satisfied for now. "All right. You take care of yourself. I'll keep the kids busy."

Karen smiled faintly. "Thanks, Daddy."

Brock stepped closer, his arm brushing against hers. "Thanks, Pop."

"Don't thank me. Just keep her safe, Bub."

"You know, I will."

When the call ended, Karen lowered the phone, blowing out a long sigh of relief. Though she'd known her dad wouldn't be thrilled with the chain of events, he was there for the family. As always. And in that knowledge, she felt just a wee bit lighter.

CHAPTER 72

The next morning, the resort atmosphere was tense as more visitors learned of or suspected what had been happening in this paradise they called the Utopia. Police tape stretched across the marina, sealing off the catamaran and the *Libertad*, while additional tape now marked Karen's former suite.

Officers lingered near the entrances. Guests whispered over breakfast, speculation buzzing through the crowd like static electricity.

As planned, Karen and Brock sat with Brady and Margaret at one of the patio tables overlooking the swim-up bar for breakfast. The bright Caribbean sun did little to ease the exhaustion etched into Karen's features. Brady looked fresh, smiling as he sipped his Earl Grey tea, but Margaret showed more concern, watching Karen quietly.

Finally, Margaret laid her hand on Karen's. "You didn't sleep, did you?" she asked softly, leaning in so Brady wouldn't overhear. The two men were deep into their own conversation anyway.

Karen forced a smile, stirring the untouched coffee in front of her. "We had a long night. We wanted to celebrate Brock's win properly."

"Celebrate, huh?"

Karen winked, a playful smile tugging at her lips. "What can I say? A wife's gotta do what a wife's gotta do."

"I'm not buying it for one minute. You're a detective. The police are everywhere. There's crime scene tape for goodness' sake."

"Could be anything. It's a resort—lots of guests. People get, you know, rowdy."

"All right, then. I won't push. But if something's wrong, you'll tell me, won't you?"

Karen's smile softened. "You're leaving. We're leaving. We'll see you back in the States sometimes soon, okay?"

As breakfast wound down, guests began to trickle out, some heading for the airport shuttle waiting by the main entrance. Brady and Margaret were among them, their bags packed and ready.

Margaret hugged Karen, and Brady and Brock slapped each other on the back.

"Take care of yourself, all right?" Margaret said to Karen.

"I will. Safe flight."

"Try to keep your husband out of trouble," Brady joked.

Karen grinned. "Impossible."

They watched their friends disappear into the shuttle. Karen exhaled, feeling the weight settle back on her shoulders. Just as she turned toward the resort lobby, a familiar figure appeared near the entrance.

De La Cruz.

He approached swiftly, his suit impeccable—not a wrinkle in sight—despite the rising heat. His eyes locked on Karen.

"Detective," he greeted, extending his hand to Brock briefly, "I was told you needed me urgently."

Her brow furrowed. "Told by whom?"

"My benefactor," De La Cruz said, his tone light but eyes sharp. "Said you were in trouble."

Brock's gaze narrowed. "You're sure it wasn't Interpol?"

De La Cruz shook his head. "As I stated, this came directly from my benefactor."

"Okay, we need to talk, but not out here. Let's head upstairs to the new suite." She turned and, without a backward glance, led the men to the elevators.

Karen shut the door behind them, locking it as Brock drew the curtains.

De La Cruz set his briefcase down, eyeing them carefully. "Did something happen last night? More trouble?"

Karen's gaze was unwavering. "We'll worry about that later. First, I need to know who's paying you to represent me."

His expression didn't flicker. "Confidentiality, Detective. You know how this works."

"Don't give me that crap," she snapped. "Someone's been pulling strings since I got here. People are dropping like flies, Mr. De La Cruz."

"Joaquin, please," he said before taking a seat. He gestured for Brock and Karen to do the same. He crossed his legs and waited.

"First, Diana," Karen said, ticking the names off on her fingers as she spoke, "then the Saunderses and the Devereauxs. Now Volkov and Ortiz are both dead too."

"Don't forget the catamaran boat captain," Brock added.

"Yeah, him too. How could I forget that? Strung up—his throat slit. Castrated, with his . . . kibbles and bits stuffed into his mouth."

De La Cruz winced at the thought.

"There's someone out there leaving bodies like breadcrumbs, *Joaquin*," she said. "And I need to know if the person covering my legal fees is the same one orchestrating this series of nightmares."

He studied her before exhaling. "I wish I could give you a straight answer. Here's the truth: I genuinely don't know who it is. Payments come through a third-party firm. Some offshore account, no direct trail. Whoever they are, they have resources."

Karen's fingers tightened around her arms. "So, it could be our Moses."

"Not sure who Moses is, but yes, it could be anyone."

Brock cut in. "If it is Moses, we need to know now. We can't afford to have Karen tangled deeper in this."

"Who the hell is Moses?" De La Cruz asked.

Karen jabbed a finger in the air. "Our killer."

A sharp knock at the door broke the tension.

"Expecting someone?" Brock asked.

Karen shook her head. She opened the door cautiously to find Montenegro, flanked by two uniformed officers.

The inspector's eyes flicked to De La Cruz, then back to Karen. "Señora Skaryd, I need you to come with me. Now."

De La Cruz stepped forward smoothly, blocking Karen with his arm. "Inspector Montenegro, my client will not be answering any further questions without my presence. If you need to speak with her, I suggest you schedule something through the proper channels."

"This isn't a request, Counselor."

"And I'm not denying cooperation," De La Cruz said calmly. "But we both know how this works."

Karen exchanged a worried look with Brock. Montenegro took a breath, then stepped back.

"Fine. I'll be waiting downstairs. Don't keep me waiting long, señora."

As the door closed, Karen groaned. "Well, that went swimmingly."

De La Cruz adjusted his cufflinks. "I will accompany you. Whatever this is, we handle it—together."

CHAPTER 73

The resort lobby was a swirl of movement—guests arriving with bright eyes and heavy luggage, others dragging themselves toward airport shuttles, sunburnt and ready for home. Below the surface of it all was an edginess, most evident in the subtle way staff avoided eye contact with the uniformed officers stationed throughout the property.

Karen, Brock, and De La Cruz maneuvered through the crowd, cutting through the noise, until they caught sight of the inspector off in a quieter corner of the lobby. He waved them on. His posture screamed impatience, and Karen couldn't blame him, really.

Like him or not, the man now had the bodies of Volkov, Ortiz and his yacht crew, and Captain Marco to his investigation. Such an undertaking would strain even the calmest nerves. And Montenegro was far from calm in the first place.

"You've been busy, Señora Skaryd," he started, his tone clipped. "Too busy."

Karen matched his gaze without blinking. "I didn't put Volkov's body in my suite, Inspector."

"So, you claim." Montenegro's lips tightened. "Still, I am not here to argue. I need statements from both you and your husband regarding last night's discovery. And sooner rather than later."

De La Cruz smoothly stepped in. "My clients are willing to cooperate, but as I've stated, any questioning will be done formally. Through the proper channels."

Montenegro's eyes narrowed, but he let it slide, shifting his attention back to Karen. He opened his mouth to say something but was interrupted by a low growl, guttural and unmistakable to Karen.

Two men from animal control struggled to control the massive Saarloos wolfdog, which strained at its leash.

The powerful animal's coat gleamed under the lobby's soft lights, thick and silver-gray. Every guest within eyesight instinctively took a step back.

"Volkov's dog," Montenegro stated. "Recovered it this morning."

Karen's brow lifted. "Really? Where?"

"We found her locked in a cabin on the yacht, sedated. Poor thing probably heard everything," he said, showing some unexpected compassion.

The dog's head jerked from side to side, nose twitching, hackles bristling despite the handlers' efforts to soothe it. The officers exchanged uneasy glances, tugging the leash to guide the animal toward the resort exit.

Karen's tapped her chin as she watched the dog, his erratic movements, trying to break free. Drool poured from its mouth as its eyes darted left to right. *The dog isn't just spooked—it's hunting.*

Suddenly, the dog forced a hard stop, refusing to move at all. It seemed no amount of yanking on that leash was going to move the animal.

Its amber eyes locked on something . . .

Karen followed its line of sight.

Chloe, mid-selfie, oblivious to the world. A few feet away, Cal, hands in his pockets, passively aloof.

But the dog's reaction told a different story.

A deep growl rumbled from its chest as it lowered its head slightly, baring sharp teeth. The two animal control officers leaned against the weight of the animal—to no avail.

"Calma!" one of the men shouted, but the wolfdog refused to relent.

Karen stiffened.

De La Cruz must have noticed her body language as he asked warily, "Something wrong?" He then turned to look in the same direction.

Karen had zeroed in on just one man—Cal. She examined him like a puzzle piece that suddenly fit. His left hand—resting near his hip—bore a distinctive ring. A silver thumb ring with a blue stone.

The ring that was missing from the body of the young Mr. Sauders, found dead in a vacant suite, along with his wife.

Her gaze shifted to Chloe' . . . her earring—an additional pierced earring dangling from her left ear. Mismatched and out of place. That same earring had gone missing from Diana's body, dead on the restaurant floor.

The realization hit hard and fast.

Cal wasn't just some quiet, forgettable guest.

He was *Moses*.

Cal shifted, and his gaze locked with Karen's. The faintest trace of a smile tugged at the corner of his mouth as he played with the thumb ring.

Mocking her.

Recognition flickered in his expression, as if to say: You know. And now, I know you know.

Karen's grip tightened around the back of the chair in front of her.

De La Cruz and Montenegro were staring at her, she could feel it. Still, she did not look away.

"Karen?" Brock's voice nudged her back to the present, but she didn't respond right away.

Cal's eyes lingered on hers a beat longer before he casually turned, drifting toward the exit. Chloe followed a few steps behind, her face buried in her phone.

The officers tugged again at the dog's leash, finally managing to drag the unruly beast forward. It didn't stop snarling until Cal was fully out of sight.

"He's leaving," Karen said quietly. "Right now."

"Who?" Montenegro asked. "What is it, Detective."

Karen pointed. "Cal. The quiet one, always in the background."

Montenegro frowned. "And why does that matter?"

"Because that's *Moses*."

Cal's figure slipped through the masses, merging with the line of travelers boarding the shuttles.

Karen stepped out of their huddle with only these parting words: "He's getting away."

CHAPTER 74

Karen didn't wait for any responses from the men. She bolted toward the exit, her flats clicking sharply against the polished tile, leaving a bewildered inspector, lawyer, and husband behind.

"Señora Skaryd—*Detective*." Montenegro called out, but she didn't stop.

She burst through the lobby doors, rapidly scanning the platform. Shuttles idled at the curb, engines humming as resort staff loaded luggage. Guests shuffled in orderly lines, chatting and snapping last-minute photos.

But Cal was gone.

Chloe, however, was standing near the shuttle queue, scrolling through her phone. Oblivious.

Maybe.

Karen strode over, her pulse pounding.

"Chloe," she said, her voice firm enough to draw not only the influencer's attention but several people around her.

Chloe glanced up. "Oh, hey, what's up?"

Karen's eyes narrowed. "Where is he?"

Chloe blinked as if confused. "Who?"

"Your husband," Karen snapped, her tone sharp.

Chloe's face twisted in mild amusement. "Oh, him. Yeah, he just, like, left. Said he had to handle something and told me to go to the airport without him." She shrugged. "Whatever."

Karen's fingers curled into fists. "He left you?"

"Yeah." Chloe laughed lightly. "It's no biggie. He already paid me."

Karen's stomach dropped. "I'm sorry . . . *Paid*?"

Chloe adjusting her sunglasses. "Yeah, I guess I can say something now. He hired me. Found me on Instagram, said he needed someone to be his 'plus one' for the week. No strings attached. Just hang out, look good, do resort stuff. Easiest gig of my life."

Karen's mind raced, piecing it together. "You're telling me you don't actually know him?"

Chloe shook her head, chuckling. "Nope. Didn't ask questions, either. I mean the guy paid a ton upfront, and all I had to do was take spa selfies and drink margaritas."

Karen stared in disbelief.

"My follower count's gone through the roof this week," Chloe said, gesturing to her phone.

"Did you post any pictures with him?"

Chloe scoffed. "Uh, no. That was the one rule—no pictures of him. Not that I minded. He's kind of a dork, you know? Didn't really fit with my brand."

Karen glanced around again, frustration clawing at her. "Did he leave anything behind? A bag, a jacket—anything?"

"He gave me this to hold." Chloe kicked at a duffel bag on the ground next to her. "Said I could keep it if I wanted. It's just clothes and stuff."

Karen crouched, quickly flipping open the bag and digging through it. Neatly folded shirts, a pair of sneakers, and a toiletry kit.

She unzipped the toiletry kit—and gasped.

Tucked among a disposable razor, a toothbrush, and a hairbrush—each potentially teeming with DNA—was a note, scribbled with the same handwriting with which she'd become so familiar: *Enjoy your trophy, Detective.*

"Any idea where he went?" Karen demanded, holding the kit tight to her chest.

Chloe frowned. "I told you . . . I don't know. He didn't say. He just—"

"Left, yeah, you said."

Brock, De La Cruz, and Montenegro caught up to her then, all out of breath. The inspector's irritation was palpable.

"What the hell is going on?" Montenegro demanded, glaring at Karen.

"That was Moses," she said, her voice steady but edged with fury.

"Who, that Cal kid?" Brock asked. "But he was so—"

"It was him, and this might be the evidence we need to prove it." she said, thrusting the toiletry kit at the annoyed inspector.

Caught off guard, Montenegro fumbled with the kit before settling it in the crook of his arm. He did not look inside, just asked, "Okay, explain to me, who the hell is Moses?"

Karen took a deep breath, her eyes blazing. "The man responsible for the murders you've been chasing. Diana, the Saunderses, the Devereauxs, Volkov, Ortiz—all of them. He's been right here under our noses the whole time."

Montenegro's brow furrowed. "And you let him get away?"

Her frustration boiled over. "I didn't let him do anything! You're the one who was too busy dragging me to the side while he walked out the front door."

Montenegro opened his mouth to retort, but De La Cruz stepped between them, his voice firm.

"Inspector," he said, "instead of pointing fingers, perhaps we should focus on processing this evidence. If my client is correct, we may finally have a lead."

Montenegro scowled but nodded begrudgingly.

Karen turned back to Chloe, her voice softer now. "Listen to me, Chloe. If you think of anything—anything at all—about Cal, call me. Understand?"

"Excuse me, Detective. If she has any information to relay, she will tell me," Montenegro interjected.

The wide-eyed girl hesitated, then nodded slowly. "Uh, sure. Okay. But seriously, the guy's a freak. Probably already on a plane back to wherever."

"We'll see about that," Karen said.

Chloe got in line to board the shuttle—*as if*—and Montenegro called over a pair of officers, just arriving at resort. Together, they stopped her.

"Señorita, por favor," the inspector said. "I think perhaps we should talk now. I have a few questions for you. We can talk back at the precinct."

"But I'll miss my plane."

"You'll catch the next one." He then ordered his officers to escort Chloe to police headquarters.

"Does this mean it's over?" Brock asked. "We can get back to our lives?"

"He's not done," Karen said, her voice low but resolute. "Not yet."

Montenegro crossed his arms. "And what do you plan to do, Detective?"

Karen's eyes burned with determination. "Find him."

And this time, she wouldn't let him slip away.

CHAPTER 75

Karen stood frozen as her mind raced. She couldn't afford to waste another second. Just as she turned to regroup with Brock, Joaquin, and Montenegro, Jose appeared, dressed in his bellhop uniform, his calm, friendly demeanor cutting through the chaos as he watched Chloe drive away in the back of a patrol vehicle.

His brow furrowed as he noticed the discarded duffel bag on the ground. As if putting two and two together, he asked, "Señora Karen, do those belong to Señor Cal?"

"Yes, why?" Karen's heart skipped. "You've seen him?"

Jose nodded. "Sí, señora. It looked like he was heading toward la marina, at the Azure Serenity resort next door."

Karen's stomach dropped. "When?"

"Just a few minutes ago. He seemed in a hurry."

Karen spun on her heel, grabbing Montenegro's arm. "We're not letting him get away."

"We'll need transport. There. There—" Montenegro pointed.

Brock and De La Cruz stepped out of the way as she and the inspector dashed toward the golf cart station, Karen's pulse pounding in her ears. Montenegro jumped into the driver's seat, motioning for Karen to climb in. He slammed the pedal down, and the cart lurched forward, speeding toward the Azure Serenity resort at a brisk ten miles an hour.

"Can't you make this thing go any faster?" Karen shouted.

The inspector only growled and beat the pedal repeatedly with his booted foot.

The wind whipped through Karen's hair as they raced along the narrow path, weaving between guests and staff who jumped out of their way with startled cries. Montenegro's jaw was set, his focus razor-sharp as the neighboring resort's marina came into view.

It was a picture of calm—too calm. Dozens of boats bobbed gently in the water, their owners milling about on the docks. Karen's eyes darted from vessel to vessel, searching for any sign of Cal.

"There!" she shouted, pointing to a sleek, low-profile motorboat gliding slowly away from the dock.

Montenegro slammed the cart to a stop, and they both jumped out. Karen grabbed a nearby dockhand. "Whose boat is that?" she demanded, pointing to the retreating vessel.

The young man stammered, "N-no sé. El señor paid me in cash. Said he w-was heading for a fishing trip."

Karen's fists clenched as she watched the boat's silhouette grow smaller against the horizon. Montenegro pulled out his radio, barking orders. "This is Inspector Montenegro. We've spotted the target heading southeast from Azure Serenity marina. The suspect is fleeing in a white, low-profile Sea Ray— aproximadamente 30 feet, dos Yamaha outboards, un navy stripe along the hull. Notify Cuerpo de Guardacostas. And have them block all outgoing vessels matching this description."

Even with Montenegro calling the Dominican Coast Guard, Karen's frustration boiled over. "He's already gone. They'll never catch him in time."

Montenegro placed a firm hand on her shoulder. "Let's regroup. Figure out where he might be going."

Back at the Utopia, Brock and De La Cruz settled at a nearby table while Karen and Montenegro spread a map across another in the makeshift command center set up at the coffee bar near the lobby.

Karen traced her finger along the coastline. "He's heading southeast, which means he'll stick to tourist areas where he can easily blend in." The inspector nodded. "Marina Cap Cana, Bavaro Beach. Maybe even La Marina Casa de Campo."

"Casa de Campo," Karen said, tapping the spot on the map. "Ortiz took Brock and me there once. It's private, high-end, and prides itself on secrecy. If he wants to disappear, that's the perfect spot."

"We'll send units to all three. If he's planning an escape, we need to be ready."

The Dominican Coast Guard coordinated their efforts with Montenegro's team. Within thirty minutes, each arrived at their location. A call came in from the group sent to La Marina Casa de Campo, the officer's voice crackling over the line: "Inspector, we found the boat."

Karen pumped her fist. "Yes!"

"Seize the boat," Montenegro ordered.

"Sí, señor." Then to his fellow officers, "You heard him, go, go, g—"

An explosion sounded over the radio. Further reports from nearby officers at the scene confirmed the boat was in flames, the boom rocking the marina and sending debris and chaos into the air.

Karen's stomach churned as she the radio went dead. Cal had a plan for everything.

He was gone.

And so apparently were Montenegro's men who had found the boat.

Frustration and exhaustion bore down on Karen as she slumped into a chair.

Montenegro's face was grim as he swiped back his hair. "He is a ghost now. But we will find him."

"Inspector, we must," she said, her voice quivering. "He's never going to stop."

EPILOGUE

Later that evening, Montenegro invited Karen, Brock, and Joaquin to a quiet dinner at Utopia's finest restaurant—the four had become a united team, after all. They were later joined by Wolfram, his date—Detective Alvarez—and Bo Laurent.

Bo revealed that he'd been reassigned to a case in Europe—another strand in the dead Volkov's web.

Karen had been cleared in regard to the Saunderses' murders. Montenegro updated her on his findings about the young couple.

"They were guests at the Azure Serenity Resort next door. It appears they were thrill seekers, spending their time breaking into various rooms here at the Utopia." He shook his head somberly. "I guess they were caught by the wrong person."

"What about Chloe?" Brock asked.

"Placed her in protective custody and putting her on a flight to Fort Lauderdale in the morning."

Wolfram, meanwhile, joked about finally taking time off, maybe opening a bar or fishing charter. All the while, he gently stroked Alvarez's hand, and they exchanged a tender look that didn't go unnoticed.

Karen learned more about Bo's backstory over dinner. The youngest of five, he'd lost an older sister, Navil, in the 1980s in NYC. A tragedy that nearly destroyed his family. Her murder inspired him to pursue law enforcement, vowing to prevent similar pain for others.

The following day, the Skaryds returned to their lives in Florida. Brock headed out on the usual service calls. Karen resumed investigating the local criminal elements—with Lion-O on her hip and T at her side, both determined to put Moses and Punta Cana behind them.

Unfortunately, Moses had different plans.

Months had passed, and Karen received a package at the station. A box of expensive Dominican cigars. The moment Woody saw the cigars lying open on her desk, he reached for one, ready to light up. Karen's sharp eyes caught the brand—the same brand Senator Ortiz had smoked.

She slapped the cigar out of her lieutenant's mouth, much to his surprise and frustration.

"What the hell, Skaryd?" Woody snapped, rubbing his jaw.

"Moses," she said through gritted teeth, holding up the note that accompanied the cigars. It read: *I hear these are killer.*

Woody's anger shifted to disbelief. "That bastard."

The crime lab discovered the cigars had been laced with concentrated Oleander nerium, the same poison used to kill Brock's fellow rosarian, Diana.

Despite Karen's best efforts, the package couldn't be traced.

Moses had covered his tracks impeccably, leaving no tangible leads. Still, the incident left a bitter reminder of his reach and twisted sense of humor.

In the weeks that followed, Karen forced herself to relax, regaining some semblance of normalcy. She went back to keeping a watchful but less obsessive eye on her loved ones, much to the relief of her waistline and blood pressure.

One night, all that changed.

Karen rounded the stadium, pushing her way through the throng, her eyes fixed on the visitors' side of the field. Her phone buzzed in her pocket, but she ignored it. She was too close.

The noise in the outdoor stadium was deafening, a cacophony of cheers and chants. She shoved past jubilant fans, apologizing tersely as she circled to the other side of the field. Ahead, a flicker of movement caught her attention—a dark coat disappearing into the chaos of the visitors' section.

"Moses," she muttered under her breath, her focus narrowing. She strained to keep the coat in view as it ducked deeper into the crowd, blending effortlessly . . . like a stone swallowed by the ocean.

The hometown crowd exploded in celebration—an ocean of cheers, the field flooded with people, high-fives and hugs all around.

Karen drew her service weapon and yelled, "Stop! Police!"

Her words were swallowed by the noise.

The visitors' side erupted as well, though their energy was less victorious and more chaotic. Karen holstered her weapon and reached the spot where she'd last seen Moses. She searched frantically, her sharp eyes darting through the mass of people. Her chest heaved as she fought to catch her breath.

And then she saw it.

His jacket lay crumpled on the ground, discarded like an empty husk. She picked it up, her fingers trembling slightly as she searched the pockets. Inside, she found three items carefully placed.

The earring trophy he gifted to Chloe.

A Polaroid of Chloe's mutilated body. Her throat was slit, and her face was frozen in grotesque smile, posed with her hand holding a phone, as if taking a selfie.

Neatly printed along the bottom of the Polaroid: *Exodus 20:17 – You Shall Not Covet.*

The third, a photograph of Bo Laurent. He was sitting at a café, somewhere in Europe, sipping coffee and eating what appeared to be a chocolate scone.

The message was clear—Moses had eyes everywhere.

Tucked into the inner pocket of the jacket was a folded note. Karen opened it carefully, her pulse pounding in her ears:

Did you really think it would be that easy?
Until next time, Detective.

— Moses

Karen's grip tightened around the note. Her jaw clenched. Around her, the hometown crowd celebrated wildly, oblivious to the danger that had lurked amongst the stands. She scanned the area one final time, hoping for a glimpse of him, but she knew it was futile.

He was gone.

Again.

Her phone buzzed in her back pocket, and she finally pulled it out. Brock's name lit up the screen. She answered with a breathless, "Hey."

"Ka? What's going on?" Brock shouted, his voice was laced with concern.

"Do you have eyes on Ellie?" she yelled.

"Yeah, Ellie's safe. She's with me. What happened?"

Karen exhaled slowly. "He was here. Moses. I almost had him."

"Jesus," Brock muttered loudly. "Do you need me to help or—"

"No," she interrupted. "Just keep Ellie close. Take her home. I'll handle this."

She hung up to his protests and stood in the middle of the chaotic crowd, the jacket and its contents held tight to her chest. Around her, the sound of victory echoing into the cool November evening. But for Detective Skaryd, the moment was anything but triumphant.

Moses had slipped away once more, leaving behind his chilling reminders. She turned and walked toward the parking lot, the sounds of celebration fading behind her.

This wasn't over.

Not by a long shot.

She would be ready for him next time. Whatever it took, she would stop him. For now, all she could do was carry the weight of his message—and the promise of the game yet to come.

The End . . . For Now

Thank you so much for reading!

If you enjoyed this story, please consider leaving a review. It doesn't have to be long—just a sentence or two helps other readers discover the book . . . and means the world to the author.

ACKNOWLEDGMENTS

As *Death in Utopia* makes its way into the world, I'd like to express my heartfelt gratitude to those who have been instrumental in this journey.

To my incredible wife, Jeanette—your endless love, patience, and unwavering support inspire every page I write.

To our four amazing sons, we are immensely proud of each of you, and your encouragement means everything.

To my wonderful friends, whose consistent support and motivation have been invaluable, thank you for being there every step of the way. My siblings deserve special recognition for their continuous love, understanding, and encouragement.

A big thanks to the Pinellas Writers and Authors Group for their insightful guidance and invaluable feedback, which keeps my pencil sharp and helps me hone my craft.

My deepest appreciation goes to Janet Fix, my exceptional editor and publisher at thewordverve. Your dedication, meticulous care, and collaboration throughout this manuscript have made all the difference.

Here's to the success of *Death in Utopia*—may it find its rightful place on the *New York Times* Bestseller List and Amazon's Top 100.

— Phil

ABOUT THE AUTHOR

Award-winning author Phillip Vega is a born storyteller who found his true calling later in life when he began putting his vivid imagination onto paper. Juggling his fervor for writing alongside a successful career in software sales, Phillip finds solace and inspiration in his Long Island upbringing, enriched by his Hispanic heritage. Now living in the vibrant landscapes of Florida, he draws upon his memories of summers on Long Island to craft gripping romantic narratives that captivate readers.

Vega's literary journey began in the romantic suspense genres with *Last Exit to Montauk* (Manhattan Book Awards Winner, 2020), followed by *The Captain & the Queen* (Top Shelf Dual-Finalist, 2020), and *Searching for Sarah* (Book Excellence Awards Winner, 2021). With the 2024 release of *Fury in Her Eyes*, he delves deeper into the intricacies of human emotion and the complexities of relationships, with even more accolades received.

Phillip's latest writing focuses on the mystery genre with the Karen Skaryd Mysteries, debuting with *Death in Utopia*. These are classic mystery novels that further highlight his talent for crafting suspenseful tales with strong, relatable characters.

Versatile and engaging, Phillip thrives in interpersonal settings, including guest appearances, interviews, and book signings, always eager to connect with his readers and share his love for storytelling.

Keep up on the latest with this author through his website: www.phillipvega.com, where you will also find his social media handles.

9 781956 856859